Sinéad Gillespie was born in 1964 in Derry, Northern Ireland. She graduated from Kent University, pursuing careers in Law and Teaching before a stint at drama school in Brighton. An M.A. in Social Sciences satisfied her enduring fascination with human behaviour, for a while.

Sinéad's writing first made a public appearance in her one-woman play, *From Within*, a story of bringing up a child with Autism.

She now writes in Somerset, U.K. where she lives with her son, his Asperger's, and her husband.

…but I love you

SINÉAD GILLESPIE

Indigo Dreams Publishing

First Edition: ...but I love you

First published in Great Britain in 2013 by
Indigo Dreams Publishing Ltd
24 Forest Houses
Halwill
Beaworthy
EX21 5UU
www.indigodreams.co.uk

Sinéad Gillespie has asserted her right under the Copyright, Designs
and Patents Act 1988 to be identified as the author of this work.
©2013 Sinéad Gillespie

ISBN 978-1-909357-07-5

Designed and typeset in Minion Pro by Indigo Dreams.

Front cover design by Bridgeen Gillespie

Printed and bound in Great Britain by Imprint Academic, Exeter.

*Papers used by Indigo Dreams are recyclable products made from
wood grown in sustainable forests following the guidance of the Forest
Stewardship Council.*

For all the wonderful women in my world

ACKNOWLEDGEMENT

My publishers for giving me this opportunity; my editor for her patient scrutiny; Imran and Brit Writers for pushing me forward; the talented women of the Mendip Writers Studio for their unending support and encouragement; Oliver and Ian for tolerating my vacant episodes, now known as 'headful of book'; readers everywhere who give us writers a reason.

for Mark,

thanks for the
experience!

...but I love you

♡ Sinéad

Chapter One

Kate and Helena

"Kiss me," said Kate.

"What, here?"

"I dare you. Come here and kiss me."

Although Kate appeared a stilted black and white animation in the strobe flashes, the glint of pure devilment in her eye was unmissable. Helena glanced around the club, quickly assessing the clientele. Groups of men, on the pull. Groups of women, dancing here, drinking there, on the pull. A few canoodling couples, pulled. They all looked pretty damn straight to her.

Helena leaned close to Kate's ear, enough to be heard over the heavy pulse of the bass, close enough to tickle her with her lips.

"It might look like a happenin' spot to you, hon, but this is Catholic Ireland! You'll have to wait 'til later for your kiss." With a flick of her tongue along the edge of Kate's soft lobe, she pulled away.

Kate faked a glare. "Then stop wiggling your arse at me. My knickers are damp and I don't think it's all sweat."

Helena laughed as she danced away, wiggling her arse once more.

Chapter Two

Andreas and Jon

Andreas Georghiades was in Dublin for some serious fun. It was his turn. He'd been on the destination end of holidays for the majority of his forty-eight years, pandering to the whims of these white Western Europeans on their desperado two-week excursions to his home in the Greek Islands. He called them desperados for it seemed to him that they spent fifty weeks of their year in their uptight, highly organised and totally reserved lifestyles, only to be bursting at the seams with a reckless desire to let their hair, and everything else, down on their package holiday.

Andreas wasn't overly handsome. He possessed his national propensity for average height, which in terms of the European stereotype made him a small guy. He'd watched his older brothers before him ensnare the holidaymakers' daughters season after season, and feared that he might be the loser of the brood when it came his turn to pull.

He needn't have worried. The merrymakers demanded a different stereotype – one that he met with ease – for to them he was exotic. His dark olive skin glowed with a depth of colour that his outdoor life bestowed, a glow they themselves could never achieve without midday madness and carotene. His rich accent curled his words with a sensuality that Essex breeding would never permit. He exuded promise.

As a young teen, Andreas had watched and learned from his brothers as they worked together in their father Elikos' traditional Greek restaurant, listening to their cajoling and smarming words, studying their glances, their enticing smiles, and the body language that assured attention. He admired their wily ways, and practised an imitation of their prancing in front of the bathroom mirror. Sometimes, he would wait up for them after he was finished in the kitchens, in the hope that they might allow him the vicarious enjoyment of their night's conquests, divulged in glorious detail.

But when he got older, well, that was when Andreas really started to make the most of the tourist trade. Now promoted to waiter, he had, by implication, his father's approval to be a sexually attractive and active young man – so long as the restaurant's customers came first.

Having spent his evening satisfying his father, he would move on to spend the early hours satisfying himself, one or two of the visitors, his ego and his growing reputation by providing his lovers with an experience they would not forget. A hot, fast, erotic sexual encounter that they would forever recall in lustful longing simply as 'Andreas'.

By twenty, Andreas was the hero of the local lads and enjoyed their idolatry. Elikos was not entirely unaware of his younger son's exploits, but as none of it had any detrimental effect on business, it was of no concern on that level.

However, at twenty, Andreas was now of marrying age. Elikos' contemporaries busied his ears with suggestions of family mergers, of the type that would be cemented in suitable nuptials. It was time to draw in the reins, and encourage him to choose of a good Greek girl. Andreas knew exactly what this would mean. It would be time to honour the Orthodox underpinnings of his culture, and commit himself to monogamous marriage. He could not hold off his father and his father's friends with their ripe daughters for long, so he decided to make the most of his last season as a free man.

He determined a new goal to make that a summer to remember: it would be the summer of virgins, acquisition of the unattainable. Andreas intended this crusade to be as ignoble as it sounded, for it was based on a bitter resentment of his early retirement, and a growing distaste for the husbands and partners of the women he so easily bedded. At other times he would feel generous and accept that the things he heard, especially about the British and their aversion to sex except as a reproductive tool, must all be true. He still felt sorry for the women, but that was well beneath the degree of his contempt for the men who couldn't perform.

Andreas believed himself a saviour of sorts. He wanted these women to know better before they even started on British men. He would have them first, and show them what sex was really about, then they might be choosier about what type of man they settled for.

If he failed in this adventure of liberation, he, Andreas, would always be the one who remained forever in their mind's desire. His immortality assured, he would then settle to marriage.

Numerous notches were struck on his headboard that last season. If his friends admired him before, they were in awe of him now. He was unstoppable. His sexual radar finely tuned, he could pick a virgin with alarming accuracy, and with his skills so highly polished, he had every one of them. Glowing with pride and an absolutely uncrushable self-esteem, Andreas almost happily gave himself up to conjugal constraint. Although plain to the eye, the baker's daughter, Theodora, had a wealth of skills in the kitchen to make her a worthy spouse. He surprised his friends, and himself, by making considerable efforts to maintain a monogamous marriage, and build a family. It seemed that in his new circumstances he adopted more of his father's ways, and he set about training the next generation of the Georghiades family.

Elikos was proud. Andreas was proud too … for a while.

14

His progress with his family was mirrored by the development of his business acumen, opening a club firmly on the pulse of the tourist market trends. At least he was still able to dance and smile and chat to the holidaymakers. After all, it was his job to coax them onto the dance floor, was it not?

His wife did not mind. He attracted good trade and made good money. Yes, Andreas could still turn on the charm like a tap, but he was conscious that there was a mould growing at the bottom of his well, a mould that grew with wisdom and awareness, a mould that was born of the knowledge that to the passing hordes he strove to entertain, he was a nobody. Oh, they valued his services genuinely, but he was no more than a service. The man started to smart, and before he knew where it began, he found in himself a new want, a want he could not explain to his accommodating Theodora. He wanted to go to Europe, no, to the British Isles. He wanted to see their lives for himself. He wanted to see what it was that they saved so hard to escape from every year. He wanted to be on the other end of this business. He wanted to be the tourist.

A wicked streak was re-emerging. Andreas Georghiades started to fantasise about his own holiday. Now he would be the one to warm to the charm of the locals and encourage their attentions, so that he too, might savour the opportunities granted him to let go of his marriage-imposed inhibitions. Yes, he would be the one to tell tales of how his wife wasn't interested in satisfying him anymore, how he was in good shape for a man of his age, how he still possessed a healthy appetite for the finer things in life.

He had no cause to feel any concerns about the women with whom he wished to play. After all his years of listening to their complaints, he possessed no misconception that the British marriage was an institution to be revered, so there would be no risk of inflicting further damage. His only small concern was for his wife.

This new fantasy held such allure that its fruition became his overriding priority, so much so, that he convinced himself that Theodora had no real reason to worry. After all, she was a lucky woman. A good-looking, sexy man like him, attracting all sorts night and day. In fact she was lucky that he had remained faithful all these years. He had been a good husband, had earned his reward. But, as she had been a good wife too, his concern was simple – that she be saved the knowledge of his little dream.

With his plan for such a holiday developing, Andreas found a new lease on life, and felt decades younger. The only initial difficulty was orchestrating an excuse for the trip. He couldn't possibly get away with saying he needed a holiday of his own, on his own. And if he did, why on earth choose the UK? It would have to be the States, or Asia, some place with something very different to offer, not a lukewarm summer, cold grey cities, and a few museums.

He thought about a 'men only' trip with a few of his pals. But that would never work. For a start, he suspected his friends didn't have the money, and then the whole 'men only' thing aroused suspicion of itself. What else would only men get up to? And more than that, he couldn't think of one of his pals who'd earned the same trust of their wife. Idiots had been caught out too often for supplying more than food and drink on their exclusive boat trips around the islands, among other indiscretions.

No, he would only pull this off if it was business, a businessman alone on a business trip.

Andreas set about studying the figures for the last few years. Nothing there. The trade was steady, constant and healthy.

Damn. Then it hit him. In the last few years there had been an increase in visitors from other European regions, France and Germany, and now the other Eastern European countries too. If he was clever enough, he could present this to his wife as a decline in their original market, a decline that should not be ignored. The best businesses knew it was important to keep abreast of changes and trends in their respective sectors, but also, it was dangerous to lose sight of the original client base, the business's foundation. In this light, Andreas could explain that perhaps they were no longer satisfying the needs of the British tourist, and what better way to establish and fully understand their needs than to spend some time among the British on their own turf?

Brilliant!

And it worked.

His trusting Theodora thought him a genius and dedicated to take such steps to procure their future security. She was much more animated in bed that night than she had been for a while. As she murmured her post-coital praises, he experienced a moment of guilt. It was just a moment.

To authenticate the plan, Andreas chose to arrange a two-centre stay. He needed an English tourist spot to see what it was the English do at home, and chose Blackpool for one week's investigation. He didn't honestly fancy the place much himself, so deliberated long and hard about his second stop.

A tune hummed around his head. He gave it air, and on hearing the words smiled to himself, for he remembered the girl who sang it.

'In Dublin's fair city, where the girls are so pretty ...'

She was a trophy of the summer of virgins, and was the only one he had cause to doubt. Oh, she played the part well, feigning shyness and a timidity about her manoeuvres, but something in her abject enjoyment of her orgasm led him to believe that it was all an act. It had puzzled him for some time afterwards, as to why she would think herself a more attractive option as a virgin. He knew, from the lads, that they were often the worst to interfere with, for they wanted your heart and soul for their precious cherry.

Over time, he had heard other things about Irish girls, how they were veritable nymphs beneath their obedient exteriors. There was a similarity to his own religious culture, and virginity was a claim they had to be seen to make to ensnare a husband.

If Irish girls were so good at playing, then Dublin was the place to go.

Five foot and two inches at the age of eleven, Jon Meredith was destined to be a tall guy. But then, everything that grew in Georgia was tall. All that heat and humidity. He was enough of an all-round American boy to pass for one of the Waltons, a fact which caused him some minor discomfort as a younger lad, except that he was actually quite happy with his world. Well, most of it.

His dad was a problem. Jon and his father just didn't have the same plan.

His dad was Robert Meredith, editor of the state-wide Southern Post, a paper he'd joined at high school, running stories of local events and visiting dignitaries, earning an apprenticeship that financed his way through college. Bob loved his work and made it his goal to climb the ranks via the local offices, and then further, 'til his name was known throughout Georgia.

Nothing gave him a thrill like seeing his name atop the Editor's Comment. He loved the power it gave him. He was the big fish in the small pond that was just one state of the great US of A. It was big enough for him. Bob dealt with news, not gossip, whatever the trends of the wider popular press. Gossip sure as hell wouldn't get any space in his newspaper.

Bob married well, and intended to fulfil his American dream: white picket fence, floral veranda, home cooked cornbread and fine sons. He got most of it. Lucy was a great woman, a beautiful woman. He adored her almost as much as she adored him. His home was everything he wanted, for she had been reared in that fine southern tradition of looking after her man. It was children that proved to be the obstacle to their complete happiness.

Jon was born three years into their wedded bliss, the bonny result of a healthy pregnancy. Enjoying him thoroughly, and the cosy dimension a child added to their home, they didn't wait long before endeavouring to produce a sibling.

Christmas came. Invitations to festive celebrations arrived on Bob's desk in abundance. Lucy's job was to look good and entirely supportive of her husband's demanding career and social importance. Even though she was some months pregnant, her dressmaker was able to accommodate her thickening waist so Lucy could maintain her acquired degree of sophistication with ease.

A good night was had, and disregarding the indulgences consumed at the Mayor's party, Bob announced his bonhomie to all and sundry, wished them all a peaceful Christmas, and drove his beautiful wife home to their son.

Black ice, loss of control. A simple accident. Could have happened to anyone. No mention of blood alcohol. No need. Trust in the revered editor went beyond that.

Tired of the restrictions on her bulging tummy, Lucy had opted not to wear a seatbelt. The spin had flung her sideways first, into the thick door handle which mercifully, didn't give.

Then full against the dash, her outstretched arms taking the brunt of the shattering windscreen. Astoundingly unbroken, her forearms required copious bandaging, but little else. Their unborn daughter died on impact.

Even when the psychological scars had healed enough to permit them to try again, the physical scars in Lucy's womb had not.

Jon remained an only child.

Jon learned about his sister from his Grandma one weekend when he stayed alone at her rambling old house some hours' drive away. He was fed up with his report cards, because they never seemed to make Dad happy.

"I got an A for PT, Grandma, an A. I'm better than all the other guys in baseball, and no one can touch my speeds on the circuit!"

"It's hard to believe you're only fifteen, Jon. You're much taller than your father was at your age." Grandma poured a glass of homemade lemonade and served Jon a piece of her pecan pie.

"He only ever wants to know about English class, and how my essays are going. I know he wants me to work on the paper. I know he wants me to be just like him. But I'm not, Grandma, I'm not."

The physical was far more appealing to Jon than the cerebral. And not just in sport. Jon had certainly inherited some of his father's characteristics: the competitiveness, the leadership. But he also had his mother's diplomacy. Jon was always team captain for the simple reason that he was bloody good at leading a team. And that was exactly what he wanted to do – but to lead a team that mattered, in a place that mattered. Jon wanted to be a Marine.

"Jon, you weren't supposed to be the only one. Your mom," his Grandma had said gently, with her soft southern drawl, "would have loved more kids, but the car accident put paid to all that. She was heartbroken, and your dad has been trying to make up for it ever since. They want the best for you."

On that point, she was right, but it only made Jon feel that his situation was more desperate than before, like he owed them, was obliged to fulfil their dreams. He went home from Grandma's with resignation in his heart that his parents, his father in particular, would never approve of his goals, his wants. As soon as he was eighteen he left home, avoiding the college career his dad had selected, and signed up.

He loved it. It was everything he was destined to be, and he gave it his all. Without the weight of his father's judgement, he grew. Flying colours, back-patted all the way. Training complete, Jon was selected by an elite corps to take a further course in diplomatic skills. He had all the qualities necessary to make an excellent strategist or negotiator. The Marines were going to take him to the top.

A remote base in the South of Ireland was the location for this further training, and Dublin, the destination for their next bout of rest and relaxation.

A love interest!

It was the thing that Jon felt he could make room for in his life right now, the thing that might ease the pathway back to Georgia when the time was right. He was aware that marriage and the services could be a tricky business, but he thought the wives of the officers had a pretty good deal, and these Irish girls were cute.

They weren't slow to befriend the American lads. Jon reckoned the old Irish-American allegiance was as strong as ever. But they weren't fast or trashy either. Yup, Jon thought he might have the opportune situation here as he downed his Guinness with his pals and headed downstairs to the bar's club.

Even on a pre-weekend Thursday, such was the fashion in the Temple Bar area, the place to be in Dublin for the hip and happenin' young crowd. Oh, and the tourists of course. Plenty of pubs full of traditional Irish music and dancing. No one caught his eye initially. Sometimes he minded the fact that he had a preferred type, although it was often easier to say what his preferred type was not, rather than what it was, as he once discovered to his detriment in a drinking game with his corps.

It wasn't that he fancied particular features in a girl. It was more an air, a bearing, a confidence that set her apart.

And there she was.

He caught his breath and quickly prayed that he hadn't drank so much that he might be a blithering idiot should he dare to approach. He watched closely, eager to assess the situation.

Mentally switching to 'first contact' mode, he scanned her environment to ascertain who she was with, and what his chances might be.

Tall and blonde, she stood at the bar placing an order. Not the bimbo image. Jon had a type, not a stereotype. Tall for a girl, but not Amazonian. He figured a metre seventy. Her hair was short with that kind of chunky cut that let the light shine through making it a myriad of blondes. Her body was long and slender, her shoulders wide and defined, a girl who knew how to use her physique. An athlete maybe. No, a swimmer. He caught the side of her smile as she thanked the barman for her drinks, and caught himself smiling at the quirky little turn to the corner of her mouth.

Damn! In her hands she held a pint of beer and a shorter drink with coke. Probably with her boyfriend.

Still, he couldn't take his eyes off her for she walked with a striking ease of gait, a woman confident in her body. He could feel the heat rise in his groin as the presumed disappointment already sank his heart.

The blonde negotiated a path through the outskirts of the dancers. He watched her as a Marine watches a target, keen to know her destination. Even if she was with her man, Jon might still have the enjoyment of looking at her and dreaming a little.

His heart leapt as she joined her friend, a girlfriend, to whom she handed the smaller glass as she swallowed from the pint herself. She turned to face the dancing crowd, and Jon thought he might die for those eyes. Large, dark, dominating her face, they were entirely disarming in their directness and innocence.

Jes—us, he thought. I'm hooked. Just reel me in!

She laughed with her friend, engaging in nightclub conversation, intimacy induced by the necessary closeness of one's mouth to the other's cheek in order to be heard. The friends appeared to be alone. They abandoned their drinks and took to the floor stopping mid-step to continue their conversation, the way that girls do.

With increasing enjoyment, he watched as a small dark man moved towards them on the floor and danced his way through their periphery. His attentions were set upon the blonde's friend, also smaller and darker, and a bit older. The man was not exactly welcomed into their midst, nor was he shunned. Getting better by the moment, to Jon's mind, especially as the man, a tourist, he suspected, was trying to talk to the friend, obliging a distance for his blonde. The man was entertained briefly before the girls re-established contact with a quick word in an ear and danced on.

On Thursday afternoon, Andreas had been lamenting his low-key success with Dublin's fair maids. The women in Blackpool had been relatively accessible, even if he had failed to perform with the second one. What an awful experience that was. Andreas was terrified that he had lost his prowess and the skills of his youth. He cursed his marriage and his misplaced fidelity, and called to the heavens that he should not be denied his natural masculinity. The rage in his response was his salvation, for the next bleach-haired, ring-indented left-hander who came round to his accentuated broken English, was fucked with a ferocity she took to be the way of all hot Mediterranean blood.

Andreas was sorted. He made the woman come, and satisfied himself. After that, self-assurance returned. But things had not been going much to plan. Pulling wasn't the problem, adjusting the age limit was. These younger women moved in packs making it difficult to engage one of them without the interruption of her friends who were more than likely to discourage his proffered dalliance with an older man. He was beginning to feel quite frustrated, too many casual rejections from women not taking the time to look at him properly, or take a drink with him. Time was running short and he desperately wanted to end his holiday on a high.

Andreas spent Thursday afternoon preening himself. During a long bath he studied his body closely, picking off hard skin here, and trimming hairs there. Everything from his feet to his nostrils and inner ears were examined and prepared for touchability. He rolled his scrotum in his fingers, congratulating himself on the weight of his bollocks, then rubbed himself to gauge the swiftness of response – hard enough, quick enough – and resisted the urge to go on. Best save it for the ladies.

His shoes were polished, his shirt ironed, his body scented and his hair oiled. A feeling of pleasurable anticipation was rising. This would be a big night.

Temple Bar.

It had been recommended by the Tourist Information Office. He'd been reluctant at first for it sounded overly young and trendy. He was not out to get his ego knocked, just his dick. But the pressure was on if his goal was to be met. He was going to have to take a risk. He was going to have to put himself out there, hence the attention to detail during the preparation process, the next stage of which was to position himself at the bar and drink up a quantity of courage. He couldn't touch that Guinness stuff. He couldn't understand the attraction of that leaden, treacly stout. Instead he stuck with what he knew, downing Bacardi and coke with a capacity that delighted the talkative young barman.

By last orders he was well-fuelled and ready for action, and happily sloped off downstairs to the establishment's club where the music and a late licence guaranteed a crowd would soon amass, spilling from the closing neighbouring pubs.

Andreas arranged himself on a barstool, giving him an excellent vantage point from which to view the dance floor, full of women, full of victims, and began the hunt for his prey.

So many young ones in their short skirts, showcasing long, skinny legs. How he wished he could still pull those. Come, Andreas, he reined in his sights silently. Choose well tonight, and have big love this evening.

There. To the left, on the other side of the tall blonde. In fact, the tall blonde ...

She was dancing with her back to him. Slender figure, narrow hips. Hmmm, he could quite imagine himself mastering those hips. In her dance, she turned so that he might see her better. Damn. Very nice, but early twenties, he reckoned. Out of his reach. The blonde moved, revealing her dance companion.

Andreas' eyes quickly refocused. Now that was more like it. Smaller than her friend, petite and curvaceous, laughing and moving her body in the most suggestive fashion, grinding her hips and shimmying her shoulders so her breasts quivered. Andreas knew this was the one. She was older, late twenties at least, maybe even early thirties, but looking good, with her long auburn hair and pale eyes. It was impossible to be more precise about her eyes from this distance, in these lights. She had a flirtatious air, carefree, almost inviting. Andreas adopted his usual process and scanned their vicinity. Only the two of them. No peer pressure to contend with, no horde of young males hovering. In fact, all he needed was someone for the friend.

He set about his seduction with a simple start; introduce your presence. Swallowing the last of his rum, he joined the floor, gyrating his hips in that small controlled Latino way, his heels clicking until he arrived beside his chosen target. Not too invasive at first, he demonstrated his confidence, dancing alone to the right of the pair. Alone, but open to company, as he suggested with his continuous attempts at eye contact, overtly illustrating his appreciation of the body beside him.

He knew the woman could feel his eyes on her, and to his pleasure, she continued to dance in her free and sensual way. That was, of course, a come on, so he edged slightly closer, then took advantage of the next break between tracks as *Ace of Base* gave way to the more melodic *Gabrielle*. The really handy thing about chatting someone up in a club was the unavoidable fact that closeness was a necessity to be heard. Permission to invade territorial boundaries was assumed.

She smiled politely as he leaned towards her ear.

"From the distance you look like Greek woman, a goddess of beauty, touch my homesick heart. But close up, you have eyes of turquoise. Exquisite!"

She tossed her hair from her face and laughed a little, before returning her attention to her friend. He could see she was flattered, and was now playing coy. The game had begun.

The *Bluebells* sang out 'Young at Heart' and the crowd pulsed once more.

He asked, "I dance here?"

She raised her eyebrows, shrugged her shoulders, and nodded. The two women shared some conversation, and the dancing continued.

From the far side of the floor, Jon had kept an eye on proceedings. The fact that the little man was still there seemed encouraging. Even if the shorter woman wasn't much interested, at least she hadn't crushed him. Then it was obvious to him, the girls weren't going to abandon one another if only one had pulled. He could, actually, be of assistance to all in this situation.

His steps manoeuvred him closer, and he joined the group of three by making contact with the man first. Male stuff. Some communication that their mutual intentions would turn them into allies.

"Your first trip to Dublin? Mine too," established the desired connection. Then it was necessary for Jon to make it clear that he was not competition, not for the auburn one anyway, so he turned to the blonde who acknowledged that it was also her first trip too. He was disappointed. An English accent, and a visitor, not quite what he'd been hoping for. He'd been allowing his imagination to run away, thinking about weekend meetings in and around the city with a local girl. Still, he could just get real and make the most of this situation. You could never know where things might lead. He pursued conversation, easy now, for they could exchange views on their explorations, and maybe share a little personal information.

The blonde was quite talkative in that stilted, over-the-music kind of way. Jon was thrilled, although there was the slight

27

question in his mind that he simply compared favourably to his shorter, older counterpart. He asked for her name.

"Kate," came the reply.

Andreas was pleased with his new-found ally, Jon. How excellent that he should distract the girlfriend in such a way. How excellent that he could now dance with his choice.

He slid in front of her, hips gyrating, a sensuous smile, and tried to engage her with some clever moves. She laughed again, before mirroring his steps, yet did not close the distance.

He performed a few more moves, as did she. In his next sequence, he moved towards her and took her hand, pulling her into a dance-partner embrace, his other hand alighting on the small of her back. She spun free of the intimate hold, turned to her friend and indicated that she wanted a drink.

Both women disentangled themselves from the males and went to the bar. Andreas was inclined to join them immediately, and pursue with fervour. But the American was playing cool. Jon remained on the dance floor. Andreas decided to hold out too, follow suit with the American.

It seemed a long drink; at least four good tunes were wasted. Then when the girls reappeared, they headed to a different part of the room, a brightly lit area of the dance floor.

Clever women, he thought. They are testing us. Now we must show them how interested we are. He shared his thoughts with Jon, who just smiled. They waited, a planned ploy, 'til the girls seemed happily dancing, then joined them again.

Jon started the conversation with Kate. "I thought the Marine thing had scared you off."

"No, no," Kate laughed, "no problem with that. Just needed to give my girlfriend a break from the Greek god there."

And there was something about the way she said girlfriend. He tried to convince himself that it was an accent thing, for it sure as hell didn't sound like the American version of girl-friend. As he made eye contact again, she was smiling as though she had read his question.

"My girlfriend, my partner, Helena," she said, and grinned with such obvious pleasure that his disappointment simply stepped aside.

Ah, girlfriend!

She was a very happy young woman, having a great holiday with her girlfriend. His ego wasn't damaged. He had embarked upon an impossible mission.

Seeing them now with new eyes, it all made sense. Their exclusive dancing that he and Andreas had just invaded, their tactile conversations, their constant eye contact. Jon thought her a lucky girl to be so happy, and told her so. Conceding defeat and in camaraderie, they continued to dance and to talk.

Andreas was yet to comprehend the truth. Not satisfied with his progress, Andreas believed he hadn't made himself clear. Delighted with Jon's continued engagement of the friend, he thought it time to declare his intentions. Capturing Helena into an embrace once more, he pulled her closer, holding her firmly against his body whilst he put his cheek to her ear.

"You are very sexy woman. You dance with your loin. You say, look at me, I am sexy, I can do good sex. I believe you."

She pulled her head away, for only her head was free to move beyond his clasp. He had hooked their bodies from hip to chest.

She looked at his face as though trying to understand him more, so he smiled and raised an eyebrow. She spoke, keeping her mouth as far away as possible from his face whilst attempting to ensure that she be heard.

"Dancing is dancing. Sex is something else altogether. Here, I am just dancing."

He felt her stiffen in his arms as though she might free herself. He'd best take this opportunity. "I too, do very good sex. You and I could do wonderful sex together."

She pushed at him sharply.

"But I want to feel your sexy body against mine."

"I am here with my girlfriend. My body is for her."

"What the hell you talking about? A young girl and a sexy woman? What are you trying to say? That you do the sex together?" He gesticulated crassly to Helena's crotch, and his own bulging trousers. "What could you do? What would you enjoy without this? It is nonsense."

She came closer to him now, closer than she had done all evening. Her eyes were flashing. Andreas saw passion. It was working, finally. He grinned and licked his lips.

She spoke firmly, clearly, and said things about loving the girl and not doing sex with anyone but her. This was no good. He had to tell her that only a man can satisfy a woman's body. It was in the shape, the design, she had to see that. But no, she said women were very good together.

"These women, they only think such rubbish because they haven't had the good sex. I tell you what," Andreas offered, "you both come to my place, you and your friend lover. I show you both a very good time. You will see what you are missing." He placed a hand on her wrist. "Both of you, yes?"

Helena snatched back her wrist. "Touch me again, creep, and you'll find out what type of woman you've crossed." Helena turned to Kate, her face afire. "I'm going to hit the little bastard."

Kate grinned proudly. "You're ready to leave, then?"

"More than ready."

Chapter Three

Kate

Kate knew she was gay when she sensed something untoward about her delight at dressing, or more specifically undressing Barbie from her Bondi Bikini. There was something about those breasts, and the way she could run her thumb over the sleek, curved bottom. She had another doll, Trudie, who was designed with a similar body, and had the addition of a special button in her tummy that made her hair grow. Kate had a game for those two. They would go shopping, and return to Barbie's house with a variety of new outfits. There they would try on the clothes helping one another to dress and undress, commenting on how beautiful the other was. Sometimes they made jokes about the attention that tiny black skirt will get, then Kate would push it higher on Trudie's bottom so Barbie could giggle at the bare cheeks now slightly on show.

Often it lead to another game of Kate's, a game of her own she discovered at the paddling pool when she was just four. Still confident to play naked at that age, she had been running in and out of the pool with her sister and two brothers. They were on holiday, though she couldn't remember the name of the place. The pool was long and shallow, barely covering Dad's ankles as he stood in his rolled-up trousers watching over them so Mum could sunbathe in peace on the grass alongside. As well as beach balls and water wings, there were mushroom-shaped fountains for the children to play with; one, she sat on by accident.

The sensation made her giggle, so she sat on it again. It was a tickle, but not a tickle, for it gently paddled at her skin in rapid movements. It tingled, causing ... pleasure. As she concentrated on the touch she was receiving, she became focussed on her nunu, where the tingling on her skin seemed to be causing a similar tingling underneath it, inside it. It was very, very nice, and a smile snuck across her face. The sight of her mother broke her concentration especially as Mum looked at her with an eyebrow raised and a most peculiar expression. Kate hopped off her happy mushroom, and chased her brother down the pool.

Something warned her not to play that game again. Anyway, by the time she was nine she was too old to run naked in the summer. Instead, when Barbie and Trudie were in their bikinis, playing in the basin at the far end of the garden, out of sight behind an old and wide oak tree, Kate would sometimes feel that tingle inside her nunu revisit. If she was lucky enough to be free of her older sister, Jo (a rarity given the sixteen months between them) and her brothers, Tom and Dan (much easier as they had a few more years on them and bikes too) she would slip her hand into her panties, where her finger could find that magic spot which made the tingle intensify so she might catch her breath. Then, too soon, she'd have to let it go, for fear of the sudden return of said siblings, or worse, her mum.

Secondary school made it all a bit insufferable. Her body was changing. So too, the bodies of the girls about her, and she found them hard to ignore. On too many occasions, while attempting to concentrate on the demands of algebra or the blank page awaiting her attempt at poetry, Kate would find herself, not staring out the window, but staring instead at the lean line of a thigh, or the inviting indentation of an inclined neck.

She'd come to with a start, furtively glancing around the room to check if anyone had noticed her distraction.

Fortunately not.

Imagine the horror that would result. She couldn't bear

to think of the labels she'd suffer, the names she would be called, the merciless teasing. She knew she had to be diligent, excessively mind-blowingly diligent, or get over it.

She'd been reading problem pages in teen magazines. They were reassuring. It was a phase, a perfectly natural phase. All part of coming to an understanding and appreciation of your own body, through admiring the further-developed female forms around you. Nothing more. They didn't really focus on the tingling aspect of one's reaction to these female forms, or how to do away with it.

Kate did her best to resist any versions of her old personal games. Something in her was uncomfortable with the fact that glimpses of Mary Osborne's navel made her want to play with it. She couldn't allow herself such indulgences.

Physical exercise. She'd read somewhere that physical exercise was a sure way to overcome the hormonal rushes of puberty. Kate possessed a fine frame. Her PE teachers had told her often enough she was broad-shouldered for a girl, and slim at the hips. They encouraged her to swim but that activity didn't satisfy her need.

She couldn't get angry in the water. She couldn't release her confusion and emotion into the elegance of the 400-metre backstroke.

Kate needed something with an edge, more aggression and sweat, where she could go on the attack and wear herself out. She began to run. Middle distance. Sprinting was no good; it was all over too fast, and more likely to leave her suffering an adrenaline rush. No damn good at all, for it brought that high. And what to do with such euphoria? Hug all the girls you've been training with? Heighten your bodily senses so you feel every inch of their touch, from chest to hips, their scent, their soft skin, their everything?

Hardly an answer to Kate's problem. Long distance running bored her and gave her too much time to think, and too much time allowed her wandering eyes to ogle the girls around her.

The 1500-metre run settled it. She had to focus her energies, and pace herself. She had to hit the rush, and then use it with a push to make it to the finish, and make it first. Perfect!

As she mastered her technique, so she mastered her mind, to the extent that after six months of training, she could look comfortably around the communal showers, jealously admiring musculature better than her own, rather than a perky breast and a taut arse. She trained nightly, tearing around the old tarmac track to the north of the park where the more serious joggers counted their laps. School put her up for the county team. The competitions numbed the need for satisfaction elsewhere.

In turn, her achievements on the track earned her a name in school … among the boys. They had a theory on athletic types. They were of the opinion that girls with that kind of energy to burn would be raring to go between the sheets. Who knows on what these pubescent boys based these notions? Some nonsense in the magazines they pored over, and hid. Come to think of it, in their situations, where did they think they were going to find the sheets to shimmy between?

'Mum, Dad, are you going out tonight? Great! Mind if I use your bed?'

Hardly. Not in this nice, Christian community.

Kate had kept to wearing her hair long, and managed to bring herself to apply a touch of make-up if she went out at the weekend: a smudge of eyeliner on the outer corners, a flick of mascara, and the merest tint of a pink lippy. So for the boys, she was quite a sight. A tall, leggy blonde who could hold her own. Kate presumed that her ability to get on with the boys was all

35

thanks to her big brothers. She'd learned to hold her own with them. She'd had to thump Tom for the safety of her dolls, or trounce Dan at arm-wrestling for her right to the garden with *her* bike, or both for her fair share of the chocolate biscuits.

Between them, Kate and her sister Jo, had mastered a range of skills which enabled them to maintain the upper hand with the opposite sex. Intimidation was not natural to them. Accordingly, Kate handled herself with ease among her male counterparts oblivious to the fact that it was her complete unawareness of their sexuality, or their perceptions of her femaleness, which removed much of the tension her female schoolmates experienced.

It has to be said that for a time, Kate's ego quite enjoyed the attention she received. She loved the adulation that her track record brought about. Her school was proud of her. Her team was proud of her. She was often to be seen on the back pages of the local paper. Her parents were relieved to find that their younger daughter had overcome her obsession with her dolls and playing alone. They were thrilled with her growing popularity. Her schoolmates enjoyed her forthrightness. You always knew where you stood with Kate. The boys took bets on which one would get it off with the amazing Kate Pearson first. And Kate? Well, Kate, after relishing the attention from the boys as she flicked her hair at John jogging by, or laughed too loud at Bobbie's terrible jokes, toyed with the idea that she might be normal after all. Or over it.

Denial is a powerful strategy. Especially when expertly and completely applied to oneself. Perhaps it had just been a phase, Kate told herself, I mean, it's hordes of boys, not girls, who are tripping over themselves for my attention, isn't it?

It was Friday night. Kate was sixteen years old. She was going out to a club with some of the girls with whom she trained.

Although the youngest, her height and demeanour precluded any problem of access to pubs and clubs. So the girls were out for a serious night on the town. She had the foresight to arrange to stay over with Linda, the only one of their group in possession of her own room, so they had carte blanche to do pretty much what they wanted.

There was nothing notable about the early part of their evening. They were dressed to kill, all heels and short skirts, or trousers and skimpy tops, hair shiny and loose, and a night free to enjoy the long earrings banned from training sessions. Kate tended towards the trouser combo because whilst having no aversion to flashing her terrific legs in a micro-mini, she did have an aversion to crushing her foot into a strappy excuse of a thing purporting to be a shoe. If her feet weren't comfortable, she could have no fun. Things were likely to get wobbly enough as the night wore on without the fear of possibly breaking your ankle into the bargain.

As was usually the case on a night like this, they had a few too many in the pub, the logic here being simply that drinks are extortionately priced in clubs, so get merry cheaply and you probably wouldn't need much else later. Secondary benefit to this logic, drink early, less chance of a fuck-off hangover the next day.

The club was one they had attended some several times before, so they knew the layout: a few tall tables for drinks around the edge of the dance floor, a couple of sagging old leather-look sofas in the shadows for snogging later, the narrow passage with the sudden bright strip-light to the loo. They knew the format. Knew all the cheesy tunes. They knew too, that the regular slow sets created the perfect opportunity to pull, to publicly snog and steal a quick grope, to choose whether to drag chosen snogee back to a dark corner for further enjoyment, or if really lucky, back to his or his mate's car for some sexual

37

rummaging; the spread of the legs determining the degree of access permitted, at the very least, the chance of a handful of boob, at best, a clumsy shag.

The only notable thing about this particular evening was that it was the first time Kate took to the floor for the slow set.

Lewis did not attend her school. Lewis was at the local sixth form college. Kate knew Lewis from their infrequent contact at the athletics track where he trained in 100-metre hurdles with his teammates. Their schedules rarely overlapped, so she had encountered him only a handful of times. But when she did, he always seemed to make time to talk to her, and not just rubbish talk about cars and TV and the latest football scores like the guys in her classes. Lewis had intelligent things to say about the activities of those around them: their training styles, their techniques of execution whatever their sport. Lewis had things to say about the world at large, political shenanigans in the US or the excitement of the Summer Olympics, and would ask for her thoughts on current affairs.

Lewis was engaging and on this very night, here he was, coming across Kate on a rowdy night out with the girls. She felt a little vulnerable at first. Her head was too lager-fuzzied to focus on worldly matters, and she feared losing her hard won credibility in perhaps a matter of minutes.

Her fear was unfounded, for as he drew nearer, his sloppier than normal smile indicated his equally diminishing sobriety. Phew! They started to chat, but kept the subject matter simple, interrupted as it was by her mates, his mates, and their own giggles. When the music slowed from *Take That* to *Mariah Carey*, they were fixed with a brief but obvious hiatus in their chatter. Kate caught his eye and he smiled again.

"Come on, dance with me."

So, Kate found herself on the floor, in the arms of a

young man tall enough for her to look up to, moving gently to the easy beat. Her friends, she was glad to note, did not cheer from the side lines as she suspected they would with wolf whistles and crude innuendoes, laughter and suggestive comments. Instead she got a more discreet thumbs up over Lewis' shoulder.

Lewis was quite a hunk, sought after by most of the girls Kate knew, at school and on the track circuit. It was not without good reason. His black curly hair topped a finely chiselled face, home to soft hazel eyes framed by the sort of lashes women spend a fortune on mascara to achieve. Then, of course, there was that smile, slow to form, almost lazy in its journey across his mouth, but once in place, equally lazy in removing itself. Lewis emanated a satisfaction with the world, an approval of all within it. Right now it was Kate's turn for satisfaction. He was quite a catch for a girl once unsure of her hook.

She took a while to relax against him, his male form unusual to her at such close quarters. Years of rolling around with your torturous brothers is not really adequate preparation for your first clinch with a hormonal hotpot on the dance floor.

They adopted the teenage pose: boy rests arms loosely around girl's lower waist; girl lays arms loosely about boy's neck. But what do you do with your head? Courting couples nestled into one another's cheeks so they could kiss one another's necks, chew ears, and generally snog. Too much of a presumption as yet, Kate held her head back and continued some form of verbal communication, confident that her flat shoes put her at the perfect height should he make a move. As the music lingered on, and the couples around them got more comfortable, it became awkward to maintain this distance, as little as it was. She lowered her head and rested her cheek in the hollow of his collarbone. In turn this drew her entire focus to the feel of his body. She could feel his heat from the length of her chest right down to her thigh.

She could feel the firmness and strength of him despite his loose embrace. His athletics served him well. From the warmth of his skin she detected a faint scent, a subtle aftershave, and the smell of a man.

Kate drew the tip of her nose along his neck, lost in pursuit of her exploration. Lewis had other ideas about the tilt of her face, and suddenly bent into it with a kiss. Although surprised, Kate resisted the urge to pull back. She wanted this experience, and leaned further into him.

His mouth was soft, a gentle pressing against hers, warm and sort of wet. He slid his tongue across her bottom lip, and she hoped his eyes were still shut and that the frown she felt erupt hadn't crinkled her face for all the world to see.

Regardless, she stayed with the kiss, determined to discover the joy of it. It seemed that Lewis was having no such difficulty, becoming more animated in engaging her mouth, and pressing his hips harder against hers. It wasn't the only hardness occurring. Kate became aware of something against her left hip, something pressing against the point of her bone.

Evidently he was streets ahead of her in the enjoyment stakes. Where was the tingle that caught her out, showering with the team after training, the one that even Barbie could evoke? Where was that old familiar warmth? She supposed it was nerves, and the unexpectedness of it all. Whatever, she just wanted him to stop, and now.

In the dimly lit club, Kate felt her disappointment duly disguised. *Madonna* picked up the pace again, and Lewis took her hand in a gesture designed to guide her from the floor. She wasn't wanting any further smooching, not yet, not tonight. She tossed her head with a hopefully not-too-obvious fake laugh and called, "Let's party!" as she eased further into the crowd, stepping up her moves.

Lewis followed.

Re-joining her girlfriends for the last lively tunes made it easy to avoid too much close contact with Lewis, although he managed to remain fairly touchy-feely for the duration of the night.

Being hauled along to the taxi rank by her drunken friends to charm and haggle their way further up the queue, there was no time for farewell snogging.

"Can I see you again?" Lewis managed in her ear.

"Yes, yes, that would be good." And she was gone.

Linda's house was their destination. At nineteen, Linda had her own room with polka-dot bed covers and striped beanbags. Her parents were lenient about her nights out and lodging friends, so a spare mattress was kept at the ready under her bed. Linda seemed more excited about Lewis than Kate could muster for herself, but Linda was contagious in her enthusiasm, and before their wind-down bed-chat had finished, Kate found herself hoping that Lewis would indeed see her again.

He called. Lewis was not unaware of the opinion held by the general populace of Miss Kate Pearson. He was more than a little proud of himself for being the first bloke to hold her attention in a physical flirtatious way, and he wasn't about to screw up his chances. He called and arranged to see her. Somewhere quieter this time, away from her pals, and his. The cinema, drinks after, this Saturday? Settled.

With four days to go, Kate felt just about as nervous as she could get before an event. In fact, that was exactly how to deal with it; treat it as an event. She got up earlier than usual, and extended her daily run to abate the threatening nausea, finally understanding that the inane ranting of her classmates about being sick with excited nerves, was not so inane after all. Kate wasn't entirely convinced it was an enjoyable experience, and presumed the fruition would make it all worthwhile.

Friday night was the worst. She occupied herself as long as possible getting her English assignment out of the way, then moved to entertainment with *Absolutely Fabulous* and *Men Behaving Badly*, but they only filled an hour.

Tom and Dan had better things to do and were gone from the house. Jo was babysitting with her boyfriend, gooseberry status disallowed. Mum and Dad tried to be kind, interesting and funny, telling stories of their early courting. But it just wasn't going to work. Kate decided that a long bath with a read of the articles in Cosmo might provide enough distraction and relaxation to warrant sleep.

Lying back in the lavender-scented water, she couldn't help but admire the body she'd developed. She'd vanished signs of puppy fat with her ardent training, and her body was defined and taut, although with fairly small breasts she feared would be inadequate, unfeminine.

Flicking through the magazine, she was impressed to find that her breasts weren't too dissimilar to some of the photographed beauties. Convenient that high fashion put the models bra-less to show off the latest jackets and sheer shirts. With little thought she ran her fingers over her left nipple. It swelled and stood pink and erect. Tracing the other with the same finger, it too, followed suit. The TV hummed downstairs and a quick glance reassured her she had locked the bathroom door. Her hand passed along the length of her midriff, across her firm stomach. She was pleased with the aesthetic benefits of her hard work. She felt her hips, strong and lean, and as her hand rested in the curve before her thigh, her crotch began its familiar tingle. She allowed her fingers to work their way through the pubic hair feeling her crotch tense in readiness. What harm could it do?

The kitchen door banged. She heard her brother's voice ring loudly over the TV. It was enough to interrupt her private musing.

She would wait.

Stepping out of the bath, she hastily dried herself off, called goodnight to her parents, and, for the moment at least, slipped naked under her quilt. In the rare privacy of her shared bedroom, her fingers played out their previous route. Writhing gently beneath the covers, she enjoyed the caress of hands on her skin, and the form of herself beneath her touch. The smooth collar bone, the weight of a kneaded breast, the firmness of a ripe nipple tense with anticipation.

As her palms eased over her stomach, her hips raised in want. She pushed on with her fingers through the curly hair until her index finger found her pleasure. Sliding the fingertip forward and back over her clitoris, her mind flooded with the beautiful images of the semi-clad women in the magazine. Sheer shirts. Nipples unconcealed. Sleek skin. Forward and back, forward and back she worked her body to climax as she imagined tracing her tongue along one of those pert breasts. With a quiet moan, the tension released.

She pushed a lazy arm out of bed to find her nightshirt. Kate wriggled into the over-sized tee, then slept.

Saturday, daytime, was a breeze. Kate thought that perhaps she shouldn't give herself such a hard time about indulging in her game when she felt the need, for she surely felt the benefit. She ceased her conjecture and had a civilised conversation with Jo about suitable attire for her date. In agreement for once, comfort and low-key was decided (it was a cinema, after all), but with a hint of sexy femininity thrown in for good measure. Kate opted for her best Levi's, perfectly designed to emphasise her neat bum and long legs. She topped them with a soft, grey jersey shirt that skimmed her waistline and buttoned low. Her hair she twisted loosely and pinned up at the back with sexy tendrils left to trail her neck. Dad told her she looked lovely as she slipped on a pair of trademark flat shoes. Unusual for him to be so vocal in his appreciation. Mum positively beamed and wished her a nice evening.

Lewis waited near the front of the cinema. He could not have been more pleased with the vision Kate presented as he watched her strolling down High Street towards him. He was going to enjoy his evening, and everything it might offer.

They opted for a romantic comedy. His mate, Angus, had recommended horror movies as a sure way of getting your hands on your girl, but Lewis thought that might be obvious, and sincerely doubted that Kate was the type to wimp out and require comforting. No, something to make them chill out, laugh a bit. That would be the perfect way to go. He complimented her liberally, bought popcorn, and guided her to a seat about a third of the way back. Lewis had a fairly sound idea of how to play a girl. Making her comfortable was the primary objective. Nothing much would happen if she was ill at ease.

He really didn't need to be thinking so hard. Kate was quite happy. Kate was looking forward to joining her friends as one half of an item, a girl with a boyfriend.

As expected, at some suitable moment during the movie, Lewis casually slipped his arm across the back of Kate's seat. She wondered with amusement where his hand might come to rest. It hovered briefly at her shoulder, his fingers barely touching the front of the collar of her shirt. Just at the time the lead actor realised he was in love, Lewis began to twirl the tendrils of Kate's hair. And as the lead actress fell head-over-heels for the brother,

Lewis followed the line of her collar along the open front, lightly brushing her skin. He had positioned himself with enough scope to slide an exploring finger further down but Kate adjusted herself slightly. She wasn't going to be as readily available as that. She wanted to feel something this time. Lewis waited a plausible period before retracting his arm. She worried that she'd offended him, and all too soon, for his hand came to rest gently on hers in her lap. She felt happier with this, and tried to return her concentration to the film and its theme of unrequited love.

It was apparent, however, that Lewis' complete concentration was elsewhere. His hand moved off from hers and onto the inside of her thigh. He was a distraction now and she was feeling mildly irritated by his persistence, so she placed her hand firmly on his to show him it was to wander no further, and to hopefully keep it in one place while she got back to the plot now that the lead actress seemed to be dating both brothers; unrequited no longer an issue.

Peace reigned, briefly. Lewis was delighted that she held his hand against her thigh. It reassured him of her reciprocal interest. The thought excited him, and he felt his jeans tighten. That would impress her, that he fancied her so.

In a swift movement, he reversed control of their hands and brought hers to rest between his legs. Kate was horrified, and could only adopt complete politeness to mask her panic. She turned and smiled sweetly, sliding her hand away. Thank God there was still popcorn in the box by her feet. She offered it to him silently.

Satisfied now that his message was clearly sent and received, Lewis relaxed into his seat to enjoy what was left of the film, and the complicated triangle, knowing that he'd enjoy the epilogue more. When the credits were done, he asked if she wanted a drink, and they walked arm in arm to a nearby pub. The atmosphere seemed to lighten between them, so Kate let go of her earlier concerns. She wished she'd paid more attention to the girlish gossip in school so she might have read the situation better. Still, all was well. Here was Lewis, charming and chatty as they had been at the track, and looking pretty good if the glances from the other girls in the pub were anything to go by. When the time came to head home, Kate mentally prepped herself to enjoy their goodbye kisses.

Outside the pub, Lewis drew her into an embrace, and into a laneway out of view. The narrow access to the back of the Chinese restaurant next door hummed with the smell of spices and grease. Lewis pressed her against the rough brick wall, splaying his fingers through her loose bun and said, "I've been dying to do this all night," as he placed his mouth firmly on hers, pushing his tongue straight past her lips. He held her to him, closer than before, his kiss firmer than ever. She tried to absorb the smell of him, the feel of him. She concentrated on his gliding hands at the small of her back, across her bum and up again. She waited for some reaction from her own body, something to confirm the mutual attraction.

It wouldn't come. Nothing responded of its own accord.

She chose to be proactive, taking the lead with the next kiss, searching his mouth with her tongue for the key to some interest.

Lewis could feel that she wanted more. He felt the same.

He took her hand and led it directly onto his hard cock. Pushing the solid mass into her grasp, he popped a few buttons on his jeans, then caught her hand again to push it down between his belt and boxers and onto his needy flesh.

Kate froze.

The action shocked her to a standstill, her lips in stasis against his. Nothing. No excitement. No want. Nothing at all.

And she sure as hell wasn't about to service his dick.

Mortified at the untimely rejection, Lewis snapped at her, arrogantly, "What is it? Don't I do it for you?"

"It seems not."

Mum watched as Kate hopped out of the taxi, alone.

"Have a good night?" she asked of her daughter.

"It was okay," Kate smiled. "Mum, I was thinking of having my hair cut. Not short, but maybe up to my shoulders. What do you think?"

Kate didn't see Lewis again. Mercifully, by the time they next met at the track, it was peak season and coach wasn't permitting conversation of any type. They waved a mutually friendly wave, and got on with their training. Kate didn't bother to show an interest in any of the boys who made awkward and sometimes comical attempts at acquiring a date. She didn't know much yet, but she did know she just wasn't interested in guys.

Kate tried to put the whole sordid business of that night out of her head. Hardly surprising really, for let's be clear on this: for a young, closeted lesbian, still unsure as to where the door was, never mind whether or not she was going to open it, she had nigh on been assaulted, forced to handle a hard cock when it was enough of a struggle to manage a kiss.

She'd been compelled to look into the face of raw and demanding sexual energy, when she wasn't even sure of her own. She was only glad it hadn't spurted everywhere. Quite traumatic, all things considered. For a while, Kate tried to convince herself that it was all just too much too soon, and that if Lewis had taken a gentler approach she would be seeing him now. She liked Lewis, she honestly did, until she started thinking of the physical, and there her desire to know more about him would stop. She made herself eye up the boys at school, especially the ones her classmates raved about as absolute hunks. Now, she could admit they were handsome, funny, clever, whatever. She could also admire their splendid forms (those that had them, that is). But when she asked herself if they were shaggable, well, the answer was technical, academic, and not personal. Kate felt sad about it, and hoped that sometime in the future she might feel differently.

That particular course of thought was boxed securely in one small area of her brain. In another, hovering on a level where she could almost deny its existence, lay the rationale for a secret search on which she embarked. She found herself constructing a library, a reference section on all things lesbian that she might happen upon. She compiled a video tape, copying any snippet of a programme or film that offered so much as half a minute of a lesbian interlude. Soap operas daring to pursue a sub-plot within a sub-plot; two teenage girls kiss. A science fiction series where alien life-forms inhabit humanoid bodies, regardless of gender; two women in love kiss. A period drama written by some early writer; an older woman and her protégée bathe naked together in a lake and fondle.

Kate would watch these moments over and over again and hide the tapes amongst her school books when she was off babysitting, and often wished, although not quite sure what she wished for.

At the Wrights' house, where Kate regularly sat, she accessed another source, an almost unlimited source. Sky TV. One evening she found an American soft porn movie, *Women Aboard*.

She popped in her tape, and wondered seriously why she was bothering to record hetero stuff. Perhaps if she could see some raunchy, lust-driven sex for herself, she might register some of the appeal. She found herself laughing at it, all that bouncing up and down, the bloke ramming the poor woman onto the floor like he had the ability to nail her to it. What was beautiful about that? What was fun, or exciting? Just as she was about to turn it off, the camera panned to two bimbettes getting ready in their hotel room for a big night out. Naturally, fixing their hair and their caked-on make-up was done in matching lacy thongs, as they pranced around the room, boobs bouncing in one another's faces. Then as one leaned across the other to fetch a plastic necklace from the dressing table, a nipple was taken into a mouth by a set of heavily glossed lips and unnaturally white teeth.

Kate uttered a moan, feeling the sudden tightening in her pelvis. She froze for a second remembering where she was, then reminded herself that she was alone. The kids were asleep in their beds. Her focus returned to the screen. It was important to explore her confusion. She watched as the two thong-clad women made love. In turn, each caressed the form of the other with hands rhythmically moving round and round, chasing curves with their jewelled fingers, flicking nipples with their tongues like plectrums on guitar strings. Their kisses deepened and grew more passionate. Bodies moved over one another. Lusty hands slipped across thighs and pushed into quivering and thrusting mounds.

Kate marvelled at how easy it was to please another woman. It was no different from how she pleased herself. It was no great mystery, no great trial. This was something she could do. This was something she wanted to do. But how? It seemed a dream. A thing only achievable in another place, another life, or on celluloid. An impossibility in the here and now, amongst the Pearson family, the girls at school, the neighbourhood, this small

49

town where her name was known so well.

It was a hard thing to humour. In a strange way, she didn't particularly desire it as her reality. In part, Kate dared to hope she might wake one day and find all this was in her past, and she would long for a 'Lewis', a man, any man. Not a woman.

But she could see no easy path with it. She wanted to try what she had just seen. Perhaps it was easier to put it out of her head than to plan and scheme and pursue. Practicalities were demanding her attention, exams loomed large, as did her final season with the county team. This would be her last summer here if all went well with her studies.

Kate turned her focus to her ambitions, channelled her energies elsewhere. University; get away, learn more, hopefully learn everything. Track work; she wanted her record to end with a bang, first place, all the way. People would remember Kate Pearson, and all her achievements would blot out memories of personal relationships, or the lack of.

Southampton was the destination for the final meet at the end of July. The team travelled with Coach Colin in their minibus, consciously and unconsciously psyching one another up for the events ahead. The anticipation was tangible. On arrival the girls headed straight to the track for warm-ups. The heats commenced.

The girls were well-used to waiting around between events. A plethora of reading material was carried with them, sources for conversation perfectly designed to abate anxiety as it rose. A favourite pastime was for one to read a letter from the problem page, and the others would take turns to offer their own personal advice to the unfortunate applicant.

This day produced some wicked and deeply sardonic

comments. Every once in a while, a truth was revealed and some fell overly involved, displaying genuine compassion and suggested practical guidance. Howls of 'over-relating' and 'good old Millie' ensued, and indeed, brief silences as thought descended and was assimilated, and then left behind.

As the clock ticked on, and stories ended, one by one the girls headed onto the track to compete. Kate and Michelle were left alone to debate the latest letter.

'Dear Millie,

I am seventeen, and embarrassed to admit that I have a terrible crush on one of my teachers. It gets worse, it's a female. I've been doing my best to get it out of my head, but the thought of her does more for me than the pathetic spotty boys around me ever could. I don't feel I can talk to my friends about this, and to disguise my feelings I am finding myself behaving rudely to this teacher, and truanting her class. She is now more attentive to me than ever because she thinks there is something wrong. I don't know where to turn, or what to do with myself! But please, don't dismiss me with the 'it's a phase' line. I need more than that right now.

Emma'

"I think I'll go straight into the answer on this one," announced Michelle. "Dear, Emma. First of all, let's be realistic. There's the real possibility that this *is* a phase. Be prepared to entertain that outcome. But of course, as that is the easier outcome to handle, you don't need my advice on it. So let's look at the other possibility – that you might be gay. I would recommend that you try to talk to a trusted individual, perhaps a good friend. Chances are, whether you realise or not, if you've been questioning your sexuality, they've probably noticed. And if they're still around, they're most likely on your side. If you can't bear the thought of opening to someone directly, I recommend contacting the Gay and Lesbian Switchboard where I can assure you someone will be able to help. Good luck, and be gentle with yourself. Millie."

The girls were silent for an uncomfortable moment, then both spoke at once, their comments tumbling over each other's.

"Well, I think that's a very good answer."

"That's a very real problem."

"I wouldn't know what to do either."

"Just as well there's a phone line to call. Imagine your friend's face."

They stopped and made the eye contact that had been avoided during their babble.

Michelle got in first. "I've questioned myself before."

Kate didn't have the opportunity to reply. Sarah's name rang large from the Tannoy. That meant Kate's race was up next.

She stood and moved from Michelle, from the questions left unasked, from silent questions asking to be answered, from the thoughts she had so carefully laid to rest, from the excitement rising in her chest that she might have someone to talk to!

Kate forced the excitement into her stride, tearing through her heats, qualifying with a personal best for Sunday's final. By the end of the day the team was well placed to walk the silver, and if they were sensible enough to calm down for the night and stay focussed, there was a high chance of the gold.

Coach Colin was very proud of his girls' hard work. He advised immediate dinner before prancing about choosing rooms, and escorted them into the restaurant at their hotel, recommending steaks and chips to replenish the day's efforts. He gave a warm and almost paternal speech at the end of the meal, but was sure to enforce a warning in a strict tone. "No nonsense tonight. You're not there yet."

He had not forgotten, nor quite forgiven, the debacle at the meet the year before when a couple of the girls had got so excited about their headway that they hyped themselves beyond sleep, and were too knackered to be on form the following day.

"You know the drill, ladies. Twin rooms. Pair up and ship out."

Michelle called to Kate, "I'm in with you, okay?"

A scrabbled dash ensued, the race to the minibus for the bags and then off for the pick of the rooms.

Quite naturally, Kate wondered what Michelle was up to. For surely, if Michelle was gay, why hadn't Kate ever noticed clues before? She wasn't butch, nor was she girly. Another fan of flat shoes over heels. But, she supposed, in the context of a girls' athletic team it was hardly the time or circumstance to concern oneself with lipstick or strappy footwear. If Michelle was gay, what would Kate have noticed? Whether or not Michelle stole sly looks at the others in the showers? Whether or not she was an avid man-hater and refused to shave under her arms? Kate could be noted for none of those things either, if you overlook the odd indiscretion in the eyeing-up department. Shit! It suddenly occurred to her that perhaps Michelle suspected, or had made up her own mind about Kate, that the whole deal was the other way around. Maybe Kate had given too much away earlier. Michelle wanted to check her out!

Okay, calm. No need to panic. If that was indeed the case, then Michelle can't be feeling too intimidated or she wouldn't be opting to share a room with her now, would she? Anyway, more importantly, foremost in her mind needed to be tomorrow's competition. She could bury anything behind that shield – temporarily.

Michelle made it to the room first and deposited her toiletries in the bathroom. "Hope you're happy with my choice. The other rooms had a fantastic view of the car park, but I felt obliged to leave them to someone with a better appreciation of cars. Do you care which bed you have?"

Her tone was very light, very normal. Nothing in it. Kate laughed at herself for having run riot from a tiny conversation over a letter in a magazine. Michelle had done a good job acquiring one of the better rooms. It overlooked the hotel's trimmed lawn, the surprising palm trees, and offered just a few centimetres of visible sea on the horizon. The walls were a bright blue, displaying seascapes worthy of the Mediterranean, and the beds were wrapped neatly in white cotton sheets and beige blankets.

"Excellent choice, girl. I'll take the bed by the window."

"Damn, I was only being polite. I wanted that one myself."

Michelle faked disappointment so heartily that in one swift turn Kate caught up a pillow and chucked it across the room directly on target, hitting Michelle in the small of the back. The pillow barely made contact before it was airborne again. Kate was foolishly unprepared for such an immediate retort and copped the squishy cotton rectangle straight in her face.

Michelle doubled with laughter, as did Kate when she caught enough breath.

"You want to be working on discus next season!"

No ice to break. Everything was as it should be.

"Go on then. As compensation for your appalling throwing technique you can have the bath first," said Michelle, and she flicked on the TV and scanned the channels.

A bath was always more enjoyable after an event. Kate liked to spoil herself by adding a couple of drops of aromatic oils.

It helped clear her mind as well as ease her body. Lavender and ylang ylang. She could taste their richness.

Water running and steam fogging the mirror, Kate pushed the door gently to, then hesitated a moment with her fingers hovering at the lock. Leaving the key unturned, she threw off her tracksuit and slipped into the warm water. In the heat and the scent, Kate began a conscious relaxation process, concentrating on separate muscle groups from the top of her neck, willing each to ease from the contracted tension of the day, stretching gently, making her body feel itself merge with the water. She was with her calves and ankles, elongating their sinewy length when she was pulled out of her reverie by the sound of Michelle singing along to a music channel. Michelle had a surprisingly good voice. Kate conjured an image of Michelle dancing across the carpet tiles, singing before the backdrop of palms, performing for her, dressed in jeans and a scant top of flimsy silk that clung to her nipples.

The satisfying stretch of her feet reverberated back up her thigh, tightening the muscles as it went, stopping only when it reached her centre. Kate allowed her hand to follow its instinct, to join that clench, but as her fingers found their destination, she checked herself. What the fuck did she think she was doing, considering a quickie to the image of Michelle who was only that door away? She'd never called upon an image of Michelle before, and this sure as hell wasn't the time to start. She tried to remember some of the neat-breasted models from the fashion magazines.

A line of stammering high-pitched 'hars', being Michelle's take on the chorus of the Bee Gees' Staying Alive, shattered the sensual moves swimming behind Kate's closed eyes.

"No fear of falling asleep in this bath with the racket you've got going out there!"

"I'm keeping Kate awaaa–aaa–aaa–aaake!" Michelle sang, with no less screeching.

To the remainder of Michelle's rendition, Kate clambered out of the bath and pulled the plug. Wrapped snugly in her towel, she emerged from the en-suite and threatened Michelle, "I'm a crap singer, so don't expect to relax too much while you're in there."

Michelle just laughed as she re-ran the water.

Kate got into her new satin pyjamas. She may not have been much into girly colours or fabrics in her outer clothes, but her underwear and her bed-wear had become another matter, in colours that would shame the autumnal efforts of mother nature; deep greens, plush aubergines, dark blues the shade of an almost winter twilight. The material allowed a glorious, impatient slither across the sheets that hinted a promise of something she was still waiting for. Her thoughts were broken by an almighty roar from the bathroom. The door flew open. Michelle hopped jaggedly across the room, arms askew, barely holding on to the towel that protected her decency, and fell indelicately onto the bed.

"Every time!" she yelled, then gasped. "Every time! Those bloody stretches! Relaxation, my arse!"

Cramps. No laughing matter in a muscle worked hard all day.

"Oh, will you do something, Kate?" she said, almost plaintively.

Kate snapped to. "Of course," and rummaged through her bag for her oils.

Michelle had rolled herself neatly into her towel and onto her front, cursing the offending hamstring all the while.

Kate was in automatic physio mode. It was a regular occurrence, a snag of their trade so to speak. All the girls had been on the wrong end of cramp too many times, and consequently learned the art of therapeutic massage. Kate sat on the edge of the bed, poured a little oil into the palm of her hand then pressed both together to warm them. She didn't need to ask Michelle where, for the offending muscle was taut in the back of her thigh.

She went straight to work, Michelle 'aahing' to every piece of pressure Kate applied.

"Oh, do give over, will you!" Kate told her, half-jokingly. Whether the pressured strokes were working or the tone had given its message, Kate wasn't sure. Michelle quieted to that assisted exhalation guaranteed by the control of another's hands on your body.

Soon there was only the sound of their breathing, and the slick glide and push of hand on skin, rhythmic and purposeful. Kate tried to focus on the task, concentrating on applying the right degree of force and weight through her thumbs here, her fingertips there, watching as the muscle started to give beneath her touch. The skin she touched was heavenly.

Michelle moaned.

Kate creamed her knickers.

Kate had to consciously control her breathing to disguise her shock. She now understood what all her earlier confusion had been pointing towards. This moment, in this room, with her hands on the body of this girl, and this reaction. It didn't really matter if she fancied Michelle or not. It didn't really matter what happened next either. All that mattered was what had just occurred. The gorgeous and amorous Lewis couldn't even make her mouth water, but one hand on the thigh of a semi-clad female and all was there for the unleashing. She gave her head a sharp toss, to push her awareness out of immediate range, lest it should be detected, only to see that her mental detour had caused her hand to hesitate, and with it, Michelle's breath hesitated.

Something hung in the air. Anticipation, expectation, desire? Did Michelle feel it? Kate eased her hands up the oiled hamstring once more. Michelle uttered a short gasp. Again, Kate pushed down onto Michelle's thigh, a quickening in her chest threatening to falter her own breath. She looked hard at the flesh beneath her, in front of her, near her, touching her, and the dark hair just visible where the thighs parted, the damp towel frightfully failing to cover anything.

Kate imagined pushing her palm right to the top of this warm leg, splaying her fingers across the buttocks beneath the towelling, tracing the crack with her thumb, easing it into the dark space beyond. She wondered how Michelle might groan then.

Get a grip, girl, Kate chastised herself silently. Haven't you learned enough for one night? Isn't your dignity still intact?

A final cursory rub. "There you go. Sorted." She prayed she sounded light. Michelle turned over slowly, casual as to the minimal coverage provided by her towel. She looked straight into Kate's eyes and held her gaze. She knows, Kate thought, she bloody well knows.

"Thanks, Kate." The gaze was maintained a second longer. "Lovely pyjamas," and she hopped off, wrapped her wet hair in a towel and climbed into her bed things.

Kate scrambled into bed. "Anytime," and was glad to hide from herself beneath the duvet.

Chapter Four

Michelle

"Tell me you love me," Damien mumbled behind her ear, and drew her back down onto the bed with him.

"You know I do," came her half-hearted response.

Milky morning light pressed through the thin green curtains of Damien's scruffy flat. Michelle was not in the mood for this game, but knew Damien must be humoured if she was to have her own way. She let him envelope her once more. His arms, he wrapped around her shoulders, crossing them over her naked breasts like some primeval safety belt. His body, he curled around her, twisting his legs about her too, so that she was entirely within his clasp.

Damien loved this manoeuvre, to physically possess and entrap this girl who could give her passion to him as wholeheartedly as she could free her mind from him. He often thought of her as two, not one. Her character, her behaviour, her direction, each could be divided, diverse, in opposition with itself. Holding her thus, he felt she was contained, and his. He needed these moments. He needed to reassert his control, his right to her, for when she wasn't there, and his view became more objective, he often queried whether he had her at all.

Peculiar, this doubt. Michelle and Damien had been together some twenty months. Though she talked of university, and furthering her running into a career, she didn't plan going far. She wanted to be near her family, her friends, him. He had nothing to fear.

He smoothed her brown hair back from her face, pushed it behind her ear, and found access to her neck with his lips. His hand returned to her breast, and pulled her body closer still. He loved that she was so lean and firm, and knew he was lucky to be finding the joy of sex with someone so physical. Manoeuvring himself further he was able to mould the curve of her tight arse into the concave he created with his groin, perfectly positioning his dick in the crack where her cheeks parted. He was almost ready to take her again.

Michelle wanted to pull away. Not through any revulsion to the physical act of screwing. Perhaps she wanted to be free of his incessant need. She sensed it. A weakness. She always sensed it, for she knew she was the cause. Should her heart, her mind, wander, he would try to reclaim her, with his body, force her back to reality, to the here and now, to him.

Just for now, she wanted the freedom to roam with her imagination, not bring herself back down to this bed. Still, she must. Edging back onto him, she pushed herself against his hard-on where she knew he might feel the warmth of her, and the wetness left from his last ejaculation. He was very needy this day, more so than most. She would have to satisfy him to earn her space.

"Yes," Damien said as she wiggled backwards and tightened around him. God, she was good, and she knew it. Michelle began to work on him, contracting and relaxing her pelvic muscles, kneading his dick, almost counting a beat in her head as she held. Two, three, four, release; two, three, four, hold; two, three …

She did not stop to listen to Damien's breathing to ensure synchronicity. There was no point. She would not come with him this time, not that he would know. Yes, she was good. She would provide what he wanted with such energy and aplomb that he would not have the chance, or inclination to wonder if it was reciprocal.

His breaths came faster now, rasping a little. She knew it would not be long and reached back between her thighs to squeeze his balls and move him along, moaning deeply to encourage him to the end.

A last spasmic thrust and he grunted his gratitude into her neck. "Okay, you love me." He was satisfied, enough to not argue when she announced she wanted a shower.

"Sure, babe," he smiled, happy to pull his quilt about him and enjoy his full-bodied release, rather than sprint into the day's events as Michelle was wont to do. Happy to believe all was well, as his woman washed herself clean of him.

Beneath the pathetic waterfall that was the shower Damien's digs provided, Michelle congratulated herself for the achievement of being not so easily read. She was proud of the expertise that kept him behind her, unable to see her open eyes, darting about as they chased her thoughts. She washed thoroughly, soaping her pubic hair then ensuring the lather made it into every crevice.

She wanted his smell gone.

Rinsed and wrapped, she sat hard on the toilet, releasing her innermost muscles once more, expelling what was left of him into the bowl. She flushed.

Saturday. Always Saturdays.

She wondered if there was life and passion, major events, celebrations, or anything on the other days of the week. It seemed that all the fun of anyone's life was saved for or shoved to Saturday. It made juggling and compromising a pain in the arse. Not much would change for Damien this Saturday. His day off from the garage, physically spent, would be enjoyed sprawling beneath his duvet. He wouldn't be wanting much more today. Just as well. Michelle kissed him lightly on the cheek, and an eye opened.

"You off already?"

"Yup. Got our presentation this evening, you know, at the clubhouse. I need to go into town, find a new top or something, make a bit of an effort for the occasion."

Damien raised his head, supporting it on an elbow. "Did you want me to come along? It's a big one, isn't it?"

"No, hon, you take it easy. Seen one, seen 'em all, eh? Anyway, ends up a bit of a girls' night, doesn't it?"

Damien was quite glad to be off the hook. It wasn't easy to act involved and interested all night when his Michelle was only a small part of it. He'd never got his head around the team effort idea. Took up too much of her time for his liking. He was glad it was the end of season party. He'd get her to himself again after tonight. Yes, he was happy for her to have this last night with the girls.

Crowded shops and malls, queues at every cash desk, queues for the fitting rooms. Was she really that keen to impress? Michelle had a simple answer. Yes.

She wasn't one for shopping. Appearance held little priority. Clothes were functional; they should fit well, be comfortable, allow ease of movement. After that she didn't much care about shape or colour. She kept her clothes plain and unassuming, like her face. Her mother often bothered her on presentation night, for she wanted her daughter to look radiant in her success, and she wanted that reflected in her attire.

"Something bright, something special," she would suggest, only to find Michelle's choice just the opposite.

This day's hunt through the shops was different, for tonight Michelle might keep her mother happy. But it wasn't her mother that she aimed to please. She wouldn't go too outrageous.

That might arouse suspicion. Just a new top. She'd been honest with Damien there. A strong notable colour for a change, and sleeveless, to make the most of her well-defined arms. That would be enough.

She discovered a lime-green number with a draped neck, hidden amongst the rear racks. The fabric shimmered silver as the light took it. Perfect.

In no hurry to be home, Michelle fancied a bit of time alone with her thoughts. She made her way to a favourite coffee shop where she knew she might be left in peace with a gossip magazine, amusing herself with the antics of the rich and famous. Placing her usual order of cappuccino and a toasted tea-cake, she arranged herself at one of the smaller tables by the wall from where she could peruse the greater part of the shop, and study the busy street beyond.

A bosomy girl passed quickly, egged on by the surge of rushing shoppers. A denimed creature with a fluffy red jumper and similar hair, paused at the window as though desperate to give herself the break a coffee would allow, but moved on, frowning. A scruffy looking man with a toddler on his shoulders and the hang-dog appearance of weekend-dad-only stomped by.

Oh, what hectic lives we lead, Michelle mused to herself. A middle-aged couple fumbled through the door, trying to look casual as they searched the busy room for a free table. "Do you mind if we join you?" they asked of another customer.

Michelle smiled to her magazine as she remembered similar words said by Claire in this very café a year or more ago. In response to Claire's question, words of polite acceptance had formed in Michelle's mind and then worked their way into the world.

"I know you, don't I?" Michelle had ventured. "'You work at the supermarket on the weekends, don't you?"

Claire let out an embarrassed giggle. "Of course, sorry. Yes, I've seen you on the kiosk. Sorry, it's town. When it's busy like this you stop seeing people."

Michelle had been aware of Claire for a few months at that point, and it had started pretty much from her first night-shift. Shelf-stacking on week nights, check out on available weekends. It was how Michelle had been earning her 'going out' money for the last couple of years.

The supermarket was an ideal place for talent-spotting. There was a lot to be learnt from trolley-psychology, and identifying the students in digs, the live-alones, the flat-sharers. It created great scope for throwing in the chat-up lines. She didn't mind that she noticed as many women as she did men. She didn't mind that she found them attractive, and she wasn't under any delusions. She knew exactly what that meant. She fancied some women like she fancied some men. If they appealed, then they appealed. It was no cause for alarm. She didn't concern herself about whether or not she would ever act on the fact. She felt most pragmatic about it all. C'est la vie, que sera sera, and all that.

It was all a matter of timing and circumstance, for Michelle. It was a happy circumstance that Claire came to work within her vision. She enjoyed the sight of her curly blonde hair resisting the obligatory hairgrips, the sparkly lip-gloss, and the cream lace that wouldn't quite stay low enough to be invisible at the V-neck of the supermarket uniform. She relished the warm buzz that their coinciding shifts brought her. It mattered not that Claire was unaware. It was not a situation of anguished, unrequited love. She had Damien, and he loved her quite enough.

Circumstances changed with that interesting turn-up in the coffee shop. Thrown together by the constraints of their shared environment. How very Romeo and Juliet!

The mutuality was a certainty: much animated chatter; many smiles, engaging, inane, unnecessary, and spontaneous; knees bumping under the table and failing to pull away; increasingly tactile. Coffees were refilled, time passed. They avoided noticing until it could no longer be ignored – the trail of shoppers thinning, the noisy cup-washing clanking their exit toll.

"Do you have a shift tonight?" Michelle didn't care how obvious her interest.

"Yes. You?"

"See you later, then," chirped Michelle, then boldly planted a small kiss on Claire's cheek.

Walking home, she didn't torment herself with questions, self-analysis, recounting their every word and movement. It was an obvious situation. Girl meets girl. Girl fancies girl. Girl looks forward to next meeting. Nor did she suffer undue angst as she prepared for work. No point when the black nylon of the supermarket uniform, with its eye-catching yellow trim, vanished any possibility of trying to look sexy or attractive. Not her thing anyway. Just be clean. Clean enough to touch. Clean enough to eat.

It must have been the most enjoyable shift she'd ever put in. For most of the time Claire was a mirage. Sometimes there, in the corner of her eye, once noticed, focus attempted, then she'd be gone. Yet the entire time, she was a presence, there constantly in her own black nylon with the hint-of-lace beneath the uniform.

Michelle took pleasure in the bizarre sensation that was almost tension. On their infrequent encounters, smiles were readily produced, banter easy. With fifteen minutes to go before the end of their shift, and as the last couples dragged themselves and their groceries away, it was Claire who took the lead.

"Fancy a drink after work? Just enough time to hit my local before the lock-in."

"Sure thing." Michelle offered no hesitation. Damien? She'd claim a late return due to PMT. He'd be glad of the reprieve.

They met in the changing-rooms trading uniforms for jeans and t-shirts. There was such a delicious normality about it. It was automatic to slide her arm through Claire's as they walked hurriedly through the emptying streets, shops lit but locked, customers tucked away in restaurants, pubs filling up. Who would question that typical action of girls out having fun?

It became necessary to exercise a degree of wisdom in the pub. It was Saturday night after all. They would be seen as fair game. Subtlety. Without killing the connection. Eyes did it. Words did it. Proximity was guarded. Gorgeously tantalising, to have to watch intently what you cannot touch, knowing the touch is desired, believing the moment will come. Distance increasing nervous tension. Craving fuelled by alcohol. The guard was dropping. It was time to leave.

Where now? Both lived at home. Where could they go that offered them anonymity, privacy, opportunity? The park. The back of the park. Obvious maybe, but in the dark, they wouldn't be the only couple heading that way. All desiring the same thing, each pair would ignore the other, determinedly looking down, away. No possibility of recognition. No one would even register that they were both female in their unisex attire.

Kissing Claire was easy, holding, caressing. For an age, against a tree, kisses ever-deepening. Lips softer than a man's. Easy too, to slip fingers along the waistband of jeans and up into shirts.

No hesitation on either part. Michelle couldn't be sure if Claire had done this before, been with a woman. Perhaps both trusted the instinctual knowledge of their own female bodies to show them the way. Hands under clothing, skin contacting skin. Delicious discovery.

Strangely, first date decency held them from fumbling into knickers. Perhaps a little decorum, a modicum of restraint and common sense, time to check out the emotional territory.

Claire was not surprised at Michelle's revelation of Damien, nor did she appear to mind his existence, for it offered a measure of protection. They developed a schedule based on their coinciding shifts at the supermarket, swapping a few duties so they might have a Thursday perhaps, and Michelle might avoid delivering too many lies to Damien.

It must have been the third time, mutuality ascertained, in the shadows of the tall Leylandii on the north side of the park, that Claire opened Michelle's jeans and pushed the whole of her hand down between her legs. The pleasure of this pressure was accompanied by a deep thrust of Claire's tongue into her mouth, sharply removed so nothing would distract Michelle from the next sensation. One finger, smooth and swift, directly on target. Michelle loved that it felt different from Damien's heavier hand. Soft and caring and no mistake with placement.

When Michelle had come, she was keen to follow Claire's instruction, and explore that which was not her own, to find it wet and wanting. Exhilarating.

Friendship with sex: sex with your friend.

Michelle liked this combination. It was an easy priority.

Until Claire wanted more.

More nights together, more activities to pursue together, more time, more adventure. But there was Damien. And something about Damien had grown to be more enjoyable now. Claire was an affair. No deeper issues, no comparisons between gender strengths and weaknesses. For the moment, she just preferred the stability of life with Damien.

Claire found it hard to accept. She wanted reasons with substance, a purpose for her pain. She lashed out with arguments about normality, and having the courage to flaunt society's edicts. It affected Michelle not in the least, for her decisions were not based on fear. It was preference.

With the summer schedules arriving, they found their shifts coinciding less often, returning to as it had been before.

Damien expressed no interest in the altering times and frequency of Michelle's absences. She could never be sure if he had suspected anything, though he was more demanding in the period immediately after Claire's demise.

Michelle shook herself back to the humid reality of the coffee shop and her chilling cappuccino. She reached to the floor for her carrier bag, and pulled out the green top to check that she didn't feel differently about it now, being out of the shop and all. It brought a smile to her face. No second thoughts. She wondered about the night ahead. She didn't have a plan exactly. There had been no obvious communication, so things would have to be encouraged to unfold. She must take care not to let the atmosphere of the evening control the pace, lest things become messy, inaccurately gauged. She was certain, at the very least, that Kate was of a like mind. Whether interested, she couldn't be sure. Time would tell.

Collecting her belongings, Michelle left the coffee shop and headed home. She was still thinking, imagining, ruminating over and over with *ifs* and *buts*. Even if she was slightly off course, the outcome didn't have to be a disaster. Mandy hadn't thought so. And in that one quick thought, her reminiscing of past relationships began again. Dear inquisitive, Mandy, whose glossy long hair, perfect make-up and tantalising cleavage all screamed hetero. In fact, they had a real laugh about it. It added another bond to their friendship, regardless that it was a one night stand, in a fit of pique. Mandy's pique, it was.

She'd been going out with a guy called Sam for a couple of months. She was into him in a big way, as he was her, when he was around. He had an unfortunate habit of vanishing, without call or contact for days on end, and just as Mandy would be coming to the point of taking the hint, he'd reappear, keen as ever. For some time Mandy had suspected that there was someone else, so she played coy and unavailable on the premise that it would provide his excuse for dumping her. When he didn't, she got arsey, and challenged him with it. He laughed gently, cajoled muchly, convincing her there was no one else. He liked his time and space, that's all. It made him miss her, and want her more. Then it would be all passion. Mandy would give in. Satisfied, Sam would go. Mandy would phone her friends and complain once more. Michelle had given up telling her to dump him. It was pointless in the face of the fickle resolve that Sam's skills could so easily vanquish.

That was until Mandy saw him one night in a club she rarely frequented, when she was out doing the sister thing with her older siblings. So this was where he got to on his away days. Lads did sessions too. She was saved the embarrassment of crossing the floor to greet him by her sister, Anna, en route from the Ladies, who had a better view of Sam's far-from-male companion. They'd exited that club, dragging Mandy kicking and screaming to one of their more local haunts.

Michelle and Damien were among the first to learn of Sam's misdemeanours. Mandy stayed furious for a week, mostly at her own stupidity, and her lack of regard for her friend's advice, as she confessed to Michelle on a girly one-to-one they were having in Damien's flat. Damien had been dismissed – not appropriate to have him around for this broken heart monologue.

"Stay at Rick's tonight. We could do with borrowing your space."

It was given, so the girls could talk as long as girls do, and drink themselves silly beyond the reaches of their family homes.

"Did you always think he was mucking me about?" Mandy was unemotional.

"Honestly, no, in the beginning." Michelle chose to be direct. "I did think his absences a bit weird, but he was always so lovely to you when he was around that I thought it must be how he was."

Shit, the words were out, and now she was afraid that focussing on the positive was not going to aid Mandy's recovery. She watched her face. It looked like it might crumple, so she added speedily, "But if it was so lovely, you'd have thought he'd start being around more, not less, so I started to wonder, like you did." Well done, nicely manoeuvred.

"Yeah. I suppose I must have known, really, for I always mentioned it, didn't I? Denial, eh? Don't know why I bothered. Bastard."

"Not worth the energy of your anger, Mandy," Michelle cut in.

"No, no, he's not." Mandy enforced bravado, and proffered her glass for more wine. "A toast. To the sisterhood, beyond the reaches of any useless man."

They clinked glasses, laughing.

Michelle clambered over the floor to the CD player. "Come on, what do you want to listen to?"

Mandy was on her feet. "Something I can dance to, girl."

Her mood had lifted, now all she wanted was a bit of fun with her friend, to shake off any last vestiges of disappointment, physically as well as emotionally. She leaned down and pulled Michelle to her feet. They started to dance around the small space offered by Damien's flat, giggling as they tripped over a pile of CDs and his chunky headphones, losing their cool stances in the tangle of wires. They jiggled about until they were breathless and Michelle gave up, throwing herself across the bed. Mandy jumped over to join her.

"Guess what?" said Mandy, slightly slurred and grinning. "Sam was crap at sex anyway!" She dissolved into laughter, shoving her face into the quilt, her denim skirt sliding up her thighs as she kicked the air.

"And you had us all believing he was God's gift, you bitch!"

Mandy laughed all the more. "I reckon they're all pretty crap, actually. Bet Damien is." She was taunting for an exposé.

"Sorry to disappoint, but Damien is quite satisfying, in a male sort of way."

Mandy rolled back across the bed, cradling her head on her elbow by Michelle's face. "What do you mean, a male sort of way?"

Michelle did not feel ready to confess about Claire, as much because of the deceit element as anything else. It wasn't really the time to admit that she was guilty of betrayal herself, never mind the rest. "You know what I mean. Men have a different approach to sex."

"Hmmm. I think women are probably better at it. Y'know, even together."

Michelle was intrigued. "Go on."

"Well, we're gentler for a start, in our touch and all."

She demonstrated by running her finger along Michelle's face. "See? Now do it to me."

Michelle acquiesced, stroking Mandy's cheek and toying with the long earring lying against her neck.

"And our mouths are softer too. Come on, for the sake of argument, kiss me just to see." She leaned forward.

Michelle kissed her gently.

Mandy smiled luxuriously. "That's really nice, that is. Do it again." Only this time she parted her lips, and pressed more firmly against Michelle's. She pulled her hair into a soft twist to one side and laid back on the bed, spreading her arms behind her head, her boobs lifting proud from her low top.

"D'you think women are better at shagging too? I mean, sometimes I have a nicer time by myself, if you follow."

Thoroughly enjoying her pal's openness, Michelle agreed. "Yup. Damien's good in one sense, but other times, I quite prefer my own company. Let's face it, we women know how to touch our bits to the best effect, don't we?"

"Yeah, but, do you think a woman would be as good at touching up another woman? D'you think she could give her an orgasm?"

Michelle wondered if Mandy had an inkling. She rolled off the bed, fetched another bottle of wine and refilled their glasses.

"There is one way to find out, Mandy. Try a woman." She smiled broadly and lifted her glass. "To women."

Mandy joined in the toast, but her face was distracted. "Do you want to do it?"

"Do what?" said Michelle.

"Do you want to try sex with a woman? I mean, me. Think about it. We've already kissed as an experiment, right?"

Michelle nodded her agreement, and sipped at her wine.

"And that was quite nice."

Michelle was still nodding.

"And we want to know, for ourselves, what it's like between women, right?"

Michelle thought it best to keep nodding, and took a deeper slug of her wine.

"So why don't we find out? Might be a laugh."

"You're serious." More a statement than a question.

"Well, yeah. I mean, we're friends, we like each other, so what have we got to lose?"

"Our friendship."

Mandy reached down to place her glass on the floor, flashing a skimpy bra. "Look, we'll experiment. If we like it, cool. We've learnt something, and it's just another secret between friends. If we don't, well, we'll probably stop and laugh about it."

Michelle's glass joined Mandy's. She leaned over pushing Mandy onto her back. "Well, with an offer like that … so, do you want some more experimental kissing first?"

"Of course," Mandy managed, before Michelle's mouth was closed over hers.

A most enjoyable experiment – for both sides. They maintained a conversation throughout most of it, commenting on touch and feel, and responses to moves.

"Oh, try circling it. Ooh … better."

"You're not going to bite? Oh, God yes!"

The foreplay was mutual, but Michelle chose to take the lead for the serious work of providing orgasm. That way she could also be the teacher, and maximise what Mandy might provide afterwards. She made Mandy stop talking at that point, telling her she would distract herself from her enjoyment.

"But I'm a bit self-conscious, now. What if I moan, or scream?"

"It's a bit late to be getting shy. Enjoy it if it's good. And whatever noise you make, I promise to do the same when it's my turn."

"Okay, okay." Mandy squeezed her eyes shut.

Michelle watched goosebumps raise the hairs on her friend's skin, and her dark nipples hardened when Michelle pushed three fingers inside her, and pulsed 'til she brought Mandy to orgasm. Mandy proved herself an attentive student, determined to bring Michelle off with her preferred clitoral orgasm. Satiated, the girls lay semi-clad next to each other in the crumpled bed. No aversion of eye-contact as Mandy began to talk.

"That was really nice. Don't you think?"

"Mm-hmm."

"You know, I might just keep you in mind if men continue to disappoint me." Mandy chuckled.

No damage was done.

Michelle returned home from shopping armed with her new green top.

"Water's hot," her mother yelled. "You'd best get into that bath if we're all to be ready in time for this evening."

"Sure, Mum. On my way."

She was washed and spruced by seven o'clock and out the door again.

On account of the team's gold win, the clubhouse had been professionally decorated with festoons of blue and yellow, the team colours. Matching flower arrangements sat on the tables, and helium balloons trailed sparkly ribbons across the ceiling. And with the excitement, everybody had made a special effort and dressed the part. Families and friends gathered around circular tables, and the teammates, together with their coach, sat at the table to the front. The girls were in high spirits, genuinely proud of their achievement. A carvery of roast pork and chicken with all the trimmings, and a free bar meant that everyone was well disposed to entertain the Mayor's speech about another jewel in the crown of his fine town, and Colin's exhortations about the efforts of his girls, the support of their families, and their entirely justified and well-earned win.

The team then took the stage to much cheering and applause, to be ceremoniously hung with their medals once more.

Once the official stuff was complete, some of the tables were moved, clearing room for a dance floor, leaving the team's table in situ where the 'honoured guests' retained focus. House lights gave way to disco dazzlers. The fun could now begin.

Michelle entertained Kate with her usual banter, enjoying how her new top slid sexily off one shoulder while her black trousers emphasised her neat bum. She failed to hold Kate's sole attention as the girls were interrupting one another's conversations repeatedly in their excitement.

"Come on you lot," Linda cut across the racket. "Are we dancing, or what?" She gave a huge whoop as they all took to the floor together. Michelle would have to give in for a while.

She was watching Kate for some sign that the interest was mutual. Nothing was forthcoming. So she chose to admire the view instead, and wait. Kate, under the absolute instruction of her mother, had worn a skirt which softly flared to just above the knee, and a body-hugging, dark blue satin top with spaghetti-straps. As usual, she'd drawn the line at heels, her long legs more than capable of carrying off flat, thonged mules. It was a sight to admire indeed.

She wasn't sure how things would play out tonight. Her hope was to corner Kate at some point, chat a while, and guess. Everything depended on Kate's response to her tonight, on a one-to-one. She was glad she hadn't made a pass at her in Southampton. It may have been too sudden. That touch on her skin, Kate's hand on her thigh, and the look on her face: there *was* something going on there. She was certain. Michelle had been unable to shake it from her mind. She had to know more.

Movement.

Some of the families with younger, or older members, were making their farewells, leaving the partying to those who were up for it.

Michelle sensed her opportunities closing in.

Kate was washing her hands in the Ladies, admiring her reflection in the skinny borderless mirror by the side of the sinks. Even though Mum had forced her into a skirt for this evening, her shorter hair took the edge off it. She didn't feel quite a tart. She was able to dance freely, so she'd get by, now that her earlier embarrassment had worn away. It threw her, to be so nervous preparing to come out tonight.

She tried to tell herself it was just because she knew it would be her last big night with the team, but she couldn't fall for her own lies this time. She had been unable to eradicate the Southampton weekend from her mind, even though Michelle had been in no discernible way different for the rest of it. Nothing more had been said. No questionable looks had been exchanged, no hints dropped for the picking. Kate's heart had been a touch unsteady since. Michelle came frequently to mind; came frequently in her mind. Kate felt sure there was more to this. She felt crippled in her inadequacy as to how to manage the next step. She was tortured with the image of Michelle's naked shoulder, begging to be kissed. She was glad that her folks had said they'd be heading off from the celebrations soon. Left more to friends than family, she could relax from her hostess duties and focus on her own fun.

She was grabbed by the elbow on the way back to her table. Sarah was leading the team in a *Spice Girls* classic and she was commanded to join.

"What, are we all Sporty Spice?" she cracked.

"Not you, love," Michelle called back. "In that little number you'd have to be Ginger!"

Kate was glad that the heat of the hall disguised her blushes.

Michelle came around behind her. "Don't take offence, I think you look great in it."

Kate felt a shiver the length of her spine. "None taken," she smiled, with a dramatized toss of her new haircut.

The girls stayed together on the floor, punching arms in the air to *MC Hammer*, hair getting sticky with sweat. Kate blew a kiss to her mum and dad as they left, waving without missing a beat.

Eventually the heat caught up with them.

"I need a drink," Kate announced.

"I'll join you." Michelle took her arm as she made off the floor towards the bar.

Beers in hand, Michelle made a suggestion. "Let's take them outside, cool off a bit."

"Good idea." Kate felt the swell and rise of anticipation, so took a mouthful of beer to swallow it down again. They crossed the grass to stand at the fence by the track, away from the noise of the clubhouse.

"So where's Damien tonight?" Kate asked, instantly angry at herself for bringing him up.

"He …" momentarily, Michelle seemed to consider a lie. Then she spoke into Kate's eyes. "I didn't want him to come tonight."

"Why was that?"

"I think you know why."

God, no. The last thing Kate wanted was to guess her way around things. Wasn't it obvious that she had no idea how to handle all this? "I might not be sure." Please, Kate begged silently, please make this possible for me.

"Well, in Southampton, I got the feeling that you liked me."

Not enough. "After three years of training together, that shouldn't be much of a revelation."

"Liked me in another way," Michelle continued, her eyes still fixed on Kate's.

Kate sipped at her beer. "And how do you feel about that?"

Michelle smiled and nodded confidently. "I feel quite good about it." She took the glass from Kate's hand and bent down putting both firmly in the grass, before returning for Kate's hand and drawing her down too. "Is this what you want?" Michelle kissed Kate on the mouth.

Kate opened her lips to speak, but Michelle returned, "Or was it a bit more?" Michelle fell almost breathless, in a heavy kiss, while her hands roamed. Kate's mind was swimming.

Her mouth.

Her tongue.

Quick intake of breath.

Her hands.

My stomach.

78

My ... oh, my God.

She's fast. Light. Lovely. Oh, God ...

Kate mimicked Michelle's moves, her desire overriding her nervousness. She kissed her in return, and just as firmly, just as insolently. She allowed her hands to move and revelled in their discovery. Yes. This was what she wanted. Michelle pushed her hand up under Kate's skirt. Her legs parted automatically and she almost lost herself as Michelle ran a finger along her knickers.

A sense of fear brought Kate to.

"No. I mean, not 'no', just not now. Not here. We'll be missed," Kate whispered, casting a glance over her shoulder towards the thumping bass, blaring from the hall.

"Then when?" Michelle kissed her again. "You know you want to."

The bass left Kate's ears. "And do you?"

"Isn't that obvious?" Michelle took Kate's hand and pushed it down inside her trousers.

Kate's brief déjà vu of Lewis and his guiding hand was promptly removed by the sensation at her fingertips; a moist invitation. She rolled her eyes to the heavens and sighed. "Tomorrow. I'll phone you tomorrow."

"Great. Now look casual."

Kate was horrified to find her family arranged in the living room on her return home – all of them. Tom, Dan, Jo too. Christ, what had happened? Had someone seen her with Michelle? Had the news made it home already? She wanted to be sick. She didn't know how to start explaining, then Mum waved a brown envelope in the air.

"God, my exam results! I forgot! I can't believe I forgot!"

"Must have been the excitement about tonight, love."

"Must have been, Mum."

Mum handed Kate the envelope with an expectant smile.

"Aw, come on, I can't open it here in front of everyone. I'm going to the kitchen. Just wait. Wait here."

Bloody hell! Michelle had proven a real distraction.

"So, girl, what's happening now?" Kate's whispered question was aimed at the envelope, her future direction. She tore it open slowly, and shut one eye as she extracted the thin white slip of paper.

"Yes! Yes!" she screamed, running back into the living room. "I'm going to Birmingham. I'm off! I'm going to uni!"

Her mother's hand extended for the piece of paper. "A, B, B. Oh, well done, love, well done." Mum turned to Dad. "That's our baby off our hands. Now how should we celebrate our good work? I know, let's be sure she's really gone. Outside everyone."

Kate was confused. They all raced out the front door dragging Kate with them.

"Mum, it's nearly one o'clock in the morning. Have you gone completely mad?"

In the drive, Dad pulled open the garage door, and vanished into the darkness. Small brake lights appeared, then reverse lights. Out pulled a scruffy little Mini in Racing Green with a tired cream stripe. Kate's mouth fell open.

Mum spoke. "I know we gave the others a cash starter, but somehow we thought you'd appreciate this more."

Kate threw her arms around her mother, and squeezed her tight. "I love it, Mum, I love it."

"Come on, then," Jo urged. "We've been waiting all night to open the bubbly. Where'd you get to anyway?"

"Oh, mucking about with the girls, living it up a bit, you know."

80

"I'll get it!" Michelle roared to the household as she raced to answer the phone. "Thought it'd be you," she replied to Kate's voice.

"Still cool to meet up today?"

"Cooler than ever, 'cos guess what?"

"Um," said Michelle on the end of the line, "your Mum said, 'I know you're gay, go out and have some fun'?"

"Michelle!"

"Just teasing. What's so exciting?"

"My folks bought me an old Mini. It was exam results yesterday. I'd forgotten. And they bought me a little car for uni. So how do you fancy being my first passenger?"

"Excellent. When?" They both understood the timeliness of this gift of freedom.

"About four?"

"I'll be ready."

Kate was thrilled with the sense of independence, of her ownness that driving off in the Mini provided. She'd passed her test as a matter of course, but had only been allowed to drive her mum out for groceries, or her dad on errands. Being the youngest hadn't paid off, for they weren't ready to give her full and solo access to the family car. It hadn't particularly mattered. She'd had no need of it. But, God, this was perfect. Here she was, winding her way out of town past the market square with the smoking school kids and the old dears shuffling to the library, and with her girlfriend (was she her girlfriend?) beside her.

Gorleston beach was the agreed destination, on the basis that the forty-minute drive would be good exercise for the Mini, and there was less chance of them running into anyone they knew. Conversation had remained stifled in the car as all efforts were focused on navigation and driving skills. Kate was glad to reach the coast, and parked the car a short walk from the sea.

Michelle had watched Kate's efforts with much interest, impressed that she herself was worth so much so soon. Now that Kate was free of the car, she was able to turn her attention fully to Michelle, and Michelle revelled in it. She was glad that Michelle had spotted her; seen the invisible veneer that separated her from the boys, noted her attractions. Attractions that she was happy to display as they kicked off shorts and t-shirts to bare their bikinis to the sun. No doubt the guys on the beach were watching them. They were a sight to be seen with their still-toned bodies and lithe runner's legs. Yet they were impervious to the stares, focused only on watching and listening to one another. Not in a way that could be construed as different. Best friends, that was all.

Until they were back in the car.

Michelle rested her hand on Kate's bare thigh. "Can we go somewhere else?"

Kate wasn't overly familiar with the territory – either territory – but she was determined to learn fast. She followed one of the narrower roads away from the little bay, heading inland towards vast green fields broken only by the farmers' gateways. Privacy to explore. Kate pulled up along a broad tied gate, assuming that the state of the old rope meant it wasn't often used, a place rarely visited.

They were alone.

Too desperate for knowledge, Kate was unable to relax enough to acquire it. It mattered not. She had the pleasure of sharing Michelle's, which in itself was satisfaction, reassurance. Michelle was forthcoming, with kisses too. Kate was made to feel some things took time, and that time would be allowed, which was what she wanted.

It was a leisurely drive back.

Kate returned home happy.

Michelle knew there would be more.

Lying in her bed, Michelle couldn't help but smile to herself. Although Kate hadn't mentioned a word, Michelle knew full well Kate hadn't been with anyone yet. It amused her that the rumours the boys enjoyed weren't true. She hadn't let any of them near her; that was apparent. No, Kate wasn't interested in boys. How delightful! And Michelle was her first woman.

She enjoyed the accolade. It wasn't the same as Mandy.

Being Mandy's first woman was just a game. Mandy was simply playing with her with no emotional wager. Yet Kate had a mission. It seemed Kate needed to know herself, and Michelle was the fortunate creature who was going to show her the way. These next couple of weeks were going to be fun.

Tuesday. Kate. The Mini. Michelle. Further west into the Broads. The countryside. Kate had been thinking for days about where they should go. She'd suggested these woods so they could walk alone together, not having to be mindful of any public about them for they were sure to spot the odd rambler in plenty of time.

Michelle got the message promptly, and as they walked she took Kate's hand and encouraged her to feel the sensation of coupledom. She underestimated how much it mattered to Kate.

They took advantage of the deserted parking area on their return, and Kate was much more eager this time in the car. She was adventurous. She was brave. Michelle wondered at how quickly eager students learnt. She'd heard it said teaching was a rewarding job.

83

When they were done, Kate rested her head on Michelle's shoulder. "I'm not the first girl you've been with, am I?"

Michelle fell for the directness of the question. "No." Then watched as Kate's face tightened, her eyes remaining fixed directly ahead.

"So, who were the others?"

No way was Michelle about to answer that. There was nothing to gain by it. "It doesn't matter, does it?"

"Well, no. But, well … I'm wondering how I compare. I mean you are unique to me. But you can measure me. Makes me a bit self-conscious, y'know."

"Well, don't be."

"But I'm interested. Call it getting to know you."

Michelle's tone was designed to end Kate's questions. "You've known me for years."

Michelle was dropped off at Damien's. He opened the door. Kate gave a perfunctory wave and drove on, not willing to witness the inevitable kissed greeting for Michelle's return.

"Kate again?" Damien asked as he raised a palm to the retreating car. "Seeing a lot of her lately." There was no welcome kiss.

"Yeah, she'll be off to uni soon. Just making the most of the last few weeks. She's getting nervous about going away and losing touch, that kinda thing."

"Right," he answered, either unconvinced, or disinterested already.

It bothered Kate, the Damien thing. She told herself it didn't matter at first. She had no need to question her own morals when

84

there were bigger things at stake. No need to question Michelle's either. But surely it was different now. They enjoyed their time together, the distance covered growing ever greater. Michelle was a bit vague about *some* things. So what?

Kate was able to ignore the lack of information relating to Michelle's past experiences. Damien, of course, was not in the past. He was becoming an ever pressing problem for her. Not that his existence interfered with their plans very much, it was ... well ... jealousy. Kate was unable to ignore the pictures that appeared in her mind: Damien kissing Michelle, Damien holding Michelle, Damien, Damien, Damien.

Watching the video *Flatliners* together, slouched on the floor and leaning against the bed in Kate's room, felt like a good opportunity to raise the question. "With things going the way they are, what are your plans with Damien?"

"What do you mean, plans?"

"Were you planning to keep things as they are, seeing both of us?"

"You knew I was with Damien when we got together. You didn't give him a second thought then. Don't give him one now."

'But I just wondered—"

"Damien is my responsibility. He has nothing to do with you."

"Not directly, no. But I am having some impact on his life, even if he can't see it."

"No, you're not. What goes on between you and me is completely separate. It has no effect on Damien and me."

Kate wanted to know how that could possibly be. She wanted to know how Michelle's feelings for her could in no way impinge on her feelings for him. She feared the answer. She didn't want to hear that she was less important, not while it was all so important to her. She changed tack.

"Okay. So long as you're sure. And everyone's happy."

Michelle took her hand and snuggled closer. "Everyone's happy," she smiled.

As the days tumbled by, Kate began to feel cheated. She felt second best, like the 'affair', the bit on the side. It hurt because she was beginning to care for Michelle. She was getting involved and already planning how they were going to continue the relationship when she moved away to university: how the move was going to facilitate their intimacy; how she might be open and come out to the new friends she would have. She knew she was dreaming in her hope that Michelle felt the same, that Damien might be on the end of his days. Perhaps Michelle would be giving it some thought now that she'd mentioned it. Perhaps Michelle would make the next move.

"I called you last night."

"I was out."

"I know you were out, and with Kate. Again."

"And?"

"And I'm not as stupid as you seem to think I am, 'Chelle."

Michelle sidled up and kissed him. "When have I ever insinuated that you're stupid?"

The kiss was not returned. "Every time you go out with one of the girls."

Michelle opened her mouth to protest.

Damien didn't wait. "The first time, I wasn't sure enough to ask. I thought I must be mad. What kind of weird idea is that to have about your girlfriend? It's not as though you had problems shagging me. So I left it. And I forgot about it. Then Mandy cracked a joke one night we were all out, something about a girls' night in. You thumped her, made like you were laughing. But I didn't miss the look in your eye. Don't forget, Michelle, I've seen all your faces."

"Damien, you have got some weird ideas." Michelle tried to laugh him off-course. He refused to budge.

"Kate was never a particular friend. You've hardly mentioned her name in years of athletics, and suddenly you're around there every other day. I followed you on Tuesday. Took Dad's car. Very cosy. What's it about, 'Chelle? What am I not giving you? Foreplay? Do you prefer girls, Michelle? Am I the bit on the side?"

Michelle had rehearsed for this moment. She turned to him, full open face and said, "Damien, you're never the one on the side. They are." She heard the emptiness of that statement.

"And just why do you have to have one on the side? A girl on the side? What kinda game are you playing?"

"Shit. It's not a game, Damien. I mean ... I'm not mucking about." She knew she was digging a hole. "Damien, I fancy women too. I had to try it out, discover stuff, you know, sort it out in my head and know what that was about."

"Mind telling me?"

"I'm trying. I fancy girls. Sometimes. But it never stops me fancying you. So I guess that makes me bisexual if you need a label. Some people can't make a choice at all. But I can and I do. Every time, I choose you, Damien. You always win."

"I'm not sure I call this winning. I don't want to worry about every girls' night out you have. Your choice needs to be clearer. Absolutely clear. So dump her, Michelle. I don't understand this, and I don't want to. Deal with it. Or I'm gone."

Chapter Five

Robin

Foul. The taste of his own mouth brought him to. His tongue was thick and mossy. A sharp agonising grind sat in the back of his throat. He tried to stretch, but couldn't. His arms were pressed tight to his sides. He twisted a wrist to find his watch. Nearly four in the morning. Unnatural light, immediate and harsh, provided more answers, no sooner in his mind than in her voice.

"What the hell are you doing in the bath tub?" Then she laughed, no doubt convinced of his inability to respond. "Well, I need a wee, and I'm not waiting to see if you can get out of there."

Robin was too drunk, and too fed up to give a shit about the picture he must have presented, fully clothed, attempting to sleep in what seemed a suitable receptacle at the time. He'd given up his room to his mates in a fit of generosity, then hadn't the sense, in his befuddled brain, to choose the sofa over the bath. No wonder she was laughing. But then, she wouldn't have noticed him at all on the sofa. The tinkle of her urine turned his head. Kate didn't care. She carried on talking.

"What's wrong with your bed?"

"Martin and Gary." His dry mouth rolled out the words, misformed.

"And the sofa?" Her irony was unmasked.

"Oh, fuck off," he mumbled.

"Vochov? What's that, Robin?" She laughed again.

Robin closed his eyes to those bare legs, lean and powerful, spread-eagle across the toilet, poking from beneath her giant Barbie t-shirt. His housemate was never self-conscious around him. Gave him plenty to look at. Right now he didn't want to see anymore. He opened his heavy eyes again and took a peek at himself. His lanky body stretched the length of the bath, grey chinos stained and crumpled. He'd taken off his shoes and socks, but kept on his coat. He could feel his thick hair standing in tufts. He'd no idea what he could have been thinking. What a prat.

The toilet flushed. In her best customer service voice Kate enquired, "Would sir prefer the light on or off for his comfort?"

In his mind he turned swiftly to grab a bottle of shampoo from the bath-side and threw it at her head. In reality he rolled over himself and caught hold of a slimy bar of soap that escaped his grasp like a demented fish to end up rammed down the side of the bath, squishing itself into his coat.

Kate pulled the light-cord and swallowed her chuckle against the sleeping household, leaving him to scuffle on in the dark. He didn't bother. The alcoholic moat around his brain swelled again. Movement was too much effort.

So was keeping his eyes open.

As they shut, he saw himself back in the first year of uni, the first week, queuing for registration in the administration block.

There hadn't been the choice of halls. UCE had a minimal allocation, chiefly reserved for foreign students. Slapped in the middle of Birmingham as it was, there had been no room for such luxuries as the old polytechnic grew into the University of Central England.

The students were farmed out amongst the less desirable streets and houses. A community awareness exercise, building ties between the city and their ever-changing student population.

Bollocks! It was just cheap. Robin wasn't fazed. He

wanted these three years to be different. He was up for a change.

A woman handed him a piece of paper with an address and a map. "Do you have transport, love, or would you like a bus schedule too?"

"No, I'm fine." His parents were in the car outside waiting to transport him and his possessions to his new abode. He re-joined them to study the A-Z.

"There it is," he announced, the first to spot his destination; a tall, Victorian end-of-terrace that looked like it had been added onto over the years. The long street seemed a continuation of this one building, its opposite side identical.

Mother had fussed, "So near the motorway. So built up."

Robin didn't mind, and knew better than to argue, let her have her say. He couldn't see that it would be so different from Reading. Bigger, sure. Rougher in parts, most likely. So what? Mother whined loudly when they found the street, adamant that used syringes lay abandoned in the gutter, and cars with darkened windows lurked on the corners. With those *horrors* Robin thought there might be hope for some adventure after all.

The house had four floors rambling in all directions. His room was at the bottom, so one of the bigger ones. Who cared if the wallpaper was something Gran would have been proud to own with its fading pattern of flowers on trellises. It was great. Bangs and clangs sounded above and next door, other new arrivals moving their stuff about. But he thought there little point in making polite conversation just yet. So many people armed with boxes and suitcases wandering about. Probably find yourself talking to the sister or the brother instead of the poor bugger who was moving in. Mother stopped whingeing when she decided that at least it was clean. For now.

It was a few hours before family members moved on and

the housemates finally began to congregate in the kitchen, negotiating ownership of the various cupboards, giving their names and checking one another out from corners of eyes. A guy with excessively gelled hair, a punky looking girl, a clean-faced blonde. Robin still wasn't sure how many of them there were.

One of the girls suggested a getting to know you session in their communal lounge. Robin looked to one of the blokes, Mick, who said, "Yeah, man, cool idea. I spotted an offy on the corner. Who's for a beer kitty?"

A touch of gender segregation threatened the spontaneity as the girls (three of them it transpired), sat themselves together on the cruddy, imitation-leather sofa, leaving the lads (four of them, and a useful majority Robin hoped) to fight over the remaining stiff-backed armchairs. Robin was happy to lose and sat on the floor. He preferred to be positioned on a different level to strangers; somewhere to hide.

Back in reality, and in the dark bathroom, Robin realised his neck had grown quite numb. Not a good thing. What if the blood stopped reaching his brain? He reached out and crashed his left arm against the bathroom wall tiles, instinctively folding his arm back as the thud reverberated from fingers to wrist to elbow to shoulder. It was the wrong bath, wrong house, wrong way.

Memories? They just do your head in.

His right arm had more success as he concentrated hard on the whereabouts of the towel rail and made contact with a handful of damp towelling. His fingers walked the side rail to the one above. It was almost wet. He wished they turned the heating rail on more often, but beer money always took priority over bills and food and books.

He pulled the first towel into the bath, scrunching it up to a rough form of pillow for his neck. His skin soon warmed the damp.

Fuck her. A bath isn't that uncomfortable to lie in.

Then he heard the joke, and laughed to himself.

They'd had a lot of laughs in that first house, starting from the night when Usha was suddenly eaten by the end of the sofa as the ancient base gave way and the seat cushion swallowed her like it was quicksand. Exotic, curvy, pink-haired Indian, impossible-to-read Usha.

There'd been a moment of collectively held breaths. Who'd be the first to laugh? What if she didn't think it was funny? In the midst of the silence Usha announced, newsreader style in her broad Midlands accent, "Promising young media student eaten alive by possessed couch as housemates freeze in terror," from between the knees level with her forehead and red Converses waving in the air. They'd laughed so much their rescue attempt failed twice and she was very nearly truly stuck before Gary played hero appropriately with his chiselled chin and sleek black hair. Gary held hero status with Usha for almost a whole term after that, though dignity was removed along with clothing in order to guarantee worthiness of the title.

Robin was surprised at how hard it was to remember that time when they barely knew one another. Intimacy had come so readily through living with them all. It was like seeing the first episode of a favourite sitcom after the fourth series when you'd totally forgotten how they started, and seemed some empty caricature of what they were to become. Bits of information were recalled with clarity, like how each took their tea, but the early impressions were completely gone.

He remembered that the girls had gone off to bed at the same time and Martin asked if anyone smoked.

Mick had looked at Martin like he was stupid, and Robin put in the explanation. "Doh! Haven't we been puffing away all night, man? Weed, berk. He wants to smoke weed."

Martin suggested that anyone interested should join him in his room.

They all went up.

The girls now absent, had made themselves the target of conversation.

Gary was cocky. "I bet I can have that Usha."

"Put your money where your mouth is, mate." Martin was always one for a fast buck that he traded in just as quickly on recreation.

"You have it," gloated Gary, slapping a fiver into Martin's hand. "Guys, you're my witnesses."

"Don't reckon that Elisabeth will survive the year," was Mick's observation.

"What about Kate?" Robin felt his face heat as he spoke, and hoped the dope would blur the perception of the others.

"Haven't sussed her yet," Mick frowned.

"She's fit," Martin cracked.

Under his breath, Robin agreed.

Drifting back to reality again, Robin heard the dull and distant rumble that was his voice ranting something about Kate. He sat upright, looking about himself frantically lest there be anyone nearby to hear him.

Fucking bath.

His neck was locked. He dragged himself over the side, falling heavily on his hip. Not thinking straight, he stood up. Pins and needles started pricking in his ankles and the soles of his feet. A strong swimming sensation welled at the front of his head, and he could feel the room moving even though he couldn't see much of it in the weak dawning light.

He threw himself onto his knees aiming for the direction of the toilet bowl. As he found it with his left hand, the contents of his stomach hurled up and out. He hadn't quite made it and his right hand came to rest in a lumpy puddle of puke. Robin found the toilet roll and wiped his hands and mouth. He was in no state to clean the floor. His eyes were rolling. Reassuring himself that no one would be up and needing the bathroom early on a Sunday morning, he flung a towel over the mess and groped and stumbled his way downstairs to fall out cold across the sofa in the lounge.

Some hours later, a slow awareness of something damp across his cheek brought him around. A flannel fell across his face. He could see Kate's silhouette on the other sofa. She was watching the football.

"So, you're alive then?" she asked. "Now is that a good thing or a bad thing? Let me see. A good thing if anyone in the house cared that you were. Hmm. A bad thing if no one noticed you weren't. A good thing if all you can remember is the laugh you were having at the Union. A bad thing if you remember what you did in the bathroom."

There was no humour in her sarcasm today, and the combination of the sour taste pasted across the backside of his teeth, and the burning in the back of his throat, corroborated her last words.

A bad thing. A very bad thing.

He tried to mumble some form of apology, knowing his every word was inadequate, and dragged himself off upstairs. He took a deep breath before he dared to open the door. The smell of bleach was overwhelming.

"Kate! Kate!" he called loudly, wracking his brain for a suitable consolation to offer.

"Oh, shove it!" she shouted back.

He crossed the landing and clambered over the huddled bodies in his distinctly odorous room. "Come on, guys. Hair of the dog?"

The three of them fought over what shirts had been lurking on top of Robin's washing basket, the more popular being those left there for the least length of time, and donned their choice of garments over copious amounts of body spray.

Robin shoved the window open. "That'll freshen up the room too. On second thoughts, a bit nippy."

He didn't have the gall to find Kate to say goodbye, though Gary and Martin did. They knew nothing about the bathroom.

"Kate not coming with us today, then?" Gary asked of Robin. She usually did, especially if there was a football match on. They'd go down to The Gate and have a few pints while roaring at the giant screen in the bar. They all admired her for that. No girly nonsense with Kate. No sulking 'cos the blokes wanted to be blokes and watch the footy in the pub. Best of all was that she was more than able to handle their behaviour or language. She could match it all. A true ladette was Kate, not one of those pretend types just trying to get close enough to snare.

"She's not in the mood today. Time of the month, probably." Robin knew he'd be skinned alive for quoting such an excuse. He didn't care. She wouldn't know. No one to feed gossip back to her so quickly this year, their second.

They hadn't been able to comfortably negotiate friendship groups to house-share for their second year. It had proved impossible to find a house to hold all seven. It seemed the university earmarked the bigger ones for the first years, and most of what was left would hold four max. For a while it looked like the boys and girls would go their separate ways. Robin hated the idea. Yeah, he'd got great mates out of Gary, Martin and Mick, but he wasn't completely stupid. Only Mick could cook, and he wasn't likely to do that for all of them too often. Whereas the girls, well, they were more likely to feel sorry for you every once in a while. And if not, they always had leftovers or food in the fridge that had to be abandoned due to excess calorific value. And they were cleaner. Robin could handle his own room being a tip, when everything beyond it was altogether more acceptable.

If Robin was pushed, he would have pronounced Kate one of his best mates, and ahead of a couple of the guys. Things were coming to the crunch when he and Kate discussed it openly over a joint in her room one evening.

"You see, I don't want to live with just girls," she'd said. "They have a tendency to get a bit male-obsessed. I can't be doing with all that. I'm not into hours and hours of clothes shopping either. I know what I like and I get it. I don't enjoy faffing with dresses and make-up and stuff."

"No, I can't see you in a dress and all dolled up," Robin had laughed.

Kate had turned on him. "Are you saying that I'm butch?"

"No, not at all." Her change of tone had caught him unawares. "No, you just, well you don't have the sort of face that needs make-up. You've got such big eyes anyway."

"Are you saying I'm boss-eyed?" She was growing quite annoyed. He wasn't sure whether to clarify his words, or shut up quick before he dug a hole he wouldn't make it out of.

"Kate, I've always thought you a lovely-looking girl. When I say you have big eyes, I mean they are captivating as they are. Don't other girls wear that eyelash stuff to draw attention to their eyes? What I'm saying is you don't need to. Doh!" Robin could see she was focussed entirely on his words, those same eyes disarmingly and directly engaging his. He was suddenly embarrassed, so broke the moment. "Of course, a short red skirt would do your image no harm." He knew he'd get a thump for such a stupid suggestion. He did. "Anyway," recomposed and dragging, "I thought we were talking about house arrangements."

"Exactly, so I don't want all girls. You don't want all boys. So what d'you say, we say to everyone that we want to share and see who signs up?"

"Sounds good to me."

It turned out similar conversations had happened among the others, though there was a general reluctance to be the one to speak up and break the group.

Usha hadn't wanted to be in a house with Gary anymore. Although their fling had been officially contained to the first term, they had a mutual tendency to seek one another out in times of loneliness, desperation, or alcohol-induced misguidance.

Usha had talked with Elisabeth. They wanted to find a smaller place of their own. Gary and Martin had been approached by some mates in their course and fancied the idea of an all-male commune. Kate and Robin were happy to assure Mick that he'd have a place with them. Most convenient, as Mick was the one with the contacts with local dealers.

No one had to take responsibility for splitting the group. On the whole, it seemed to work out. New accommodation was relatively centrally located. No one seemed more than five minutes from anyone else. Ties were maintained. In their own little house, Robin was happy with the way things went. Kate was easy with the lads hanging about so long as they were particular in the bathroom and kitchen.

"I will not wash with your shavings or pubic hairs. Got it?"

More often than not she'd join them in *Championship Manager* or *Soulblade*, and beat them to a pulp with her female digital dexterity. On the days when she tired of them, she'd head over to see Usha and Elisabeth, returning when she was all perfumed out.

Sometimes Robin wished she'd head out more often. It gave him a break. He needed space from her, to detach himself from her. But only found he was glad to see her more each time she returned.

And today, he was glad she was in a mood. It made it less of a chore to stay away.

Pie and chips, with lashings of gravy, absorbed last night's beer fermenting in their guts, still swilling and rising in rancid waves; fatty foods settling the fresh pints taken in an attempt to kick their brains into order, and lining their stomachs in readiness for the long evening ahead.

"Our place for the Playstation? Most of the gang are off shagging this weekend." Gary knew it was a sure thing. They'd hired a huge TV on a student deal from a High Street company. The accompanying washer/drier wasn't utilised to its full benefit quite as often, but it impressed the visiting parents.

They restocked at the off-licence and settled into Gary's living room with its mismatched sofa and armchairs from the Oxfam shop ready for a tournament to the death. By ten o'clock stomachs were calling out for more than beer.

Martin had an idea. "Call Mick. He can pick up kebabs on his way round and get his hands on some puff for later."

It was Robin's job to call the house. Kate answered the phone. He was overly careful with his enunciation, to disguise the continued imbibing.

"You alright, Kate?"

"Enjoying the peace, Robin. Mick's asleep in his room."

"Would you wake him for me?"

"Sure thing. But any temper's on you."

He waited out the silence as she went upstairs to wake the sleeping lump. He smiled to himself as he heard her call to him through the door.

"Mick, your drunken mates are on the phone. Want you to go and play."

Mick was up in a shot, on the phone and agreeing to the tasks requested of him.

"You coming, Kate?" Mick asked.

"Did Robin ask?"

Robin could still hear their conversation

"Don't he always?"

"Well, not interested. And be warned, any vomit tomorrow and you're all dead."

"See you soon, then," Mick said into the phone.

Mick delivered the kebabs. "Doners for all of you, mates," and had to down a few swift pints to catch up. Too much like hard work to be the sober one.

It wasn't long before they wanted to move on. Mick had made the arrangements. The stuff was dropped off, and Gary got out the makeshift but extremely effective bong.

Robin was happy for the heady slowness to settle on him. He felt he wasn't fighting himself so hard. The thoughts about Kate and him and what he wanted would still come, but without jarring as they usually did. Martin and Gary were slunk on the sofa. Mick was lying across the living room floor. Robin was arranged in the old armchair, legs dangling over the side. The silence was upon them, each lost in the profundity of their thoughts, trying to manoeuvre the time shifts of their brains, unable to breach the lost link between mind and mouth.

Robin loved it when the present world stood still like this and time suspended itself in peace beside him. He wished it was a magic that could be called upon at will when necessary, to hold a moment, or to avoid the next. He knew, of course, that beyond the realms of his conscious awareness, time raced on as always.

Bloody White Rabbit was right. But not in here, in this room.

He gazed at his friends. Gary was smiling to himself. Martin's eyes were fixed in amazement at the lunacy of the *Road Runner* beeping madly on the cartoon channel, fantastic viewing from an altered mind-state. Mick studied the carpet with intent. They were good mates.

Suddenly he was in the school playground playing tag with Georgie Bradshaw and Kevin McCool. Jesus, he'd forgotten he'd ever known them. Childish happiness suffused his body as he felt again the freedom of a six-year-old, and the physical abandon of running around a playground, throwing himself about with full force, grabbing onto others in unabashed, unashamed full-bodied tackles. No boundaries of social etiquette. No fear. None at all. No fear of Fiona Greenwood either. Not the day she pulled him behind the sycamore beyond the mobile classroom and asked if he was big enough to kiss yet. He was ecstatic beyond imagination. All the boys went soft around Fiona; blonde curls and big eyes. He'd thrown his arms around her and kissed her heartily on the mouth, too young to know the word technique. Fiona stood and smiled, then leaned forward to kiss him herself. Her face became Kate's. She kissed him.

Robin drew his focus back to the room. He thought about getting up. He needed the toilet. His legs did not agree. He stared down at their length, stretching on and on beyond the arm of the chair, and out of sight. Their mass merged with the cushioned fabric. They were one. He couldn't extricate what could be his body from what might be the chair. He didn't fight it, remembering Usha in the quicksand of the old sofa. Instead he wallowed in the sensation, allowing it to move up his body so that the rest of him too, was sunken, boundaryless into the spongy mass.

"We are a couple already," he announced to the wall.

"She just hasn't seen it yet. It all fell into place right at the start. We even chose all the same units on our course. That shows how much we are alike, the same units in the same order. That's more than coincidence. That's destiny laying her hand. That's what she does, destiny. It's not fatalistic as some think. It's not determinism in a pure sense. No. The paths are there. Determined in so far as they exist. Sure. But not in control. Ultimately not leading the life that happens upon it. That's where destiny plays her role. She shows you the paths. Different ones, here and there. And it's up to you to recognise them. It's up to you to see what is in front of your face then choose to follow or not. She is my path. But she's not looking yet."

Robin's philosophy was no clearer to his mates for his efforts.

"So the woman of your dreams, yeah, is she determined by fate?" Mick said, looking a bit lost. "The one and only that you're supposed to end up with? Or is destiny throwing you a whole bundle saying 'loads to choose from, mate', in which case, it's not fate at all."

"Of course there are choices," Robin replied. "That's what I mean by the different paths that lay before you. But they lead to different places, don't they? One might lead to suburbia and two-point-four kids. One might lead to divorce and acrimony. One might lead to a trek around Nepal and six months of great sex. But if you're paying attention to the signs, if your eyes are open, one of them is the one you're supposed to find. So you choose the best path for yourself. Got it?"

Gary tore his eyes away from the *Road Runner* to stare questioningly at his pal. Robin knew Gary was quite happy to shag anything on offer really, and that he couldn't stay faithful for longer than a fortnight. And he knew that privately Gary blamed Usha for that. But the look on his face told Robin he was second-guessing where the blame lay. "Perhaps Usha is my true path and that's why destiny keeps pulling me back to her."

Martin started to giggle. "Get a life, Gazza. You haven't found anybody better in the sack yet. That's what you told me, you horny fucker."

Mick rolled over on the floor. "What, she's better than that Sally, the one with the big tits? I heard she was a right goer."

He rolled back onto his stomach and made like he was humping the carpet, before rolling back and spreading his legs and shouting in a high pitched voice, "Oh, Gary, oh, yes, right there, oh, harder, Gary, harder."

Martin was still laughing, and so now was Mick, all from his exhortations on the floor.

For a second, it looked like Gary wasn't going to crack up. Then he did, screaming at Mick through his laughter, "You had her too, mate?"

Robin was the last to let go. He didn't like to laugh at girls. It wasn't very nice. Then he remembered the same Sally, leaning over his table in a pub, a skimpy red top inadequate for the containment of those boobs, asking him to walk her home. She was a terror. She'd eat them all alive. And the image of her devouring them caused the eruption. They laughed 'til they ached, 'til Mick shed tears and Martin's jaw clicked out of place. They laughed until they were done, the energy gone, the silence upon them once more as the bong was circulated again.

Gary turned to Robin. "Who's a couple then? You said, we're a couple. Who is?"

"Me and Kate." Robin was quite factual.

"But you've never gone out with Kate, have you, or have I missed something?"

"No—"

Martin cut in, "Jeez, don't give him that bong any more.

102

He's lost the plot."

Robin was undeterred. He took the bong and sucked hard. Exhaling, he continued. "Kate hasn't gone out with anyone else either. And that's my point exactly. It's like it's all falling into place, ready for the right time. We are a couple already on other levels. Look at all the things we do together naturally. No politics or debates, just naturally do the same things together. Look at last summer when we both worked as runners for the Travel Channel. They kept us working as a team the whole time 'cos we do it so well. Remember she stayed at my house, with my family too? And she just fitted in there. Like she belonged. My mum thought she was great."

"So?" said Mick with boredom in his voice.

"So what?"

"So why are you not shaggin' the woman, then?"

"Kate hasn't realised yet."

"So make her realise, man." Mick was on his feet, acting out his lines. "So, honey, you and me, yeah? We've been friends for a while now, so you must have noticed how good we are together, right? So what d'you say we take it a stage further, y'know. See how good we are at other things. You know what I'm saying?" By this point Mick had himself embraced in his own arms, lips pouting, ready for his 'honey'.

Martin had started to laugh again. "If Robin came out with something like that, Kate'd floor him."

"So would any girl with half an ounce of sense," added Gary.

"Well, you'd be the one that'd know, mate," and Robin laughed with them. It really couldn't be helped.

Mick and Robin made it home at four in the morning after an interminably long walk avoiding the cracks in the pavement. It was Mick's hang up, but much easier to go along with him, dancing about like a deranged ballerina, than fight the emerging demons with him.

They went straight to the kitchen. The munchies were maddening. They found cheese and ham in the fridge, enough for sandwiches.

"We've no bread," Robin told Mick as he opened both of their cupboards.

"Check Kate's," Mick suggested.

Great girl. She had half a loaf, and crisps too.

They took the lot, made their feast and headed into the lounge. Mick turned the telly on. It kicked in on full volume.

"This fine digital watch, only thirty-four ninety-nine!"

"Shit, Mick, turn it down!" Robin whispered, rolling his eyes skyward. "No point in pissing her off before we eat all her food."

Their stomachs were their priority. The telly went off.

"Robin! Robin!"

He could hear Kate calling. He half opened an eye and saw the streak of daylight between his curtains, relieved to find himself in his bed for a change. His head was too thick to work out anything else. A thud, and the door was open.

"Why aren't you up yet?" She gave him a nudge.

He couldn't manage to open his eyes for longer than a second.

"We have to finish our treatment for our short film today. It's due in at twelve. And you're just not going to be there, are you? Robin, this is all getting out of hand. Smoking's one thing, but every bloody night? What's got into you?"

Robin buried himself in the duvet unable to face Kate, angry at his stupidity. No less angry than she.

104

"Well, you can be the one to explain. You can negotiate the extension … if you can. And fuck you if I get no marks for this, Robin. I used to rely on you, you know."

She was gone, leaving the door open to annoy his cocoon, thumping her way out of the house.

It was nearly five when Robin finally felt he could move at will. He sat up in his bed and looked at the mess that was his room. He creased his nose at the smell of it all. If it was a stink to him he could only imagine what it was to Kate. He got out and waded through a week's worth of worn clothes strewn across the floor.

He shoved a hand through his thick short hair, leaving it standing in tufts. Who was he trying to kid? Why the hell would Kate look at him twice? He was a skinny mess. And he knew why.

He shook his head. He was afraid. He was afraid that in all this time she had never seen him as anything but a brotherly mate, too comfortable with him. Or that she didn't see him as a bloke, didn't see him as a potential boyfriend any more than she saw the other blokes who eyed her up and asked Robin to put in a good word for them. He never did. If she didn't notice his competition, why bring it to her attention?

He wanted to ask her straight out if the thought of anything beyond a friendship ever crossed her mind. But he was too afraid that she'd laugh and take away his hope. That was his dilemma. That was why he got wrecked with the lads at every chance, instead of facing her. He looked at the clock. She'd finish at six today. Even if she came straight home it'd be a quarter past. He had just over an hour to do something to impress her.

Shower first or clean the room? Clean the room. No point washing the smells away only to walk back into them. He bundled a wash together and shoved it in the machine in the kitchen. Across the fridge she'd arranged the magnets B R E A D.

He'd put that right too, with a quick dash to the Co-op.

Back to the bedroom. Curtains drawn, windows opened. Not Lynx this time but fresh air. He stripped the Superman duvet cover off his bed and cursed his efficiency as the laundry basket filled immediately.

Coffee mugs spawning green fungus and plates splattered with crusty remnants of God-only-knew were gathered off windowsills and the desk, and even from floor amongst stray pants. A lone sports sock was used to dust off the computer and stereo, his TV and his one bookshelf. Filthy, he forced it into the basket with the growing mountain and shut the lid.

"So that's what my room looks like," he announced to no one.

Now for the kitchen. He took his dirty plates and mugs downstairs and filled the sink. The carnage from their munchies was scattered about the Formica worktops. They hadn't put the cheese away, and its remains lay sweating in the last sliver of the sun from the slatted window. Despite his returning fear that it was way too late, he pushed on until the dishes were done and sat gleaming on the drainer. Bench tops were still wet with actual kitchen cleaner. The table was cleared. Grungy food removed from the fridge. Rubbish bin emptied.

Now his turn. The shower.

Hot water washed away his own grime, in turn clearing his nostrils, and with that he discovered the fresh citrus scent of his shower gel. He scrubbed down over his ribs and his concaved belly, refusing to be drawn into his usual self-deprecating analysis of his inadequate body. He was long-limbed, wiry, and he hated it. He wished he was bigger, more of a man than boy. He'd reached his full height two years ago, five-foot-eleven. His mum had reassured him he would fill out when the vertical growth was over. He didn't.

106

He dried off quickly, sifted through his cupboards and drawers and found something clean to wear. He layered up to give bulk to his frame: loose checked shirt, baggy jeans, chunky fleece jacket over the top.

Quarter to six. Time to shop.

Robin ran to the local Co-op and bought cheese and ham to replenish the late-night scavenging. Bread, of course, and cake – Kate's favourite cake, the one with the chocolate marbling.

He contemplated flowers, but knew she'd think he was taking the piss. One slip would undo all his efforts. No. He wanted her to see it was genuine. Too much would be like contrition, and contrition never lasts.

Six-thirty. She hadn't appeared.

Seven o'clock. Still no sign.

He paced the kitchen, boiling and re-boiling the kettle, wiping the worktops again, spraying a bit of air-freshener. She must really have the hump with him.

Then he remembered – the treatment. Shit! He was supposed to have gone through the script and worked out the most effective camera angles and cuts. It had totally slipped his mind. He didn't know what his chances were of contacting the tutor at this time, but he had to try.

He waited for the monitor to flicker to life, and opened his mailing program. He was in with a chance if their tutor, Steve, attended to his mail in the evening. He'd have to claim to be ill, of course. A lame excuse, especially for a Monday. Robin knew that it wouldn't do by itself, so he mentioned Kate's hard work and how aggrieved he was to be jeopardising her grades. He hit 'send' and stayed online in hope.

Yes! Two minutes later a reply arrived. Short and to the point.

Noon tomorrow – for Kate. And no messing.

107

Robin rummaged through the disks on his desk and found the started project. He put it in, pulled it up and set to work. Fast and furious. Focused and fastidious. A great job, he thought, when he heard the front door open. He could tell from the sounds that it was Kate. Lighter on her feet than Mick, bag to the floor first, then the metallic rattling of the studs of her denim jacket as she hung it behind the door. Her footsteps travelled into the kitchen. He heard a distinct 'hmm' as the direction of the footsteps changed.

Kate came upstairs. Finding a tidy room and Robin typing away on his keyboard, a look of surprise brightened her face.

"Guilty conscience, I see."

No point in lying. "Yes. And I've talked to Steve. He gave me 'til noon tomorrow. I've got the work here. How do you feel about spending an hour pulling it together?"

"Well now that I can breathe in here, I feel fine about that."

She pulled up a chair, free of its usual pile of clothes, and they got busy.

Robin was absolutely right on one thing, they were a good team. They agreed on the lighting, the point of view shifts, even the close-ups. The piece was finished in no time. He was glad to be redressing the balance.

"Cup of tea?" he offered.

She mocked him briefly. "Tea? Not going for something stronger tonight?"

He refused to bite. "Tea. I got your cake." He was standing.

"I noticed," she answered with a wry smile, and stood with him. She leaned forward and gave him a peck on the cheek. "You clean up alright, you do."

Smiling to himself, Robin cut two chunks of cake while Kate made the tea. It may not have been what Robin intended, but it was best that way. Robin usually made a rotten cup of tea. They put the TV on and sat in amiable silence while watching some re-runs of favourite comedies on UK Gold, classic *Only Fools* and *Horses* and *Fawlty Towers*. The odd chuckle broke the peace, and before long they were chatting again. An ad for a travel agent came on, flashing images of New York, Geneva, Barcelona; all city breaks.

"Weren't we supposed to go on holiday last summer?" Kate asked.

"Yes, until work experience was demanded of us and our free time became free labour."

"Oh, yeah. Well, what about reading week, Easter?"

"What about it?"

"Why don't we look into it, see if we can get a cheap deal somewhere. What's a student loan for? Paris. I'd love to see Paris. Isn't there a song? Springtime in Paris, or something? And we could do with spending some quality time together. You've been such a moody sod lately, and too much time with the lads hasn't been bringing out your good side, you know."

"I know. Just got carried away. Sorry." Robin's imagination ran wild with the possibilities of having Kate alone, without the lads or anyone else, subjected to the romance of Paris. He could really be in with a chance. "You're still prepared to put up with me for a trip then?"

"So long as you're on your best behaviour from now until then." She was on her feet, flicking through the football calendar on the wall. "It's only three weeks away. What d'you reckon? Shall we check it out tomorrow … after you've handed in our treatment?"

"Sure, let's do it."

Charles De Gaulle airport was impressive in its steely calm. Hi-tech and efficient was its message. Robin wondered where the people were. It reminded him of Stansted, too quiet to be a convincing hub of international activity. Still, it was of benefit to have the space to gauge their next step, catching the Metro into the centre of the city, which is where L'hotel Beau claimed to be.

Finding the right train line wasn't as easy as they'd hoped. Kate was beginning to doubt her recall of French, when a helpful character beneath a floppy hat and raincoat, and sporting an American accent, cut in and showed them to a line that would take them within a five-minute walk of their hotel (they hoped). The heavy glazed door sucked to a close and the double-decker train moved off. Robin pulled out the information he'd received from the hotel. According to the map it was just off La Grande Armée.

He and Kate had agreed that a twin room would do them just fine and he was glad he'd be so close to her. He fought the rise of nauseous anxiety, worried the place might be a dump. The only problem with booking through an excursion agency was that they told you very little about your accommodation.

His nausea was unnecessary. L'hotel Beau was compact but plush, decorated richly in warm colours and deep carpets. The concierge patted his wool jacket and smiled kindly at the young English travellers as he gave directions to their room.

Pulling open the lift's wooden door to reveal the latticed metal within, Robin felt like he'd stepped into another century, another world. Lift secured, they travelled the three floors to their room.

"I think I'm going to like this," he told Kate, pushing open the door marked '316' and standing back to allow her the pleasure of experiencing the room first.

"Oh?"

110

Definitely positive. Robin looked over Kate's shoulder. Heavy damask drapes framed the tall window. The walls were finished in a fabric that had the touch of fine suede. An ornate dark-wood table stood silhouetted to the window with curving armchairs beside. To the right, the bed was a mass of lace and cushions.

"Oh!"

A hiccup. The bed. It was a double. No twins.

He stammered. "I didn't book a double ... it said twin on the receipt ... I'll go downstairs."

Kate laughed. "Well someone thought we were a couple. Oh, it doesn't matter. It's not like it's the first time I'll have had to put up with you in a bed."

No, thought Robin, just the first time sober, a whole other ball game. "Seriously, though, I'm happy to go down and have a word, or try to."

"It's not worth the bother for two nights. Just promise me you won't fart in your sleep."

He saluted her order. "Will try, Ma'am."

"Sorted, so come on then, let's go while there's still plenty of light." She dumped her bag and rummaged for her camera.

"I take it you have a plan?"

"Yup. Up the Grande Armée and on up the Champs-Elysées, all the way to the Louvre."

"You're joking!"

"No way. Three days. Heaps to see. Let's go!"

It was a gorgeous afternoon, warm for early April. The great tree-lined avenues glowed in that soft orange light of a low sun. Paris was truly as beautiful as Robin had heard. Little wonder it was the seat of romance. He watched the crowds bustling about him. Walking the Champs-Elysées was very much

111

the thing to do. Couples, old and young, passed by. It tickled him that the older women were so well turned out, very chic, very Chanel. It was almost surreal. And there was Kate, chattering happily alongside him, stopping at random points to photograph the elegant buildings dappled by the sun through the tall trees out front.

Any weariness from their early start melted away as the fresh foreign breath of this remarkable place enthused them. Robin grew aware of the distance involved in trailing Kate's plans. The look of excitement on her face kept all his protests at bay.

"It's so beautiful here. I know people say it all the time, but I've never believed it so completely. And look, oh, look. It's the pyramid, the Louvre! Can you see it?" She skipped off to clamber up a wall from where she had a better view. "Come on, sit up here!"

They let their feet, hot from the hurried walking, dangle a while as they watched the activity of the park. It seemed most tourists marched to and from the museum. An ice-cream vendor was parked under a large tree. Robin hesitated, daunted by the thought of attempting communication in his altogether dodgy French.

Kate had read his face. "I'll go. What do you want? Deux chocolats, s'il vous plait? Easy!"

She bounced from the wall like a delighted child. It seemed to him that even her step was lighter as she crossed the grass. He didn't take his eyes off her.

"Ah, Kate, Kate. Surely this time you'll figure it out."

As soon as the ice-creams were gone, Kate was off the wall again, raring to go. She wanted photographs, and lots of them. Using the timer she caught them both posing beside the pyramid, seated before the fountain, with the Louvre as a backdrop. All of it.

"Do you want to go in?"

Kate looked at her watch. "Don't be daft. You'd only get an hour for your money. We'll do it in the morning. Early. Straight after breakfast."

At last she agreed it was time to turn back, get to the hotel, freshen up then find somewhere to eat. She wanted to do 'really French', which was fine with him. Anything she wanted would have been.

Kate had brought a dress for the occasion, tiny printed flowers on a navy shift, with dark ribbed tights for the cool evening. Her camera hung, ever-ready, on her shoulder. Robin wore his sand-coloured chinos, with a smart grey blazer. The sun had waned and the top of the Grande Armée was lit by the Arc de Triomphe. What a view!

"Let's find somewhere that looks over this, shall we?" Robin ventured.

Le Jardin Des Champs seemed authentic, down to the snails and horse on the menu displayed on the stand outside. Already busy, they had to make do with a table near, but not in, the window. It was enough. They could watch the Parisians walking briskly by on their business, or the tourists stop to admire the view, or check the menu. From everywhere came the call, 'Garcon!' to the busy waiters.

"Do you fancy champagne, Kate?"

"Isn't that a bit extravagant?"

"Well, yes. But how often do things surpass your expectations?"

113

"True," she agreed. "Let's have it."

She insisted on the snails too. Robin couldn't bring himself to try one.

"You're such a wuss sometimes, you know," she challenged.

"And sometimes that's just fine with me." Robin couldn't remember feeling happier; no one to take Kate's attention from him. And there was still the bed situation to come at the end of the evening. He couldn't remove the thought from his mind.

He'd run through a scenario, several times, as they'd walked the parks to the Louvre. He would whisper to her as she lay beside him, and caress her gently, tell her how much he wanted her. In his version, she would turn to him, threading her limbs through his, drawing her face close saying, 'I know, Robin, I know'. Then they'd kiss, deeply, longingly, until desire could be contained no more.

"Tarte Citron or Crème Caramel, Robin?" She looked hard at him. "Are you miles away?"

He faked a laugh. "Probably tired. All that walking you made me do."

Dinner was finished in easy banter, revisiting highlights of the day. The short walk back to the hotel taken as a slow meander.

The concierge beamed at them. "You are enjoying our beautiful city, non?"

"Oh, definitely," Kate responded. "Absolument."

The concierge nodded. "Bonne nuit. Sleep well," and winked.

Kate got the giggles in the lift.

"D'you reckon they presume everyone's a couple?"

"Probably," his sigh inaudible to her.

She raced him to the bathroom with, "I'm first," and was in the bed three minutes later.

Robin took a little longer, conscious that he wanted to be clean beside her. He lathered himself carefully in the shower with the musky French soap they provided, ensuring not a bit of him was left unwashed or unready.

When he came through to the room he found Kate had claimed the right side of the bed, curled up with her back to the middle. He climbed in. She turned her head towards him.

"Robin?"

His heart skipped a beat. "What?"

"You know the problem with snails?" A pause, then a muffled sound beneath the duvet. "They make you fart!" Kate exploded into noisy laughter.

He shook his head.

She turned away quieting herself. "I won't do that again, I promise. Night-night."

Robin rolled away too, lying a distance away, giving her space to relax. His body was rigid, too conscious of the sweet scent of Kate's shampoo as she turned on her pillow and the quiet whisper of her breathing slowing to rest, too worried that he might seek her out in his sleep, find her and hold on to her, blowing his cover before he had a chance to tell her …

He spent the night drifting in and out of a twilight zone, at times unsure of where he was, and what time it was, what day it was, dreaming he was holding Kate, kissing her. He'd wake sharply, relieved to see she was at the other side of the bed, and the cycle would begin again. He wanted Kate badly. But it would not come to be. Not tonight.

Tiredness must have got the better of him eventually, for when he woke from a deep sleep it was to the sound of her voice, singing in the shower. A few minutes later she surfaced already

115

dressed. Those bathroom walls were going to hide a lot of what he had hoped to see.

He followed suit.

Breakfast had been delivered and Kate devoured a pain au chocolat while scanning a large map. She decided that a combination of the Metro and scenic walks would take them around the key tourist spots in a day. And off they headed, armed with plenty of francs and a camera.

The top of the Arc de Triomphe, with the insane circles of traffic below; a thorough visit of the Louvre, looking over the heads of the Japanese tourist-party to note the disappointing size of the Mona Lisa; the Notre Dame with its grand towers; the site of the Bastille, no Bastille, just a site; back to the Musée D'Orsay, and a fruitless search for the tomb of Napoleon, which left them hysterical. Robin was of the mind that it was exhaustion setting in and begged to be allowed back to the hotel to regain some strength for the evening.

"But we haven't done the Eiffel Tower."

"Aha! I have an idea about that. Let's do it in the dark."

"A sterling idea from you, young Robin," and she linked her arm in his for the walk back.

Already a couple, he thought.

In the twilight they worked their way through the smaller streets of Paris, en route to the tower. Despite adhering strictly to the map, they found themselves clear of the shopping district and amid tall apartment buildings, shuttered up against the chilling night air. They couldn't find it.

"This is ridiculous," said Robin. "According to this it should be right in front of us."

No tower. They tried again, turning the map upside

116

down, reading it the other way round.

Still no tower. Just like the day's search for Napoleon's tomb.

Robin's temper began to fray. He had hopes for this evening. He needed his strength, his composure, his courage. They tried to regain their bearings. Kate laughed.

"Can you imagine," she started, "going up to some passing Parisian and saying, excusez-moi, s'il vous plait, où est La Tour Eiffel? Wouldn't they just piss themselves laughing trying to work out how some dumb English tourist couldn't find their giant creation?"

She was right. He softened. "Let's forget the map. At times like this it's best to be sheep. Follow the crowd … well, that couple there."

She took his elbow and *baa-ed* quietly as they fell into step behind the two in their warm coats with turned up collars, hugging tightly to one another.

The couple raised their faces to the sky. Robin and Kate imitated, and there it was, larger than life, the steel giant, astounding in its intricacy, overwhelming in its strength.

Kate stood open-mouthed.

"At last," Robin gloated. "Kate Pearson is lost for words."

She hit him a playful thump. "Come on. We are going up aren't we?"

They hurried to join the throng of tourists, all undeterred by the sharp drop in the evening temperature, holding fast to their places to be the next on the way up. Robin stood in the line while Kate purchased lift passes.

It was bitterly cold at the top. The wind tore across the sky. But nothing could mar the view. It was spectacular. The whole of Paris lit up below like Christmas in heaven. Robin wanted to pull Kate into his arms, use the pretence of offering

117

protection from the biting wind. He would cradle her, rub her arms, her shoulders. She would fold into him, lift her chin, look to his eyes. Romance. This was the place. Should he try? Was it time?

Kate overrode his hesitancy by standing tight alongside him.

"Fucking freezing," she said.

"Fucking gorgeous," he answered, mimicking her candour.

"It is that. It is," her voice fell away, wandered like there was something on her mind. "Robin."

Another skipped heartbeat. "Yeah?" He forced his voice to remain light, despite his racing thoughts. Did she have it now? Had she finally woken up?

"We are good mates, aren't we? I mean *really* good mates?"

"Sure."

"Y'see, it's being up here. Seeing this stunning scene, from up here, virtually in the sky, and there's Paris, all of beautiful Paris below."

He didn't recognise the tone in her voice, but he wanted to. Oh, how he wanted to.

"It's very moving, isn't it?" She was quiet. "Beauty like this is for sharing, in a special way."

"It is, Kate." He could hardly breathe.

"I was wondering how many of these couples are proposing at this very minute." She didn't look at him. "It's the perfect place."

"It is."

"And then I was thinking, that even though we're *really* good mates, I've never dared to tell you. I thought you'd worked it out a while back, then I wasn't sure anymore. Well, if you're my

118

mate, and I know you are, you'll understand. I want to come back here one day. I want to propose, up here, when I find the woman I love." She cast a glance from the corner of her eye. "You don't think that's stupid, do you?"

Robin felt the blood drain from his arm as it went limp. He felt his heart drain with it.

Kate seemed to notice his change, and held tighter to his arm. "Robin, do you?"

"If it's the person you love, Kate ..." he started, then paused before trying again. "If it's the person you love, how could it be stupid? Come on. Enough of this soppy stuff. Let's find something to thaw us out." A perfect excuse to knock back a few stiff ones, deal with the shock, occupy his mouth.

Kate gave him a hug under the duvet. "I'm so lucky to have a mate like you."

"You're worth it, Kate." He kissed the top of her head before she rolled away.

Robin listened to Kate's breathing deepen beside him. It didn't take long for it to slow further, even out. She rolled back towards him. He stared hard to make out her face in the dark. It bore the innocence of a child at slumber. Totally secure. At ease with the world, at one with herself, her heart.

His chest tightened, his eyes squeezed shut. He cried, silently. With one finger he reached out and traced the side of her face, barely making contact with the skin, lest she move. "But I love you, Kate."

Chapter Six

Helena

Tucked away in a quiet corner of the institutional-green staff room, coffee mug cradled in both hands. Now that was a woman with a comfort craving. Tessa watched as her friend swallowed hard on the coffee, assumedly to force the lump back down her throat.

Tessa scanned the room. Margaret was across the other side in a high-backed armchair like you'd see in a care home, her reading glasses teetering at the end of her nose, intent on the Journal of Abnormal Child Psychology. Natalie was at a desk, head down, scribbling case notes into a folder. Satisfied the two women were too absorbed elsewhere to be listening, Tessa encouraged Helena to carry on.

Helena did. "So, right now, he's packing. The gracious David took the day off work to get it done while I'd be out. Compassion for me, he said. All heart, isn't he?" Helena raised her eyes, their ice-blue shining turquoise behind the veil of tears she somehow managed to suspend from falling. "And, do you know the worst thing? All night, I thought it was going the other way. I'm so embarrassed. I feel such a fool. There it was, ultimatum time, and I was convinced he was going to get his act together and choose me, choose to go for it, for good!"

"So what did he say?"

"Well, we'd agreed to be civilised about it all. So, he'd said he'd get some Chinese food, and we could eat and talk. We opened a chardonnay, and he was very relaxed, smiling and sweet. You know, it was like how we'd always wanted it to be, together in our own place, surrounded by our joint-purchases over the last couple of years, his videos lined up with mine, his books amongst the shelves. I was just noticing the other day, how he had permeated every corner of every room. His Assam beside my Earl Grey in the kitchen. His aftershave beside my moisturiser. His unopened cardboard boxes beside mine in the spare room." Helena made a small, sharp wave in front of her face, swatting the thought as you would a fly. "It felt cosy. Right. And we got talking about the good times, the fun things we did together. I still didn't see it coming. It felt so positive. We opened more wine, lit the fire. And I know, so don't shout at me, we ended up making love. It was so beautiful," she crooned, almost apologetically. "I felt so close to him. It was the best we'd had in ages. All I could think of was how perfect it all was, and how this was how I wanted things to be. Then I walked into it. Lying in his arms, staring at the fire, I said to him, full of presumption, smiling at him, 'So you've come to a decision'. I felt his shoulder stiffen under my head, and he said, 'I thought you realised that'. I hadn't realised anything."

Tessa reached out and stroked Helena's hand. "You poor thing."

Helena sniffed back the emotion. "So there I am, lying in his arms, having just given the man what he wants and more, and he says, 'You deserve better than me, Helena, someone who will love you like you need to be loved. I'm too fickle. You're right. I'm not ready for commitment. I wish I was. You're a wonderful woman', blah, blah. All meaningless crap. Sorry."

The staffroom door opened, snapping Helena from her melancholic dwelling. "Oh, my eleven o'clock!" She stood up in a hurry, and tried to smile at Jackie who'd just walked in. "Tessa will fill you in, Jackie. I have to get organised. Still have a job to do."

Jackie poured a coffee and sat down in the vacated chair.

"So, how'd it go?"

"He's a slimy bastard, that one. He even wangled a farewell shag, the pig. I'm glad she's rid of him, not that we can tell her that yet, love her. That woman could have her pick of any man, and she just doesn't see it."

"Sounds like a girls' night is a major necessity. Let's hit the town, get smashed and chat up random hunks."

"Sorry, did she look she was in the mood to party to you?"

"It's what I'd do," Jackie defended herself, shoving a hand through her black hair to re-spike her choppy cut. "Tequila, noise, boys! Our Helena really needs to be reminded that she's bloody gorgeous and deserves a bit of fun."

"Helena is so not you. But perhaps you're right, if we're to stop her from wallowing. A night out might do it, something that keeps conversation to a minimum."

"Let's check out who's on at the NIA, and see if we can grab a few late tickets."

They reconvened at lunchtime over their sandwiches, the staff room lively with the break from clients.

Jackie laid on the drama, her voice a deep tenor. "Now, ladies, contain yourselves because I have discovered, for your complete enjoyment ..." her voice crumbled into a wary question, "the Riverdance Tour?"

Tessa winced slightly, awaiting Helena's reaction.

Helena retained the art of surprise. "You know, I'd be quite interested in seeing that. Something different."

"Consider it done. Saturday okay with everyone?" Nods all round.

They'd decamped to The Colonnade Bar after the show. The NIA was way too brightly lit to hang about in. Tessa and Helena were still poring over the cocktail list, distracted from the choices by intermittent comments on the show.

"Pleasantly surprised. Seriously," Jackie announced. "So what's the order?"

Tessa started again. "I loved that bit where the—"

"Not another word until drinks are in hand," Jackie cut in.

"Okay, okay. Cuba Libra," said Helena.

"Brandy Alexander for me," requested Tessa.

Jackie headed to the bar and Tessa continued her appraisal of the show, "... where the dance steps echoed the drums, and as the music grew more complicated, their feet kept up."

"I know. Amazing. How fit are they?" said Helena.

Jackie was back.

"That was quick," said Tessa.

"Yeah, and the cute barman will deliver our drinks, ladies," Jackie winked. "But back to the show. Bizarre way for those Irish to dance," she said taking her seat. "Completely upright and stiff and legs flying every which way. Don't you think? All lined up and kicking like a centipede on speed."

Helena gave a half smile, barely acknowledging the humour. "Incredible composure. It's a wonder they keep it looking so elegant."

The drinks arrived and Jackie smiled overtly as she tipped the cute teen-barman generously – too generously.

Tessa was quick to check her friend. "Girls' night means girls' night!"

"Shame," said Jackie, watching the retreating young butt. But Jackie toed the line and continued the conversation. "The finale did it for me. How many people did they have on that stage? At least thirty I'd say, and every one of those legs kicking in time. Wasn't the sound of it powerful? I mean really powerful, like a huge march, a million footsteps keeping time. I suppose that makes a lot of centipedes." She shrugged and smiled.

"Quite moving, really." Helena was on the brink. "That piece with the pipes, it was haunting. It jarred my heart and made me want to weep, though I couldn't say why."

Jackie patted Helena's hand. "Darling, of course you could say why. That's why we're out to play. It's meant to distract you. But none of us are pretending it's all fine."

"Thanks, girls," said Helena, sniffing back her melancholy, then took a good swallow of her Cuba Libra. "Come on, let's do a bit of people watching, some Desmond Morris versus Johnny Morris."

Tessa ran a fantastic murder plot for a table in the far right consisting of older looking men, slightly too-heavily endowed with gold.

"So, you in?"

"Dunno. You gonna kill my bruv?"

"That'll be extra. I'll need me mate Johnny for that."

"Don't care who you need. Take 'im out."

"You after 'is missus, then?"

"None o' your business, mate!"

"Orright, orright!"

Next, she teamed up with Jackie to provide a running commentary on an all-girls table eyeing up the talent of an all-boys table.

"I like the look of the blonde one meself."

"Look again, Chardonnay, he's wearing mascara!"

"He isn't!"

"He is. And 'is hair's sprayed stiff."

"Might not be the only thing."

"Yeah, if you're a cute bloke giving 'im the eye!"

"What about the guy with the afro?"

"Doll, you are way too high-maintenance for him!"

"Cow! I bet you'd do alright wiv the tattooed fella."

"Not sure he'd be man enough for me, you knowotimean?"

Helena brought it to a giggling conclusion by taking on the thoughts of a particular boy who was actually eyeing up one of the lads on his table, then went solo on a couple keeping to themselves in the corner.

She started with a serious, *"I might be pregnant."* Then gave the bloke a high-pitched Geordie accent. *"Ma mum sez yeh can't get preggers joost kissin'."* She fell back into her own voice. "Actually, do you know who he does look like? Remember Richard?"

The women nodded.

Helena was recovering from Richard when she'd joined them at the Youth Mental Health Team at Sutton Coldfield. "Yeah, he looked quite like that. Now there's a blast from the past. I never did tell you all of that story, did I? I didn't really know you well enough."

"Hold it right there," cut in Jackie. "I don't want any interruptions for this story so I'm going to get us a bottle of wine. Yeah?"

Jackie and Tessa had often debated the Richard story, intrigued by Helena's silence on the matter. They'd invented some outrageous scenarios themselves at times and suspected that the truth may not be so exciting. Nevertheless, they wanted the real thing. Who didn't love gossip?

The cute teen-barman looked even younger as he delivered a bottle of sauvignon blanc and three glasses, with a wide smile to Jackie. She ignored him, waiting intently for Helena to begin her story.

"I met him in my final year at university. Edinburgh, we

were. A fancy dress party. Rocky Horror Show of all things which was probably why he managed to get in. The only bloke with the nerve to wear a lab coat with suspenders and heels. A friend of mine, Mel, had arranged it in connection with the Fine Arts Society and set it to coincide with an exhibition of life drawings. It was supposed to be exclusive to final year students but a few opportunistic second years fancied their chances of a night with the big boys. He was such a charmer. I swear the man should have become a TV interviewer or journalist. He so quickly engaged people in conversation about themselves that their egos were enjoying the massage too much to question his legitimacy. It only came out when Mel and another girlfriend, Perry, and a few others got talking in the Ladies comparing notes, that someone registered none of us knew who he was. I offered to flush him out, thought I'd rope him in with my womanly wiles, then out him as an impostor once he was vulnerable. Of course, it didn't happen that way. You think it would have occurred to me that the girls weren't comparing notes without reason. I'd never met anyone so entirely beguiling, and it had nothing to do with his taste in shoes." Helena laughed softly, then turned serious again. "I haven't since, actually. He had a presence, a stirring bearing about him that was palpable. He was in no way dominating or pushy. He was just so *there*. Most of all though, was the eye-contact. He had this way of paying total and complete attention to whomever he was speaking with. It made you feel like you were the only person in the world. Nothing distracted his gaze. It was thoroughly disarming, without appearing intentional. I was hooked, much to my embarrassment. I made up some story to the girls that he was legit, and on some obscure course that we had little contact with. It didn't take long for us to become an item. On one level, I didn't want it to happen at all. I'd had a good time at university. I had my fun, ladies, but I was avoiding serious attachment. I've heard too many stories of these couples who are all over one another at university then rapidly go their separate ways when the demands of career-climbing become an issue. I thought I might keep it light then move on. Somehow it just grew, and he didn't want to end it when I graduated, even though I landed a post back down in Oxford near Mum. We didn't see one another much that last year of his. He said it was perfect. He could focus on studying, without me to distract him, and I could focus on making an impression at work. It was still a bit of a surprise when he wanted to job hunt around Oxford. He got an assistant editor post in an academic publishing house, and we found a flat. It was all very easy. One step followed another, and by the end of two years we were engaged to be married. We planned the wedding for the best part of two years further on down the line, and spent the time organising a mortgage for a better place of our own, and doing lots of family stuff with his and mine, in preparation for the big day."

Tessa interrupted. "I didn't realise you two were married."

Helena smiled a wide-eyed smile. "I'm not finished yet."

"Oh, come on, what happened then?" Tessa topped up the girls' glasses.

"In a nutshell, my dad and mum actually came together to finance this huge 'do' for their one and only, overcoming their own differences to give me the reception I apparently deserved. They were fantastic about it all. We had a beautiful hotel booked and ready, dresses were bought and lovely, guests were invited and presents arrived daily. I remember arguing with Richard about a week before. He was supposed to have arranged for his best man and ushers to have final fittings for their morning suits. I was tense and Richard was as calm as ever. I did lose it a bit, so he promised to sort everything before the guys were due to head off on the stag weekend. Apparently they did, 'cos I had a call from his mobile on the Friday afternoon to tell me sweetly, that everything was fine and there was no problem with any of the suits. He told me he loved me, and not to be too worried about the stag thing as he trusted his friends to give him a really good time, but to return him safely home. And that was it."

"What do you mean, that was it?" Jackie asked.

"I never saw him again."

"What?" It was Tessa's turn to ask. "You mean he went off on his stag do, never to return?"

"Yup, that's exactly it. Richard didn't even call his parents. It was a case of getting too late on Sunday night, and worrying that they hadn't got back. Ironic as I'd no idea where they'd gone in the first place. All a big secret and surprise for him. Nobody else knew, as I was to discover. On the Monday, I had to start contacting the housemates and girlfriends of the guys he'd gone away with. Everyone else had made it back, and they believed all had gone their separate ways after leaving London. No one had heard from him. Over the next couple of days no one had any unusual events to recall, no strange or out-of-place comments over the weekend which had apparently been hilarious fun. My poor mum took it upon herself to contact his family. They thought we were joking, you know, giving them a last minute fright. It took quite some convincing to put across the few facts we had."

Jackie threw back a drink. "You must have been in such a state. I can't begin to imagine—"

"Don't even go there. I think fear that he was dead somewhere dominated at first, blanking any possibility that he'd just changed his mind. Finally, on the Thursday, with just forty-eight hours to go, an orchid was delivered to the flat with a note saying, 'I'm sorry. Richard'."

Tessa's jaw hung agape. "Not even a phone call, no explanation?"

"No." Helena was factual. "I never got an explanation."

"What, never ever?" asked Jackie.

"No. I did the hysterical bit of calling his family, then calling all his friends, asking them all if they had any idea what happened, why he'd changed his mind, where he'd gone. Nobody knew a single thing. No one. At least we were all reeling in shock. Then of course there was the mortification of contacting everyone to tell them the wedding was off. I hated him for that. My parents had to do his dirty work without any sort of excuse from him. His family apologised a million times for him, and carried their share of the expenses. I felt for them on that, 'cos they only did it for me and still without a word from him."

"So how was it all left?"

"On a very practical level. Everything cancelled. Presents returned, ties severed. Just like that. He never wrote or called. To this day I don't know what happened, why he made such an about-turn. All my psychology training has entertained me with a few theories, but never knowing why was pretty hard to bear. It was a long time before I could believe it wasn't fundamentally my fault."

Helena turned away from the 'I'd never have guessed that was in your life' and the 'my God, I couldn't have coped' looks. She spotted two men looking roughly in the direction of their table and put on a gruff voice, again playing the game. *"Quite like the spiky haired one myself. You take the blonde. But how are we going to get rid of that middle one? Looks too intense for me. I'm just up for a one-nighter."*

She had them laughing again.

"You did the right thing, moving away and making a

fresh start," announced Tessa.

"Absolutely. I came up here and found two like-minded lunatics to play with. I even felt brave enough to get involved with someone again, albeit an erroneous choice. But that's fine. It's all growth, all progress. But I do believe I've done enough personal reformation for the time being. So I'm going to have a rest. I am going to spend some quality time with myself for a while. I change too much when I get into a relationship. I spend too much time and energy trying to be everything the other person wants, and ultimately, I lose sight of myself. I want to find it within myself to enjoy being alone for a while, relearn my childhood skills."

Jackie and Tessa burst into mini-applause.

It was Jackie who delivered the accolade. "A perfect client, wouldn't you say, Miss King? Write up the process notes."

Chapter Seven

Hal

Hal sat in his impeccable lounge with a large glass of full-bodied claret, catching up with the world's financial market on his wide-screen TV when the phone rang. He stepped into the hallway, pristine white with a large, ornate mirror above the only piece of furniture, a neat ebony table on which sat the shiny black phone.

Natalie, his younger sister by two years, sounded animated. "I have some news."

"And what news might that be, Nat?"

Hal watched his reflection as he spoke, quietly admiring the image he'd perfected over the years. A keen climber from the age of fourteen, the development of strong pecs, biceps and the ever-enviable abs, was a happy consequence rather than a painful teenage austerity. He'd maintained his physique by taking a position in the forces in the Physical Training Corps. Though he hated army life, it was the perfect springboard for a career in the real world where he was snapped up by the Moorfield Community Sports Facility close to the family home in Solihull. He was the instigator of several exciting projects directed at a wider spread of the community. His speciality had become team-building weekends for corporate bodies, and abseiling events for local and national charities.

Yes, he looked good.

"Your favourite fantasy has just come back on the market," announced his sister.

"No way! Did she finally dump the loser, then?"

"I think *he* dumped *her* actually."

"Shit, is the man blind as well as thick?"

"Hal, if you're going to gush, I'm going to hang up."

"Aw, come on. I'm sorry, sis. Fill me in."

Natalie Preston provided what information she could from her eavesdropping in the staffroom at the Youth Unit. She had little, if any, direct contact with Helena, as Natalie specialised in counselling children, and Helena was the Clinical Psychologist attached to the young adult bracket.

Natalie wasn't sure she actually liked the woman herself – one of those with the ability to attract too much attention without any apparent effort. She could see that Helena possessed a natural charm, and a great figure, but she lacked something that Natalie couldn't quite put her finger on. That wasn't Hal's opinion after he'd met her. Well, to say 'met' would be an exaggeration, but Hal liked to see it that way.

Natalie had recommended Hal, as a little sister does, when the unit's new Senior Psychiatrist had taken over last summer and wanted to participate in a getting-to-know-you-out-of-the-office thing. They ended up with a day of assault courses and abseiling from the fire station training tower. Natalie knew her brother too well not to notice how he'd clocked Helena within the first two minutes. She made light of it, teasing him for his *Lara Croft* fantasy, and that only fuelled his lust, for in his reply he explained he hadn't registered any likeness, but now that she pointed it out …

There was Helena, in her combat style shorts, sturdy hiking boots, and a tight t-shirt accentuating her perfect bosom. To top it off, she'd plaited her auburn hair out of her way. Hal had to work hard to divide his attention evenly among the group that day. Natalie cringed more than once at the speed of his assistance when Helena looked like she might require some.

Helena was just as speedy in telling him she didn't. Assertive little madam. Hal liked her all the more for it, even if it cut short any legitimate touching as she ascended the climbing-wall.

That evening Natalie hadn't even made it to the shower when the phone rang. "Christ, Hal, you're embarrassing me now," she'd told him.

"But she's gorgeous," he'd whinged.

"And cohabiting, brother dear. Get over it. My shower's running." She'd left him hanging. As she stood beneath the hot spray, she asked herself why she felt so narked. She knew that some part of it was a jealousy of Helena, but she chose not to look at it that way, deciding instead that she was just possessive of her handsome big brother, as he always was with her. It was like that every time he started seeing someone. It didn't matter. Helena hadn't been available then, so end of story.

That was last year. Now Natalie had the opportunity to inform her brother of Helena's availability. She could have said nothing, but if he ever found out she'd known, she was afraid her silence would damage something between them.

"Natalie? Nat? Are you still there?"

"Sorry, Hal, distracted by the cat. Mmm, where were we?"

"When did all this happen? When did the louse cut loose?"

"Before Christmas, actually back in the beginning of November. I held off telling you a while because I didn't want you rushing in with your size-twelves to get rejected out-of-hand on the rebound."

"That's very thoughtful of you, sis. You going soft on me?"

"As if! Just fed up with you asking me about her all the time. I'm giving you the chance to do your own dirty work. And of course, I'm trying to find some hapless female to take you off

133

my hands."

"You sweetie. So what gameplay should I employ this time?"

"Oh, please, Hal, I'm drawing the line there. You're a big boy now. Just remember she's been through a hard time. Try being romantic."

Hal lifted the claret to his lips. As he did, the light from the table lamp passed through the fluid, the colour intensified in its luminescence. "Roses. Deep, red, beautiful roses. Come around tomorrow, sis, I owe you one."

Helena had just brought a young man of seventeen to closure. It hadn't been an easy case and she was feeling justifiably satisfied with herself. He suffered Borderline Personality Disorder that rendered him incapable of maintaining meaningful connections with other people. His family had failed to notice that there was an identifiable problem, and found him awkward and unloving, slowly rejecting him as a social outcast. He hadn't fared much better with his peers, taking the brunt of much physical bullying in his young years and emotional exclusion in the last few. Helena was pleased to have diagnosed his condition relatively early in their sessions, and had worked hard to build a pathway forward for him. He was leaving her armed with a strong network in place, externally and internally, to embark on the next stretch of his life.

It didn't always work out so positively. A high proportion of the younger clients were inclined to drop out of counselling after only a few sessions, unable to face their difficulties, or unwilling to take the necessary measures to break free of their limitations, preferring instead to blame their parents, their peers, the world.

No matter what the reason for their failure, Helena took all these cases personally, like somehow she had failed to make a connection or provide the right hook for these people to grasp, a shred of hope that things really could change. She understood that to be there and to listen was invaluable of itself. Nonetheless, she was happiest if she felt she'd helped someone one step further on from where she'd met them. Her mind was elsewhere as she walked into the staffroom for a well-earned coffee.

Several faces lifted towards her. She looked down over herself quickly fearing a burst button, an undone zip, or a streak of toothpaste on her black top. Finding nothing immediate and eyes still on her, she began to flush. "What is it? What have I done?"

Her supervisor, Brian, watched her with a smile. "I didn't realise it was your birthday, Helena. I'd have bought you a card."

"It's not my birthday. Why?" It was then that the flash of colour on the counter caught her eye. Two dozen identically-shaped red roses sat in a haze of gypsophila. They glowed blood-red, wine-red, and were beautiful.

"Well, aren't you going to look at them?" asked Jackie.

"What the roses? They're gorgeous. Who owns them?"

"You do, you dark horse. What haven't you been telling?"

No reply.

"You could stand there and guess your way around your known universe, or you could read the card," Jackie coaxed.

Helena reached forward, and withdrew. "What if it's—"

"Mr Ultimatum? I'm pretty sure that's a closed deal."

"A grateful client?" Helena posed tentatively.

"Only if you're shagging them in the armchair, love."

"Okay, okay!" and she reached her fingers forward once

more.

Hal was chasing overweight estate agents up the climbing-wall. Physically, he was behind them. Vocally, he was egging on their every move. Mentally, he was watching a film wherein the beautiful woman who'd captured his heart was flushed with pleasure as she gazed upon his message attached to a bouquet so glorious it conveyed one word, 'love'.

He was besotted. He didn't mind. It was what he had expected one day, an attraction to someone beyond pure lust. A vision of a woman whom he'd know was all his from the outset, and one he was sure to win, eventually, for she'd know she was his too. Adoration, control, obedience. Hal's love.

"Hal? Hal Preston?" Helena looked around the room for his sister, Natalie, but she was nowhere to be seen. "Why is Hal Preston sending me roses?"

"Let me read it." Jackie tendered a palm for the card. "'You are never far from my thoughts. I would love to see you again. Hal'." Jackie's face cracked into a wide grin. "I should have seen that one coming on our team-building weekend. He couldn't take his eyes off you. Mind you, what poor man could with that t-shirt clinging to your tits? And I had him down as one of those physicality-equals-lust types. Oh, the poor bugger. That's been ages. And he's been watching and waiting patiently ever since." The grin dissolved into a soppy, gooey-eyed smile.

"Get a grip, Jackie." Helena was sharp in tone.

"Oh, come on, aren't you impressed? Slightly?"

"Well, it's a text book move. I presume he expects a text book response."

"And what will that be?"

"I haven't decided yet." Helena tried to absorb a share of Jackie's enthusiasm for the romance of it all. She tried to let a little warmth into her bones. Yes, she'd been aware of Hal on the course. He wasn't one to be missed. And yes, she'd noticed him giving her the once over, more than once. That was something she'd become used to. It wasn't something she liked. Anyway, she had not long been kicked out of what seemed a stable relationship. She wasn't in the frame of mind for playing with anyone. "I'll think about it."

At home, she had trouble finding a space for the glass vase housing the bouquet. She wanted the blooms in a corner, only somewhat in her vision, so as not to harass her.

Nothing worked.

The bouquet was too generous. It demanded the centre of her circular table. She shook her head. The roses would obliterate the view of anyone who might be at the table with her. In fact, they obliterated her view of the rest of the room. She crossed to the sofa, and looked back. There was no question as to their beauty. But how they dominated the room.

How dare they dominate *her* house with *their* question!

How dare Hal dominate *her* thoughts by imposing *his!*

She could feel him waiting, pressured by his generosity (must be forty pounds worth, at least) and his public declaration of his interest. Even all the staff at the unit were on his side, demanding compliance in their romantic pipe dreams. They would be keenly waiting for her answer. The answer – how was that to be given?

Helena had no number for him, no address. So she was drawn into the game. She would have to pursue him in some way to provide a response. Even a negative would require effort, involvement. Very clever, Mr Preston, she allowed. You demand that I work on this.

Helena was angry. I could track you down via work, and make my statement as you have, she planned to herself. Except that's not quite how you did it, is it? No, we have a sister involved. Jesus, there are already three people in this relationship and it hasn't even started! And what answer? What are you expecting of me? If I say no, Natalie will know, and word will travel that the cold-hearted Miss Helena Callender wouldn't grant the romantic sod the grace of meeting for a drink. So maybe I should meet you for a drink. Then what? Two dozen red roses don't say, I'm vaguely interested. No, they say, I fancy your arse and I want to get into your knickers. They're a deposit on a sure thing. Kinda, owe you a quickie for a gesture so grand. How dare you be so bloody presumptuous! I didn't even talk to you.

Helena caught her mental breath, fully expired after her silent tirade. She paused, then burst out laughing.

"What is the matter with me?" she said out loud. "Some poor man apparently languishes with overwhelming feelings for me, and when he finally gets the opportunity to make his move, I curse him to hell for his rampant chauvinism. I spend years hoping someone would take such a romantic step, and when it happens, I see it as some form of manipulation."

She made herself a large cup of tea, and settled in front of the TV to give her mind a rest. After a soap and an episode of a docu-drama, she was able to take a step back from herself, as she had been trained to do, to view the interaction objectively. She decided that Hal's desires and attentions were irrelevant in this whole scenario. What was interesting was the ferocity and negativity of her reaction. She did not fully comprehend it. What she did know was that this was no time for her to be in a relationship. She'd had enough of the games, enough of the power struggle. She was not enjoying the male-female dynamic.

138

It had become too much like hard work and she no longer trusted it. She had no faith in it.

And that's fine, she started silently again. I actually mean that. It's fine. I do not have to live in search of the perfect man any more, or in search of the perfect relationship. It is irrelevant. All that matters right now is that I find my own happiness in being me.

She sent him a note. Gratitude. Flattered. Rejection.

Chapter Eight

Caroline

Some kind of progress was finally indicated in the case notes. It had come about slower than most. Caroline had resisted taking responsibility for her anger, choosing to see it as a result of her situation rather than an integral cause. Caroline believed that her aggressive outbursts were entirely attributable to a build-up of frustration at her mother's insipidity and weakness. She'd had enough of her mother's inverted sexism, and was fed up trying to balance the household herself. So she struck out.

She'd slapped her mother hard in the face, and her mother had immediately cowered and apologised. Furious at this further display of weakness, Caroline had punched her in the stomach repeatedly, until one of her brothers heard the commotion and intervened. All the way to the hospital, her mother still excused her, saying how she was just upset and didn't mean any harm.

It was three weeks ago that Caroline had left for school before her father or brothers made it downstairs. Ridiculously early it was, but she couldn't face them. She was still angry. Fire and fury pulsed through her veins. She kicked the living daylights out of cans and stones as she walked along the unevenly paved street. She glowered at people passing by, daring someone to pick on her so she might vent this rage. She begged she might fall prey to the girl gangs that hung around the unused garages, loud-mouthed girls calling out obscenities to passing lads, waiting to torture the younger kids heading to school. But no luck came from that wish. She was too big for them to make her a target.

A hundred yards from the school gates, she dropped her

bag to the pavement, drawing her army knife from her coat pocket. She flicked the blade, clenched her fist, clenched even tighter, then clenched her teeth.

It hurt.

She found a handkerchief in the other pocket and packed it into the palm of her hand. She laid the strap of her bag across the top of the new wound then raised her arm to let the hand take the weight of the bag.

At the end of registration, Caroline held back to see her form tutor alone. With only the two of them left in the room, Caroline extended her hand. The saturated cotton unfolded like some exotic blossom. "I need to talk to someone."

And she did.

"We took the train into town. I bunked a day off school to do it, 'cos she wouldn't have gone on a Saturday. Too busy. Too many people. Mum doesn't like being in big crowds."

Helena watched as her client described her day out with her mother. Caroline had made an obvious effort with her appearance today. Her hair had been tied back during all of their previous sessions. Left loose, it was feminine, falling in soft blonde waves. It added another dimension to her character, her sexuality. Helena thought she could see a hint of blusher on those broad, high cheekbones, and a touch of mascara on her lashes. Helena didn't want to look too hard. She didn't want to inhibit this natural development of her sixteen-year-old client's journey of self-knowledge. Changes in her image were a natural part of the course. She wished it wouldn't be unprofessional to comment.

"I suppose it went well while we were in the shops. We picked things up, said things about them, admired colours, even kinda complimented one another. Stuff like, that blue jumper would really suit you. That kind of thing. I'd thought a long time about being kind to her, like you said, kind but not pitying. So when we were in Boots I got her to smell their fancy bath range. I chose one, lavender for relaxing, and bought it for her. She didn't say a lot, but she smiled. So I suppose that's good.

"It was harder when we went for lunch. Maybe that was pushing it a bit. For a start, she's not dead familiar with foreign food, and that includes lasagne and bolognese. So she was a bit worried about finding something she liked. It was okay, though, 'cos they had battered plaice with fries. That was one hurdle. Then we had to sit there, facing one another over a tiny table and make small talk. That was really hard. The two of us have only ever been together over chores, so it's all instructions and teamwork. It's not conversation. She asks how school is, of course she does, and I say fine.

"I know it's been my snobbery. She left school so young I presumed she knew nothing. I didn't even allow her the dignity of an opinion. I've been a right cow, haven't I?"

Helena permitted Caroline a long and apparently painful pause.

"I've been just like my dad."

Her eyes were wide and moist as they focussed in trust on her counsellor. For a moment the beauty of realisation radiated in her face. Helena wished she could tell Caroline of it. It would not be appropriate. If Caroline maintained course, it wouldn't be long before she might see her beauty herself.

"How has it been with your father since our last session?"

Caroline's radiance was reabsorbed, a harsher edge to her bones again. "Men! They're so pig-headed!" Caroline looked directly at Helena again. "Don't *you* think?"

"That's a generalisation, Caroline. But it may be your experience."

"Well, you know that's the case. This one time, we went on holiday to Greece. Bit of a joke really. Foreign country, big resort, full of English pubs and restaurants. Mum agreed to try a real Greek place one night. She ate pie and chips. But the waiter, first he's chatting up Mum, in front of Dad, said his name was Andreas or something. I almost admired his nerve. But when he got no response, he followed me when I went to the loo and asked if I wanted to do something afterwards, with this big sleazy smile. I mean, the man was short, ugly and well into his forties. Who wants that?"

Caroline had a different note in her voice, one Helena hadn't encountered before and didn't recognise. She made a mental note to rethink it later.

"Tell me anyway," Helena coaxed, "how's your father?"

The session ended.

They were on tri-weekly sessions now so that Caroline could do some quality homework in between. Most of the dirty work was done: the pain, the fear, and ugliness raked up and over. Caroline was rebuilding, and for the time being, her mother and father appeared to be assisting, in their way. To Caroline, her brothers were irrelevant. She lived quite independently of them, and seemed to be absorbing nothing of them. The relationships, or lack of, were of no detriment to Caroline, and were of no immediate concern to Helena.

As she drew the notes together, that tone in Caroline's voice rang in her head. It was the way she said, don't you think, with the emphasis on 'you'.

Me.

Helena.

Directly asking me to agree that men are pig-headed.

She thinks she has something on me, decided Helena. She thinks she's found a connection, a connection of experience.

Helena flicked through the notes of earlier sessions, when she herself spoke more openly to encourage Caroline to open up. She searched for hints at what she might have said. Had she been personal? She was certain she had not. It simply wasn't how she worked. No. Page after page evoked nothing. No compromise. Helena continued writing up the day.

Again, Caroline's voice, 'well, you know' … the same emphasis on 'you'. Different meaning this time, not the 'girls like us' feeling, something lighter, a hint of something amusing … playful … flirtatious.

Caroline was flirting with her!

How did I not see that one coming? The traits are all there, she chastised herself. Weak, victimised mother, rampant sexism and male dominance, over-relation to male parent, adoption or exaggeration of male gender traits. The girl's gay. Caroline is gay. And she knows it. Or is coming to know it. That's the vague sexual-type vibe I felt today. She's working on it. Well, good for her. Hmm. That could be part of the suppressed energy behind that temper too. I can't believe I almost missed that.

Helena finished the notes with a comment about her expectation that Caroline may feel ready to raise the issue soon. She'd prepare, read up on some of the more recent research in a few journals, be ready to guide the girl properly.

Reception buzzed through to tell Helena that Caroline was waiting. She had decided to draw Caroline away from talk of family today. She wanted to explore her other relationships, get more of her take on gender issues amongst her peers, if she'd let her.

Caroline's long hair was loose again. She wore a skirt –

casual, denim, and long – not what you'd describe as girly exactly. Definitely female though. In light of her present theory, Helena found it an interesting position to take. It was more common for girls who understood their lesbianism to reject the overtly feminine, at least for a while. Hair was often cut short or kept unkempt, skin make-up free, and trousers adopted. All rejections of the stereotypical male expectations of female attractiveness.

"I want to look a bit further afield today, Caroline, if that's alright with you?"

"Sure. What are we looking at?"

"Relationships with others generally. You're making great progress at home. Let's look at extending it." A professional white lie. "Let's start with early friends, primary school, that sort of age."

Stories of childhood games with children playing in the streets flowed thick and fast. Physical games. Much running and pushing and chasing. Adventures too, in gangs with the freedom to clear off for a few hours from under parents' feet. Caroline was animated, smiling at the memories. Helena pursued more detail on the friends.

The majority were boys, and the games never included playing house, or mummies and daddies.

"Doctors and nurses was one game I played but only with nurses. I remember thinking it was an exciting game. Not scary-exciting like climbing onto the roofs of the garages at the flats. Naughty-exciting." Caroline blushed.

Helena smiled, serene. "Most children play it at some point. So where were the doctors?"

"On call," Caroline laughed. "No, not really, we weren't that clever. It's the only time I remember getting 'in' with the other girls. We didn't want the boys in on our game. It was a novelty for me. We didn't do anything really bad." She was suddenly defensive. "We took turns pulling down one another's knickers and examining bums and things. Each one of us was as interested as the next."

"How did you feel about that?"

"Never really thought about it. Didn't play with the girls again." Caroline broke her usually consistent eye contact indicating a degree of untruth, in some part of that statement at least.

"Take me forward a few years," Helena invited.

"When I think about it, I spent a lot of time playing with boys. I put it down to William and Des. They always had mates dropping in. There were always blokes about. I got the feeling Dad told them to watch out for me. So it was easier for them to teach me boy games and make me fit in with them. It was fine. I liked it. Gave me a sort of superiority over the girls in our street, 'cos I was involved in stuff they weren't. Then Mum blew it by sending me to St. Mary Magdalene for secondary."

"You've not mentioned your mum's religious affiliations before."

"That's because she didn't have any. No. She started to get particular about the time I spent with the boys, with the threat of puberty coming up and that. She suggested to Dad that I be sent to an all-girls school, and he actually listened to her. That was a first.

"You have to laugh. Mary Magdalene wasn't exactly the best behaved woman in the bible, was she? Oh, it was all right once I got over the shock of seeing just girls everywhere. You know, there were hardly any male teachers, half a dozen at most. Yeah, it was a nice atmosphere once I got used to it. Not the same kind of aggro and competition that you get from boys on just about everything, including pissing and eating. I stopped

146

spending so much time with the boys from then. It was weird, hard kinda. Part of me wanted their physical games, yet the rest of me became aware of their stupidity, how they never really share stuff in a deep way. And then it was weird on the other side 'cos the girls would get all deep and I hadn't a clue what to say. I just didn't know how to at first. And they were stupid another way, spending ages talking about their hair and make-up and clothes like it was really interesting. Anyway, I got used to being around them in the end. I suppose I started to quite like it." Caroline threw a look, quickly connecting with Helena's studious gaze, and then it was gone again.

Helena was cool. No mistaking it this time, a definite flirtation. Caroline didn't add any further conversation. She stared out the window, lost in thought. Helena watched her closely. Her face appeared unemotional, no flashes of pain or traces of rising tears. Her gaze ambled over the lawn, up and down the trees, around the shrubbery. The traffic of the nearby motorway hummed quietly in the background as the minutes eased by.

Finally, Caroline's focus returned to the room. "I am a lesbian," she stated calmly.

"I'd like you to tell me how you reached that conclusion."

"I realised pretty quickly at secondary school. I knew I liked the girls, just not necessarily in the way they liked me. I had a crush on my form tutor for three years! So much is put down to puberty, rampant hormones and all that. I waited. I watched how I was feeling. Hormones settled and I still felt the same. I thought about boys too. I've spent enough time with them, haven't I? They're great mates, and some are probably my best mates. Maybe that's why, 'cos when it comes down to it, I'm a lot like them. I fancy the girls too." Caroline smiled.

Helena was impressed with the girl's composure. It couldn't have been easy. They'd been seeing one another for two months now, and there'd been no hint of it before. Perhaps she'd thought her counsellor a bit useless and unintuitive. Regardless, she'd made her move. She'd come out.

"How do you feel about me now?" Caroline put to her.

It wasn't Helena's place to express feelings about her clients. Emotional detachment for objectivity, care for the individual's growth from a professional base. Nothing more. She wondered if she needed to spell this all out to Caroline. It would sound cold. It wasn't what she needed. But what did she need? Caroline's question was so unusual of her. She had rendered herself vulnerable. Not her style at all. Helena was aware she was taking too long to answer. Play it safe, she thought. If in doubt, use ultimate professionalism.

"Caroline, I am very proud of you, your self-knowledge, your courage, your composure. Well done. Well done." Helena caught sight of the clock. "We can continue to talk about this some more when I see you again, if you wish."

"Yes, I'd like that."

Aspects of the session continued to sit uneasily with Helena. She decided to sleep on it, knowing that the peculiarities would soon work their way free of the rest of the mass, highlighting themselves for her attention. It took three days, and ended up hinged on that one question. How do you feel about me now? At last it was clear. She had read Caroline's earlier flirtations as experimental, possibly subconscious as she prepared to come out. But it ran deeper than that. Caroline had developed feelings for her. Not the oft-encountered over-attachment on a dependency level, but feelings. An emotional attachment. A sexual attachment. More than that, she wanted them reciprocated. That's what the question was about. A subtle proposition.

Damn it! This could, no, this *would* compromise their working relationship, ruin it completely. What to do? A meeting with her supervisor was in order.

Brian perused the case history before meeting with Helena. "Come in. Tea?"

"Coffee, please."

Brian gestured towards the soft sofa and Helena smiled. "Not putting me in the client's chair, then?"

"Do I need to?" he joked back bringing two mugs to the table.

"No, it's nothing serious, just need a sounding board, that's all."

"I believe that's in my job description. Share."

"I think my young lesbian is coming on to me, and I'm checking my mirror. I'm concerned that maybe my body language or expression is somehow leading her on, giving her permission."

"When I first brought you onto my team, your clarity of boundaries was one of the things that stood out about you, Helena. I have no doubt whatsoever that you're not misleading her. The fact that you are here now, corroborates that. But I have to ask, given that this is a first for you, do you have any issues discussing homosexuality?"

"Goodness, no. You know me, Brian. Live and let live."

"That's what I thought. I'm behind you to continue with the sessions."

Helena's brow furrowed. "I don't know. I'm concerned she's going to say something she can't retract. We might be risking further damage to this girl."

"If you transfer her to another counsellor, she just might choose to construe that as rejection of her sexuality. That in itself would set her back." Brian sipped his tea. "This is what we'll do. This interview will be noted on the file, and your questions recorded. My recommendation is to continue. Tread carefully. Deflect any perceived declarations of affection. Try to keep her on track. And if she instigates anything else, the responsibility for the impact on her therapy would be hers."

Two weeks passed. It was that point in March when winter's back felt like it was well and truly broken. The air was softer, and natural light visited both ends of the working day. Helena liked to park her car out on the hill so she could walk a little to work. Fresh air and budding trees had a way of instilling hope in her every step. Winter invariably got her down, and when she'd get to thinking that all good things were out of her reach, the light would hang around a few minutes longer in her day, thrown to her that she might hang on.

Her spirits lifted and she felt like she'd really turned the corner from her miserable Christmas as a recent 'ex'. She found a fresh energy, one that had been missing a while and she took that energy to her clients that Thursday morning.

Thursday wasn't her favourite day, for it was a long one. The unit ran a drop-in facility every weekday evening from six to nine. The counsellors covered the shifts on a rota basis. Until Easter, Thursday was Helena's. Expect the unexpected had become her mantra for the drop-in sessions, and was adopted as policy. Often it seemed that drop-in meant drop-out. That quaint old phrase once used to label the poor buggers marginalised by society, depending on perspectives. It wasn't always that these individuals had a problem they needed to talk about, more a need to talk and be listened to, and treated as visible. No one was turned away, unless there truly wasn't a counsellor available.

This Thursday was no different. A woman contemplating suicide had to be sectioned, Helena holding her hands for comfort and safety until the ambulance arrived. An elderly man grieving desperately for his wife who passed away thirty years ago, needed TLC and tea, and a carefully boundaried response so he wouldn't switch his attachment, but rather, try to process it. A lot of coaxing was needed to convince a bi-polar patient on a high, wanting to share his manic elevation with everyone who would listen, to take his neglected medication. A quiet man with a severe stutter, homeless and hungry, just wanted company. And then, with only an hour left in the shift, there was a racket at the front desk. Terry, one of the regulars, was yelling at the receptionist, evidently heading for a psychotic episode. Helena intervened, hoping he would still recognise her in his heightened state. He didn't at first, screaming, "I want the bloke with the bow tie! Brian. He's my mate, he is. He knows how to fix me!"

"Terry. Terry, look at me. Remember me? I'm Helena. Brian isn't here. He went home earlier."

"You're hiding him from me!" he accused, and made for the office door.

"Terry, no, I'm not." Helena stood alongside him. "Come on, Terry, what do you say to a nice cuppa?"

Peace and nine o'clock came with relief. She was free to go.

No more than three hundred yards from the building, she heard her name.

"Helena."

It was a command. She hesitated, unsure whether it was wise to pause and identify the speaker, or walk swiftly on.

151

"Helena, it's me, Caroline."

"Caroline! You gave me a fright!"

"I'm sorry."

"What are you doing here at this time of the evening?" she asked, her mental file rapidly confirming Caroline's address, a train journey away. "Were you wanting to call in? It's too late now."

"No, no," Caroline reassured. "No, it's nothing like that. I wanted to talk to you. I phoned a while ago. They said you were on tonight."

"Why didn't you come in? Or wait until ... Monday, isn't it?"

"I didn't want to talk to my counsellor. I wanted to talk to you."

"Caroline, this is not a good idea."

"I need to," Caroline begged.

"Okay. I'm not totally comfortable with this, but ... let's find somewhere quiet, so I can listen."

Café Rose was spacious and only a few guests sat at the bars and low tables enjoying an evening drink. It seemed a sensible choice. Helena could order coffee, set the tone for this interaction.

"A beer, please. Stella Artois," Caroline demanded of the waiter.

Helena wanted to reprimand Caroline. She could certainly pass for eighteen, but that didn't make it right. Helena decided to pass on playing parent. She ordered her coffee.

Caroline began to prattle about the unusually mild weather, that *The Bodyguard* was still on at the cinema, and not being keen on *Madonna's* new single. Questions peppered her chatter.

Helena held back, unwilling to divulge anything about

herself to her client. The beer was downed too quickly and another ordered. They increased Caroline's gregariousness. The subject shifted to her day at school, her studies, ordinary stuff that rarely got a mention in their sessions. She was light in her delivery of the trivia. No unnecessary self-analysis, no heavy realisations. Abruptly, she became serious.

"Thanks for being so understanding about the gay thing."

"No reason not to be."

"Not everybody thinks like that."

"No, of course. I'm sorry. Have you been having trouble?"

"Not *that* kind of trouble."

"What kind of trouble, then?"

"The emotional kind. I know what I am. I know what I want. But it isn't always easy to tell if the person you want it from is interested." Her gaze was direct now, staring searchingly into Helena's eyes.

Helena had to look away. "No, I don't suppose you can just walk up to a girl and ask her if she's straight or not?" She tried to inject humour.

Caroline declined it, moving her hands and her glass an inch further into the centre of the table. "That wasn't what I meant."

Helena knew what she meant and was already regretting her agreement to this meeting.

"I'm pretty good at spotting the girls who are up for it, even when they hide behind a boyfriend. I've been with a couple of girls at school like that."

"It can't be easy for all teenagers to be certain of their sexuality." Helena drew her cup closer, swirling the coffee around like a mini whirlpool, keeping the flow just short of the lip. She was not enjoying the sensation of being preyed upon. In her growing discomfort she began to wonder if somehow Caroline felt she'd let her down. Nothing she had said indicated it, but why else would her back feel plastered against the wall?

Caroline looked displeased with the comment. "Don't treat me like a little girl, Helena. We are on neutral territory. We are equals here, right? So no more games. Are you in love with anyone?"

Helena hesitated. "No, I'm not."

"Well I am. I want to talk to you about it."

"Perhaps we should leave this chat until Monday."

"No, now." Caroline finished the last of her beer with a long swallow. "You know, don't you?"

"Caroline, I ... please be clear ... I'm finding it very difficult to follow you."

"It's you, Helena. It's always been you."

Helena lifted her cup to her lips, slowly, eyes fixed on the table.

"Did you hear me?"

Helena nodded.

"I always fancied the look of those girls in school, and to tell you the truth, it was fun to get a bit of enjoyment out of them. But it was nothing more. I knew the minute I saw you. I knew that was it, that you were the one for me. You're everything I've always dreamed of. Your eyes, your hair. Why do you think I've worked so hard to improve myself, to impress you, to show you that I'm not immature? I'm no child, Helena. I hated it when you pulled our sessions back to three weeks." Caroline pressed her lips into a fine line. "I thought you'd worked it out, that you were subtly saying no. But you didn't change. You were as warm as ever. As beautiful as ever. That's why I decided to bring up the subject of lesbianism. I needed to see your reaction. It was exactly what I'd hoped for. You congratulated me, approved of me. And that's how I knew you'd been thinking of me too. I saw that you noticed I'd changed my hair, and then you noticed my legs when I wore my skirt. Though you were too clever to say anything. I know it wouldn't have been right in those circumstances. That's why I waited for you tonight, to give you the opportunity to talk without being the counsellor."

Monologue complete, Caroline gazed adoringly at the object of her affection, awaiting a response.

"This is very inappropriate and—"

"But I love you, Helena."

"I'll be honest. I did know you held some sort of feeling for me. That is why it's unforgivable of me to let this happen, to let you say these things. Don't get me wrong, I do approve of you and your choices. I am very proud of you, of how hard you have worked. I don't think of you as a child. I'm so impressed with the maturity you display in handling your sexuality issue. That's very rare, Caroline, special."

Caroline seemed to hear the praise loudest. Her face was aglow, radiating hope. Helena had no choice but to crush it.

"I am touched by your feelings for me, but I cannot, do not return them. I am not gay. And if I was, and if I had feelings for you, it would be totally unprofessional of me to counsel you. And that's the problem we now face. Our professional relationship is breached. I'm sorry, but you know it means we cannot continue your therapy."

"Are you not only saying no, but also that I can't see you again, at all?"

"Caroline, you must have realised that this would compromise things." In that moment Helena saw Caroline's pain, saw she was dealing with a tender young woman, who, in the urgency of her passion, had only envisaged the best possible outcome. She wished she could reach her hand across the table, place it on the girl's, offer consolation. She could not. It would only make matters worse.

"I'd better go now, Caroline. I'll get the bill. "

"Don't patronise me!" Caroline slapped a ten pound note on the table. With tears cascading down her cheeks, she grabbed her coat and ran from the café.

Helena hesitated, allowing a minute to pass so that she might not find herself catching up with Caroline. Outside she was glad of the cold night air. It cleared her head, and helped squash the distress rising inside. She felt wretched to be the cause of the girl's pain, however unintentional.

At home, she poured herself a brandy and switched on her PC. She began to type:

Memorandum
To: Brian Sharpe
From: Helena Callender
Re: 'Caroline'

Further to our meeting on Thursday. I am applying
for the transfer of the management of this case to another
counsellor on the grounds …

Chapter Nine

The Client

"I went to the newsagent in the end, found a section in the Birmingham Post. It lists all the gay-friendly pubs and clubs about town, and specifies their male-female orientation too. I took it from there really. I wasn't madly happy about it. I was a bit afraid of going out on my own. What choice did I have? I didn't imagine my straight friends would be too keen to support me on this one, not in the practical sense anyway. Talk about an education! Made me feel quite naïve in a way. Didn't know I had so much to learn.

"The first pub was a disaster. I walked up and down the street a couple of times, trying to be discreet and not look like some perv. I tried to get a glimpse through the window, ascertain the clientele. I couldn't see well enough. So I had to take a deep breath and walk in, you know, straight up to the bar, like I knew exactly what I was doing, like I was meeting someone. I swear my legs were shaking. How embarrassing is that? The pub itself was totally ordinary. I don't know what I was expecting to be different. It was a bit like the Queen Vic in *Eastenders*. Lots of wood and pillars, cosy sofa-type corners and all that. Then I dared to notice the women. Shit! Sorry, but honestly, most of them were so ugly. I mean, I know that's a stupid thing to say. A lot of men are bloody ugly too, aren't they? I suppose it was different for me to be looking at women this way, you know, as objects of fantasy, lust, someone to fancy. I mean, I had looked at women that way for a long time, but without engaging myself, my feelings. This was different because ... well, if I'm honest, because given the chance, I was on the pull.

"I find that so hard to say. I was on the pull. It makes me feel like a bloke. That's the really hard thing, still feeling like a woman when you want a woman. It can be a bit confusing in the head sometimes.

"Anyway, this pub. Well, let's put it like this, there was this woman sitting at the back. She must have been fifty-something, not that age itself is the issue. She was quite fat, wearing combats and a vest. She had no bra on. Not really a surprise, except that she had these huge saggy tits that the vest wasn't up to supporting, or concealing. It wasn't a pretty sight, if you get me. As well as that, she had bushes of grey hair under her armpits. The hair on her head wasn't much better. It was long, scraggy and grey, worn in a loose plait. Needless to say, no make-up. Not that I can talk, I never wear it either. But she was scary. And she was sitting with a bunch of mates who were all similar; drooping boobs on one, not a hint of make-up anywhere, and definitely the work of barbers rather than hairdressers. Now, I know that shit about men determining what female beauty is, and all that. I know there's a lot of strong arguments there. We talked about it in college. But you can go too far the other way. I mean, picture it. If a fat fifty-year-old man was sitting in the pub with his flab hanging out of a vest, and his hair all long and unkempt, we'd have him down as a pervert for sure. You definitely wouldn't fancy him for being a 'natural man', would you?

"But they weren't all like that. There were some younger girls. I don't know, maybe I picked a bad night or something. They were more stereotypes than anything else. Punk hair, body piercing, boyish looking and aggressive. It made me sad really. If I had dragged a straight pal along, I would have fed all their worst nightmares. You can see where the media gets their negative gibes on lesbians, can't you? The worst were sitting around me.

158

Nothing I was interested in.

"I waited a couple of weeks before I ventured out again. I read about a new bar, not too far from Chinatown. It was described as a male-female combo. I thought it might provide a better balance. Well, believe me, it came as a relief, I can tell you. It's called Babes. I suppose that in itself would insult the academic lesbian contingent. But it was cool. Being a new place, it was pretty funky, all yellow and oranges, upbeat, but warm and welcoming. It wasn't that busy when I first walked in. I had a magazine, and took a table by the window so I could people-watch on all sides. As it started to fill, a couple of guys asked if they could sit at my table. Course I said yes. Turns out they were really friendly. We had a good talk. They gave me the download on a lot of the clubs and places around. Always better to get that kind of information first hand, isn't it? They laughed at my experience at the Queen Vic. Told me they'd been in it themselves once with some lesbian friends, and they were 'frankly terrified, darling. Butch? They were monstrous!'

"I lied a bit when they asked me about my girlfriends. I suppose it was a compliment that they thought I must have had several by now. I thought I must be coming across quite confident. That made me feel good. I lied anyway, said I was recently out of a heavy stint and fancied a bit of fun. They liked that and suggested we go out somewhere some time. Gave me a phone number. Okay, so I wasn't expecting to pick-up a few guys, ha ha, but it's a start.

"I haven't tried to call them yet. I was enjoying finding my feet on the pub scene alone, so I thought I'd work on my basic security first, before trying any clubs. I have it in my head that they might be more predatory, if you know what I mean. I'm preparing myself for that one. I've been back to Babes a few times. I decided it might be an idea to make myself a regular face, more chance of getting noticed. It's been fine actually. I established my routine. Magazine, *Diva*, to look the part, window seat when possible, and sometimes I scribble in a little notebook, to come over a bit intellectual. I made a point of chatting to the bar staff, who were so friendly it was easy. Didn't want them thinking I was a voyeur and not up for any action. And then, last Tuesday, I got my first break.

"I'd been studying all day, well, in between morning telly and *Countdown*, and I fancied a break for the evening. I didn't take anything to read this time. I was feeling brave. I thought I might make the effort to really chat to some people for a change. No, I wasn't setting myself up to pull, I haven't seen many singles there as yet, and it's not always clear if girls are together or not. I mean, there are some who are all over each other, snogging, constantly touching the other up and that. I enjoy watching when I think I can get away with it. No, it's the groups or pairs that I'm guessing are lesbians, but they're intense and into talking and tactile and that, but it's a bit different, and I can't be sure. When I say chat, I mean I wanted to pluck up the courage to ask to join some people at a table and maybe make friends, some contacts.

"I timed it so Babes would already be busy and it would be more likely that no free tables would be left. I got that bit right. I lurked at the bar for a good twenty minutes. I wanted to make the right move so I wouldn't look like I was coming on to someone. There was this group of three women, mixed ages. One my age, and two were older, maybe by ten years or so. I was pretty sure they weren't paired off. Eventually I plucked up the courage to ask if I could sit. That was no problem except that they kind of turned away to finish their conversation. I wanted to die. All I could do was try to sit comfortably and look nonchalant until my lager was finished. I was nearly done when one of them turned to me and said, 'Been stood up?'.

"I hadn't even thought about that, how I must have looked that way. I swear I blushed scarlet as I said, 'No, out on my own this evening'. They probably didn't believe me. She went on, 'I didn't mean to embarrass you. Sorry. Look, this is Christine and Ariadne, we call her Ria. I'm Deborah'. She offered me a handshake.

"They were fascinating. Christine is two years older than me. She has a girlfriend she's been seeing for a couple of months. It's her first serious girlfriend. I enjoyed listening to her. She was talking about things like getting over the lust and passion stage, and moving on to the nights-in with a DVD and a bottle stage. And then, whether that meant the excitement was over and they'd start getting lazy with one another and not dress up any more. I loved it because it was exactly how I'd heard girls at school talking about their boyfriends. It sounded so real, so normal. Ria is thirty-two. She's a big woman, immaculately dressed. Her clothes are totally colour-coordinated, expensive looking, perfect make-up and bleached blonde hair in amazing condition. She radiates complete self-confidence, and although feature by feature you wouldn't say she was a beautiful woman, her attractiveness is undeniable. I mean, I don't fancy her myself. That sounds arrogant, right, like I'm gorgeous or something? Well, that's not what I mean. I would say she's not my type, if I knew what my type was. Maybe I should start at those points: not big, not blonde. Deborah is something else again. She's thirty-five, doesn't look it, light brown hair, wears it short. She's one of those women who's definitely female, but gives off a very male vibe. It's hard to pinpoint. It's not body language exactly, or speech. But there's an abruptness, a directness that comes across quite mannish. What's amazing about her is that she is married and has two kids. Married, not divorced or even thinking about it. She says she likes having this normal, acceptable life where she can toddle off to the school gates and not attract the attention of the other mums for being different. She says her husband rarely wants sex, so while she doesn't enjoy it much, it's not too awful to put up with. She reckons he has no idea how to make love to a woman, hasn't found her G-spot in ten years! He doesn't know she has lesbian affairs. He's happy for her to go out with her mates. He knows Ria, but not that she's gay. So off she goes on dates and what have you, and enjoys the best of both worlds.

"I get such a sense of well-being around these women. I feel able to be me, drop my guard. You know, we had a real laugh too. So much that we stayed 'til closing time. That's when it happened. We were shouting a last drink and Ria decided cocktails were in order to mark our new friendship. One of the barmaids brought them over. She placed my Margarita very carefully with a napkin, and bumped my shoulder as she moved away. She turned back to me and rested her hand on it a moment, with a very deliberate, 'Sorry'. So I had to look up at her. She smiled at me and Christine kicked me under the table. She went off. I lifted my napkin and there was a number written on it. The girls thought that was great. A real smooth move. I got a better look at her while she worked among the other tables. She was alright. About twenty-five, sallow-skinned, dark hair tied up in mini-bunches with a colourful scarf wrapped around her head, not a bad figure either, lean, small boobs. She was chatting with the punters. Friendly, happy sort, confident. Deborah was egging me on, telling me I had to ring her, that I had nothing to lose. She was right. I had nothing to lose, and quite a lot to gain.

"Then I got impulsive. Probably the extra Mojitos. I dunno. I felt it was more to do with the assurance the evening with these women had given me. They'd made me feel better about myself, more at ease. So I told them I was going to talk to this woman, there and then. We exchanged numbers and I had to promise a blow by blow account. I told them not to wait, that I'd ring. And off I went to the bar.

"Her name was Tani, short for something foreign and exotic, and impossible to pronounce. She told me she'd seen me in the bar a few times, checked out I wasn't with anyone, apologised for being forward insisting it wasn't really her style, but when she saw me chatting to the others, she thought she'd better make a move quick, before it was too late. All very flattering, believe me. So I ran with it. Cool as, I said, 'Doing anything now?'. 'No,' she said, 'and finishing in twenty minutes. Have another drink while you wait'. She made me a Tequila Sunrise and I sat there watching her collect glasses and clean tables while the stragglers left. I found myself watching her ass as she bent over, then down her top at her black bra when she was facing my way. I started to feel really turned on. Is it okay to say that? I guess it had been an emotionally satisfying evening, and I felt ready to take it further. I wasn't judging myself.

"Tani finished and said her car was in a side street, not far. Not allowed to drink on the job, she wanted to know if I wanted to come to her place, have a late one with her. We didn't make it that far before we were all over one another. I think she moved first, in so much as she put her arm around me as soon as we walked out of the bar. I felt the heat of it and thought, fuck it, and slid my hand into the back pocket of her jeans. As soon as we turned off the main street, she swung me to her and we started kissing. Nothing delicate, full on stuff, let-me-at-you type snogging. I'm not going to romanticise or anything. I know I was dealing with lust at first sight. But it was great. She wanted me. This good-looking, normal woman wanted my body. We pulled apart to get to the car, though she kept turning her head to catch my mouth time and again. We were both panting by the time we reached the car, and it wasn't the distance. Sorry, is this too much information? Okay. Tani opened the car and pulled me by the waist. 'In the back, please', she said. We had it off in the back of the car. She had her hands in my jeans, under my top. It was great. I felt like I was having real sex for the first time. It wasn't embarrassing. It wasn't one-sided. We did eventually get into the front of the car and drove to her place. I know the town well now, so I wasn't worried. I knew where I was. She shares the flat with another girl, a friend, so I gathered. We locked ourselves in her room and basically kissed and fondled and had sex all night. All night! I don't think we talked at all. I took a taxi home at five. I didn't want to sleep there.

"Tani phoned up the next evening. She wanted to get together again. But I didn't. This sounds awful, but she'd served her purpose. I knew she wasn't my sort of person, that I didn't want a relationship with her. I used the same lie again, that I was recently out of a heavy relationship and that I didn't want to go steady with anyone for a while. I should be so lucky. I ought to be careful with that one. I might end up jinxing myself.

"I guess I felt I needed to get that first encounter out of the way. I should clarify, it's not the first ever. The first one happened in an easier way. It sort of grew around me. I didn't have to take any action myself with that one either. But I can't wait for life to come and find me, can I? I knew the time would come when I'd have to make the first move if I saw someone I wanted. So that's what Tani was about, a practice run. Am I making sense? Good. I'm not very proud of it, using Tani like that. It's not what I'm about, really. I was … testing myself.

"Can we stop now? No? Okay, you're the psych. I think the reason I'm still nervous is because of the things you hear. Straight people, normal people are supposed to find their partner for life and live happily ever after. Despite the divorce rate, people still get married in that hope, that hope they might be the lucky one-in-three, or is it one-in-two these days? I want that too. Not children or a family. No, not at all. But a true love. That loyalty, that commitment. Someone to share my life with. And then everything you hear about gay couples is that they never last. That makes me sad. It scares me 'cos I'm left thinking I don't belong in either of these groups, 'cos I want the straight thing. But I'm not, and I don't want the gay thing. But I am.

"I'm nearly twenty years old and I haven't had a relationship worth the name. I tried the boy thing first. I knew in my heart that it was a waste of time. I'd always looked at girls, always. I suppose I thought I had to give it a go. Partly to keep everyone off my back. Parents, friends, schoolmates. I knew too, that being gay wasn't going to be the easiest path in life, and let's face it, who's going to choose to make life any harder? Right? It wasn't going to happen, not with a bloke. I snogged a couple on nights out. It was horrible. Honest. A warm wet mouthwash, only without the fresh aftertaste. Nothing sexual about it. I couldn't understand how friends of mine could tuck themselves away on a lap in a dark corner and mutually lick out chops with some bloke for up to half an hour at a time.

"I got a bit closer to one. He was gorgeous according to all the girls I knew. Yeah, even I would say he was good-looking. I'd known him a while, liked him as a friend, thought it might be a good bet. He was too forward, too fast, wanted me to touch him. I have to say the thought of playing with that thing repulsed me. That was when I gave up on the boy business.

"It wasn't so very long after, that I had my first girlfriend. At least, that's what I thought was going on. I liked her a lot. I could feel myself getting hooked. But she had this boyfriend that she just wouldn't drop. At first I thought she was scared, socially, and needed a smoke screen. We saw one another quite a lot. I thought it had potential. I wasn't in love, but I thought I could be, given time. Not that it was reciprocated, as it turned out. She dumped me. No warning, no explanation, except that she decided to be with him. Didn't do a lot for my self-esteem, that one. It wasn't that I was broken-hearted over her, it was the circumstances. I was dumped for a man. That made me feel unworthy, truly not good enough, second rate.

"Sometimes it's so depressing to have dreams. It's like you can invent this ideal world, or this ideal situation in your head, or worse, in your heart. And you want it so much. But reality fails to meet it. Constantly lets you down 'til you wish you had no dreams, 'cos they make reality miserable. So you stop wanting and start compromising, knowing that's not going to make you happy either.

"Do you have dreams?"

What an intriguing young woman. Remarkable. Helena could not get the girl out of her head.

Chapter Ten

Counsel

Setting It Up ...

    Mike Brown and Janis Dickinson, winners of last month's 'Meet Your Match' talk to us, separately, after their dinner date in Soho's trendy new Thai restaurant, Bambu.

The article went on to tell how Janis worried about what she would wear (she changed seven times!) and whether her nervous giggle might get the better of her and cause Mike to think her an absolute airhead. Then the cab Janis ordered failed to show, so a friend was enlisted at the last minute to deliver her late to the restaurant. But of course, not only was Mike more handsome in real life, but an absolute gent. From Mike's perspective things weren't so rosy. His manners may have been such not to let it show, but his pet hate is tardiness. So disrespectful. And that laugh. He spent the entire evening painfully conscious of the turning heads every time Janis guffawed like a braying donkey, which was often. In conclusion, poor Janis had gone off quite impressed, despite finding Mike quieter than his questionnaire had indicated, and anticipated hearing from him again, while Mike was so glad to see the end of the date, he phoned a friend and redeemed the evening in a club.

    Painful. Public and painful!

    Helena reclined on her sofa, reading her monthly *Marie Claire* with new eyes. Her new client's eyes, she told herself.

    Another article was running in the same issue taking the whole matter to another level. The dating agency supreme. This particular agency, based in London of course, was aimed entirely at the successful and beautiful. Helena wondered how such a thing could get away with its inverse discrimination. She also wondered that it didn't occur to them how they were imposing limitations on taste and desire. In the natural way of things, do not opposites sometimes attract? Might the successful wish to nurture the struggler? Might the beautiful not want the competition from an equally or more beautiful partner? It seemed to her a pitiful way of narrowing options, in the distant hope that it was for the better. Interestingly, the journalist taking part in the introductions offered by the agency was unimpressed by the clientele. Not physically. She readily acknowledged the abundant gorgeousness of the guys and girls. But beauty does not guarantee chemistry or attraction, and it certainly doesn't guarantee personality. Helena was dismayed that these amazing young folk felt the need for an agency, blaming busy lives, demanding careers. No time for fun and making friends. How could they possibly believe that a line-'em-up and date-'em-fast group would solve things? You might as well choose a partner mail order.

Helena put the magazine to one side and reached for the remote control. She wanted some trivial telly to wind down with before bed. *Street Mate* came on. It wasn't something she'd seen before so she laid her head against the arm of the sofa to observe at leisure. The presenter explained something about the city she was in then announced she was off to find a man, whereupon she pounced on random young men (favouring 18-30s), asking if they were single and whether they wanted to join her in her game of finding a date on the street for dinner the next night.

Helena shuddered at the crassness of it, presuming that the people who agreed to take part must be in it for their fifteen minutes of fame. What was the programme trying to prove? Helena was sitting up straight now, jaw agape at the embarrassing assaults on passers-by, or shop girls, based on the man of the episode's directions of 'in there … her … she's fit'. By the end of Part One a pairing was made. In Part Two, they went out for their date, filmed doing their getting-to-know-you thing in its entirety. Then there was Part Three. The presenter returned to talk to the individuals a month later to see if love had blossomed.

"Love?" Helena said to the television. "How the hell could love have blossomed out of such a set up? Are people so hard up these days that they've completely lost the knack of getting to know someone? Are we truly that busy? I suppose it's on a par with *Blind Date*. No wait, that's even worse. Imagine applying to sit in a line-up behind a screen, tarted up and spouting cheesy one-liners designed to show your wit and humour, and not just your desperation to end up with Mr Ugly with the gorgeous voice who'll be a pain in the arse on the date anyway. And this is normality? This is straight people. Loads of choice. Not a minority."

Helena's thoughts took a serious turn. If meeting a partner had become such a major enterprise for the so-called mainstream of society, it was no wonder her gay client was struggling to make her way. Hardly a surprise that your sexuality would be difficult to confirm and be comfortable with if you can't find a way of meeting your own kind. It made her feel sad, for the first time feeling the loneliness that struggle must be for a teenager who knows they are beyond the norm. It took enough guts and courage to make contact with the opposite sex within societal norms when you were fifteen and terrified. How much more so must it take to find yourself a whole new world aside of that? She cast a cursory thought over her own relationship history. Hadn't had too much luck herself really, and she was supposed to be quite eligible.

Helena decided she owed it to her new client to go out on a limb with her research. Firstly, she had a good look through the TV guide. There was barely a mention of anything homosexual. None of the soaps were running a side-line gay story at the moment. Channel Four was looking a bit thin on the weeknights too. *Sex In The City*, all straight in the key roles. There was *Graham Norton*. Helena made a note of the show's scheduled time and stuck the reminder on her fridge.

On Friday she finished work at four. Always did. It seemed people didn't want to talk much about their problems on a Friday, holding on to the dream that the promise of the weekend might just change all. Unsurprisingly, Monday was often their heaviest day. She was about to pass the newsagency on the way to the car when a thought struck her. If she was going to do TV research tonight, then she might as well go the whole hog and find some reading material as well. It took a few minutes to locate anything, and she felt a touch foolish not knowing what titles to search out. The gay men were spotted in a corner just beneath the porn. A tad ironic to Helena's mind.

On the verge of settling for the *Pink Paper*, a title caught her eye. *Diva*, subtitled *Lesbian Life and Style*. Great! That was the one her client mentioned in her session. She pushed some magazines about in the hope there might be another issue.

"Can I help you there?" The newsagent was a man in his late fifties. Helena spoke to him maybe once a week, when she chose a paper to keep her mildly abreast of the news. She felt herself blush, and was immediately angry for such a petty response. She took a few steps towards him and held the magazine up so he could read the title.

Moving his eyes from the magazine title to Helena's face, he recognised her. "Oh, hello, love."

"I don't suppose you have any other editions of this

one?" She heard the rest of the sentence form in her head, *I'm doing some research on lesbianism*, and imagined how lame it would sound aloud.

"Let me go out back a minute."

At least there was no one else in the shop yet. Helena took the remaining steps to the till and busied herself in finding her purse from her bag.

"The new batch has already come in. Not due on the shelves 'til next week. But as it's for you, love, you can take them both now." He spoke as though all of a sudden they shared something. Helena could feel her face heat again.

"Thank you." She paid up and left. That was painful. How the hell can anyone be out and confident?

Graham Norton wasn't due on 'til ten, considered too risqué for an earlier audience. Helena mused at the prudery of the British. After eating her pasta, she made herself comfortable with some cushions on the lounge floor, a large glass of Australian chardonnay, and her two copies of *Diva*. She scanned them first for visual imagery and was disappointed to find numerous photos of boyish women in sports gear and jeans, and none of the most attractive mould. Come on, they can't all look like this.

She pictured her client. Okay, so she was in jeans, and trainers, and had a narrow-hipped athletic sort of body. But it didn't have that male edge to it. Probably wasn't kosher to call it that. No, she had that urban-sports chic, with the sort of trainers that certainly weren't used for training of any sort. She wore fitted tops too, that showed off her high perky breasts, unlike these flat-chested women in the pictures here, or those who disguised their womanly bosoms under voluminous shirts. And her hair was chin-length, cut in layers so it fell softly and feminine. No make-up. But then, few of her work colleagues bothered with make-up during the day either. No, she was certainly prettier than anything Helena had seen so far, and she found it bothering that the girl's choices should be less so. She opened the other copy. It was almost a different publication. Beautiful models, very sexy ads for videos, and a better-looking bunch of readers photographed for some event they'd run. Helena was inspired to find this wider selection of availability.

Only eight o'clock. Helena homed in on the classifieds. At first glance, the majority read as slim, attractive and intelligent. This was positive. She laughed at her own naïveté. Of course it was positive. It was advertising! She read again, more closely. Now they all blended into one, barely a syllable to set them apart. 'Seeks friendship, maybe more', was a key phrase. Age? She supposed it the most obvious credential to work from; seemed women were more open on that one. And geographical location? It wasn't like there were a whole load of women on the doorstep here. Then again, shagging away from home might have its advantages.

Helena turned the page. The ad took a moment to figure out, all shiny, silver and high-tech. A website. Of course, the bloody internet. Why do I never think of it?

Helena tripped off to her little box room. She called it her study, though it was barely large enough for the desks (one for the computer, one to write at) and the laden bookshelves. She turned on the machine, and wandered back to fetch and refill her glass while it booted up. It was ready by her return. Helena decided to have a little fun first and typed the word *lesbian* into the search engine. It pulled up hundreds of sites, maybe more, certainly more.

She chose one at random and nearly spat out her wine as the image came to life. Two women having sex on the floor. One breast, belonging to the woman on top, was in the mouth of the woman on the bottom, and the fingers of the woman on the bottom were very clearly inserted into the vagina of the woman on top.

Approaching from behind the top woman's raised ass, was a large and very red cock.

Helena hit the mouse to eradicate the scene. Uh! That can't be right! She clicked on another site. This time the man was lying on a bed, rubbing himself off while two women leaned across the top of him to share tongues.

She tried another, and then another, and then another. It was all just bloody pornography. For men.

She played it safe and typed in the address of the site from the magazine. To her relief it was indeed lesbian-related, and offered much to choose from. Travel, insurance, eating out, fashion, sport, health and so much more there could never be time to read it all. Helena printed off a few pages to browse later. A couple of links caught her eye so she explored further. Who'd have known that the words freedom and rainbow could have such particular symbolism? She thought them rather poetic. Though the American link, *The Knitting Circle,* surprised her somewhat, as it no doubt did the many unsuspecting needle-wielders who sought it out in good faith.

Her printing finished, Helena was about to close down the site when two words shouted at her: Chat Room.

Helena felt surreptitious, naughty, a voyeur at her desire to click on the link. Oh, what the hell, I've got this far. She went for it.

A page of badly presented and misspelled text appeared. It was a fairly pathetic weakness of hers to judge on the basis of poor spelling and even worse grammar. She tried to suspend it as a sentence walked its way across the screen. There was a pause, almost a whole minute before another appeared. The pattern repeated until it became clear that three women were talking. The women were talking about television programmes, or more specifically the characters in them. It amused Helena to see only women spoken of – that fit new bird in *Corrie*, the sexy nurse on *Casualty*, even the BBC newsreader – and described in terms of their attractiveness, both physical and sexual. It was almost normal to her. She'd often discussed the beauty of other women with her pals, though it was never intended sexually. That hadn't crossed her mind. Another sentence was forming: 'Anyone else listening in tonight?'. Helena pulled away from her PC with a start. Shit, can they tell if someone else is online, like a kind of warning against eavesdroppers?

She scanned the screen for some minute icon that might indicate presence in the chat room. Nothing she could recognise. An answer: 'All off to watch *Graham Norton*, I think'. Helena laughed at herself, her jumpy stupidity. She felt like the kid in the back of the classroom who'd almost been caught copying the girl in front. "What are you like, girl, honestly? *Graham Norton* it is."

She switched off her machine, gathered her print-outs and her wine glass, almost offhandedly ignored, or perhaps refused to acknowledge, the tinge of excitement in her crotch, and returned to the living room. The papers were dumped on the floor with the magazines. Herself, she dumped on the sofa, curled around her glass, and with an inexplicable enthusiasm, awaited her further education.

Graham Norton proved a colourful character. Flamboyantly dressed, but not in a *Liberace* way. More a nineties tasteful flamboyance. He was outspoken, not crude, and very quick-witted. Helena was most entertained. He had guests and games and internet activities. It all made Helena feel quite hip. During the commercial break, Helena remembered her reason for watching and queried the gayness of it all. Sure, Graham was gay, in a confident, out-there sort of way and that was great. An excellent role model. The guests were mainstream, universal, certainly not chosen to appeal to a gay audience exclusively. Not that on appearance, the studio audience was exclusively gay either. In fact, it appeared remarkably diverse. Helena decided that was the point exactly. Here was 'gay' as just another segment of a diverse, multicultural society, all part of the fabric, all normal. Oh, that the world would reflect television once in a while.

Helena's phone started to ring. She glanced at the clock, Ten forty-five. She chose to let the answering machine pick it up, until she heard Tessa's voice, and Jackie's.

"We've been to the pictures. Wondered if you were still up, you raver. Could we call in for a night cap?" Helena jumped to the phone. "Hey, you two. Course I'm still up. Come by."

Ten minutes later they were all in Helena's kitchen debating the wisdom of a coffee over a small Baileys. "So long as they're small, Helena, one won't hurt," Tessa chided.

"Are you sure it was just the pictures. You two are a bit lively," Helena teased.

"We spent an hour or so in the pub first. You'd have laughed." Jackie was in full story-telling mode. "There was a bunch of American squaddies in. Bought us drinks and everything. Lovely guys. Oh, we should have phoned you and got you to come down. Apparently they've been doing manoeuvres in the hills. Top secret training, they said."

"No secret now," Tessa giggled.

"Anyway, they put a song on the jukebox, that one from *Top Gun*, you know. Then they all started singing, doing that scene where Tom Cruise and the other guy ..."

"Goose," Helena prompted.

"Goose, yeah, him, were singing in a bar. It was really funny. Where's the Baileys?"

"Here. You pour them if you think I'm too generous." Helena handed over the heavy brown bottle.

"Hmm, a fresh one," Tessa mocked as she weighed the bottle. "Finished the other one already?"

Helena threw a slap that just caught Tessa's thigh.

"My, my, you fiery thing," Jackie teased them both and skipped off to the living room, only to stop at the sight of papers everywhere. "Working? On a Friday night?" she exclaimed in genuine horror. "We should have dragged you to the pictures. What are you working on anyway?"

Helena felt her face heat, and began stuttering a reply when Tessa squeaked behind her, "Oh, *Graham Norton*. He's hilarious. Damn, is it nearly over?"

Jackie was sitting among the papers on the floor. She turned over a magazine first, then rifled through some of the loose pages, examining the headings. "What's this all about, Helena?"

Tessa heeded Jackie's tone in time to notice the *Diva* title. A small query raised one eyebrow.

"It's this client I've got at the minute. She's a lesbian. Nineteen. She reminds me of someone, something. Anyway, being gay isn't her problem. It's relationships, getting into them that is. Real ones, not just girls who are playing around or curious, that sort of thing. I'd never really thought about it, but do you know how hard it is to find another lesbian out there who is like you, similar interests and all that? I mean, look how hard it is to find a man you actually like, as well as want to sleep with."

"Too true," said Tessa raising her glass. "Any of this help?"

Helena was on the floor in a flash, selecting a few pages

176

of her own to look through. Her focus flicked from one heading to another. "Sort of, I guess. Well, it's broadened my outlook, my understanding at least."

Jackie looked at the crease on her friend's brow. "This one's really getting to you, isn't it? Sure you're okay with it? Something you need to take to Brian?"

"Yeah. No. It'll be fine. You're right. How sad am I working on a Friday night?" She gathered the paperwork into a bundle and shoved it to one side of the table. "So what film were you watching? Have you terrified Tess?" Conversation was rounded off with milky coffees and the visitors were gone not long after midnight.

In the taxi home, Tessa took Jackie to task. "Something you need to take to Brian? You weren't very brave, were you?"

"Aw, come on," Jackie shrugged.

"I thought we'd agreed that at the first hint she'd give, we'd make it easy for her."

"But look at her, Tessa, she's getting close, yes, but she hasn't twigged."

"Do you think we should give Brian the heads up?"

"That wouldn't be fair. She'll go to him when she's finished analysing any transference."

At two, Helena lay wide-eyed in the darkness, the images of her dream still crystal-clear as though on celluloid. She'd been in a forest, by a river, in beautiful seclusion, easy in the company of a young woman who walked to her side. Deep in quiet conversation, the mood was warm. She was blonde, this young woman, with large eyes, vibrant features, and the smoothest,

177

most beautiful skin. They were standing face-to-face when Helena saw that the girl was dressed in a type of toga, tied over one shoulder and falling diagonally beneath the opposite breast, a breast bared to the air.

The woman leaned forward and kissed Helena on the lips, a brief and gentle meeting. On parting, the eyes searched hers, and she came forward again, pressing firmer this time, longer, on her mouth. Helena's lips did not move in response. Instead, she took her body through a half-turn to stand with her shoulder facing the girl. Looking over this shoulder she could see fresh tears dropping onto the girl's flushed cheeks. She spoke. "You said you would love me."

It was Judy Brenton's face, Helena's science partner in middle school. The voice was her own.

Now awake, Helena moved her hand across her breast to find the nipple erect. Her crotch was hot. She smoothed her other hand down and pressed hard onto her tingling mound. She worked a finger through and the muscles contracted in anticipation. Then she withdrew, shaking her head in the darkness, and got up to fetch a glass of water.

Chapter Eleven

Friends

It was Wednesday before she saw the client again. She'd forgotten her dream by then, lost as it was to the shadows of the night, the unconscious state. Kate was in a positive mood, strong, buoyant. Helena enquired as to the reason.

"I decided to take your advice. I decided that this would all feel a lot less dramatic and painful if I was sharing it with someone. That's not to undermine you in any way, truly. I mean, someone to talk to as though it was all ordinary, you know, so I can talk like regular people about who I fancy, and how it's all going. So I decided to come out to my friends."

Helena applauded Kate's courage.

"I talked to Robin first. That was cheating really, 'cos I had sort of told him before, two months ago when we were in Paris. But I'd done it in that 'I'm saying, but not inviting conversation' sort of way. We haven't ever talked about it since. I kept it all really natural and told him that I'd been trying to pluck up the courage to do the scene, that I'd been finding it hard to make my way, and really wanted to be in a relationship, that sort of thing. He was totally sweet about it. Said he'd wondered where I'd been getting off to on my own, thought he wasn't my favourite mate anymore. And get this, he said if I ever wanted company, if it wouldn't bugger my chances, he was more than happy to come out for a drink in a gay pub.

"That really gave me a good bit of pluck. So the next night I went round to see Usha and Elisabeth. I have to say, I was nervous that night. I think I was afraid that my girlfriends would see me differently, you know, worry about all the times they undressed in front of me or slept in my bed after a night out. We'd been watching *Point Break* and smoking a bit of pot. I eventually felt I had enough nerve. I started with the 'I have something I want to tell you' line and Usha immediately came back with, 'Shit, you're not pregnant?'.

"It nearly stopped me, but I used it instead. Told her she couldn't be farther from the truth. Liz saved the day. 'No offence, I did wonder. In two years you've shagged no one, not even poor Robin who drools when you enter a room'. It was such a relief!"

Kate prattled on excitedly to explain how they, like Robin, thought it only right that they should support her on a night out. Kate told them about Babes, how nice it was with lots of tables and stools in the open, not a sleazy tucked-away place, and what a mixed crowd. They'd suggested to line Robin up too, and all go out, maybe choose a nice date for Kate.

"I'm not sure Usha's a hundred per cent happy with it. She said, 'No one's going to chat me up, are they? I wouldn't know what to say'. Liz laughed at her and told her no self-respecting lesbian would fancy her anyway and to shut up. So, we're all going out at the weekend."

Helena told Kate how happy she was for her, and so proud that her bravery paid off. Kate said that perhaps now, she would not feel the need for her sessions any longer, at which Helena was obliged to smile – and agree.

Lumpy cheese sauce. Helena pushed it around the pan with a wooden spoon, cursing its congealing mass. Steam shoved the lid off the broccoli.

"Great. Bet you're soggy now too." The limp stems confirmed her fears. "Great, just great!"

She threw it together in a bowl, giving up on

presentation in acceptance of the demise of her general mood. She plonked her miserable butt on the sofa, wondering if some rubbish TV followed by a long bath might help lift her from her melancholy.

Over coffee in the staffroom the next morning, Helena was still trying to shift gear. "Jackie, to prove I'm not a sad loser, fancy going out on the town tomorrow night?"

"Wahay! That's more like it, woman. The usual threesome?"

"But of course."

"Fancy Chinatown? I'll book."

Elisabeth stayed true to her word and organised Usha and Robin for a night out to support their friend. They gathered in Elisabeth's room, sharing hairdryers and lip-gloss while Robin sank a few beers.

"I can't believe you want us to go to Babes," said Usha.

"Doh!" Robin interrupted. "What's not to believe? Where else would she want to go?"

"I told you, it's a nice gay bar," Kate explained for the umpteenth time.

"I'm not worried," added Elisabeth, rolling across the top of her bed in search of a pair of shoes hidden somewhere beneath layers of bedding. "You can pretend to be my partner."

Kate laughed.

Usha whinged. "But I won't know what to say to anyone."

"I'm the one that should be worried," Robin teased. "As the only male of the party, it's more likely some guy will feel the need to rescue me."

No matter what was said, Usha needed two whiskeys before leaving the house, straight and on the rocks, and she sunk them back pretty quickly.

Alighting from their shared cab on the corner, Elisabeth broke the building anticipation by demanding a group hug. "Come on, you lot," she announced loudly. "Let's find a gorgeous girl for our Kate."

Kate didn't know whether to laugh or cry, their support was a great thing, but she prayed they wouldn't blow it by embarrassing her.

They were lucky to find a table, and a good one to assess all the clientele. The lights may have been dimmed, but the wall of mirrors compensated by allowing plenty of viewing time.

Despite the need to order an initial double, Usha relaxed quickly. "Aw, they all look harmless really," she announced on her first sip.

"Actually, they are pretty damn gorgeous from where I'm sitting. Are you sure they're all gay?" Robin asked Kate.

In return she gave her theatrical patronising stare. "I'm guessing not everyone in here is gay, present company and all that. But I'm sure as hell hoping. Did you see the red-head with the gorgeous butt at the bar when we walked in?"

Kate had a brief flash of the Eiffel Tower, minus dialogue, an expression on Robin's face, or a mood, that she'd missed. She didn't want to think about it.

Curiosity and alcohol were getting the better of Elisabeth. She had been buzzing with questions of the more personal kind since Kate had come out. She wasn't quite ready to ask about sex yet, not in detail anyway. What she was dying to know was Kate's taste in girls.

"Right, Kate, come on, who do you fancy in here then?"

Kate, as was her usual habit, had been making discreet mental notes on who was about, relieved that Tani didn't have tonight's shift. "Well, I'll only answer if you swear to be subtle when you look."

"Of course," they hissed back in unison.

"Okay. Table directly behind Robin, far side, the dark-haired girl in the blue top."

Three heads turned simultaneously, Robin included, who nearly pulled off an *Exorcist* style spin.

"Fucking hell! Thanks guys. Subtle, my arse. I'm telling you nothing more!"

Robin laughed. "Oh, Kate. We're sorry. That was so dumb. D'you think she noticed?"

"Doh! No idea," Kate answered sarcastically, refusing to look and find out for herself.

"Let's try it another way," said Robin. "Why don't we take turns pointing out someone that we think might be cute, and you can give scores?"

"Sounds like a good game to me," announced Elisabeth, swivelling in her chair. "I'll go first. Ooh, blonde with the bling handbag."

Usha cut in, "Tight ass brunette with the flowery clip thing in her hair."

"Seriously?" Robin questioned. "Ms Sensible there in the navy shirt with the lovely boobs."

Kate hadn't enjoyed a night out so much in as long as she could remember. Every muscle in her body was letting go of the barriers they'd held high for the last two years; the weight of it all was rolling away. As the tension evaporated, the beers soaked in and her ease was paramount.

No one they chose scored more than six. Usha thought Kate was far too picky.

"I might have a minority to choose from, but that doesn't mean I should lower my standards," Kate retorted haughtily. "Not until I'm really desperate, anyway."

"Okay then," Usha went on. "Ignoring sexuality for the moment, let's look at female celebrities and see who you think is hot."

Kate wasn't given a chance. Robin created a list of gorgeous creatures: Meg Ryan, Angelina Jolie, Christie Turlington, Naomi Campbell. The girls were more particular in their selection in the end, opting for three categories: a) beautiful in a stunning sort of way; b) attractive in that could be stunning/could be ugly sort of way; and c) shaggable.

Robin was astounded that women were so fussy in their categorisation and, God, getting them to agree on one person for each category was nigh on impossible. Still, they were dragging a bit more information out of Kate, who was now slurring a list of quite shaggable actresses.

"We've already said Meg Ryan, so, back to real life," probed Elisabeth further.

"Well, that counsellor I was seeing. I'd do her."

"Is she gay, then?" Robin pounced.

"Dunno. But there's a first time for everything, right?" Kate swallowed the question with her beer.

Blinded by the coloured dragon lights, Tessa tripped on the metal staircase that wound its way out of the first floor restaurants.

Jackie mimicked Tessa's earlier voice, "Another jug of sake, please, another jug of sake. That's the last time you're in charge of ordering. I can't see straight."

"Yeah, yeah," Tessa rolled the words off a clumsy tongue. "You say that every time. Didn't see you refusing any."

Helena took Tessa's arm, and burst into giggles as they both swung off heavily in her direction.

"Thanks for the help, Callender, much appreciated."

A mere five hundred yards to the taxi-rank. They'd need to navigate a few crowded pub doors and other groups of merrymakers stumbling and swaying similarly to themselves, and then they'd be right. They could manage that, couldn't they? They made their way along the noisy street, cheerfully ignoring the suggestive remarks of guys too far gone to carry out their pledges of sexual excesses.

Jackie laughed. "Just as well I didn't want a shag."

Helena tripped over the feet of another late reveller stepping out of a pub doorway. She automatically put her hand onto the girl's shoulder and mumbled an apology. As the face came into focus, she smiled widely and kissed her on the cheek, delighted to find herself face-to-face with Kate. No sooner was it done than Helena realised the inappropriateness and stepped back, again apologising, but for an altogether different reason.

"It's fine, you didn't hurt me," claimed Kate with a suave smile.

"I'm just so surprised to see you," Helena babbled. She became suddenly aware that they were entertaining a circular audience.

"Not a bad surprise, I hope. I've been out for a drink with my friends," Kate explained. "You too, huh?"

Looking up, Helena spotted the name of the bar flashing in neon pink lights. Babes. The place Kate spoke of in her sessions. Her ex-client was out on the prowl.

"Yeah. Me too," she answered with a slur, embarrassed to be drunk in front of the girl.

Kate didn't flinch, her eyes fixed on Helena.

"Maybe next time we'll bump into one another early

enough to have a drink together."

"Yeah, we just might."

The two groups moved on.

"Who was that?" Jackie asked.

"That's the client I've been telling you about." Helena looked back over her shoulder at the disappearing silhouettes.

"Who was that?" Robin posed. "She seemed awfully pleased to see you."

Kate giggled. "She did, didn't she? That's that counsellor I told you about."

Kate went to bed a happy girl, full of gratitude for her great friends, and flushed with fantasies based on her chance meeting with Helena. It was that smile, genuine and unaffected, that warmed her heart. And a kiss! Kate was sure that was not how Helena would greet all her clients, ex or not.

Maybe. Just maybe.

Chapter Twelve

Helena and Kate

Across town, despite the girls' night out, Helena put in another wakeful night. She found herself thinking of Kate, a lot. "I'm over-involved. I've lost my boundaries. I'm … I'm … I'm trying to kid myself. I fancy her. Dear God, I fancy her, a woman, a *young* woman, an ex-client!"

She awoke the next morning to find herself further out of sorts, too aware the excessive sake could not wear all the blame. When she felt fit, she took herself off towards Dudley and the hills. Maybe the fresh air and the trees would go some way to restoring her balance. It didn't work.

She remained agitated, cursing the springtime overgrowth as she tripped her way through the paths, scowling inwardly at the couples she passed. She quizzed herself ruthlessly. What the hell am I going to do? Gay? Because I have a crush on one woman? School mates don't count, right? Even if I am – Kate? She's too young, impressionable, I could damage her. But, dammit, I *really* fancy her.

She knew what she had to do.

Helena felt a heavy hesitancy with every ring trilling in her ear, and was on the verge of hanging up the phone when Brian's easy tone offered greeting.

"I'm sorry to call you on the weekend, Brian," Helena began.

"Is something wrong? Are you okay?"

His concern brought a lump to her throat and she coughed it down to speak. "I'm okay, well, I mean, nothing's wrong. Nothing serious. But, something … or I wouldn't be ringing. Would I?" She tried a chuckle.

"Helena, take a breath and tell me what's up."

She stammered something she knew was unintelligible, and assumed Brian would suspect it was work. A counsellor's load could get heavy and the emotional dam sometimes refused to hold against the torrent of human struggle they supported and waded through daily. They often needed to offload, take care of themselves and protect their own psychological wellbeing.

"Just sounds like you're a bit overwhelmed, Helena. It doesn't have to have a reason, nor does it have to mean anything. A bit of time out, I'd say. I'll handle your caseload. Take the week."

On Sunday she slept long and late, surfacing only to fetch a few papers which she took home and spread about herself. It kept the day at bay. The evening would not be held off so well, the agitation and melancholy swimming together amongst her disconnected thoughts. Helena decided she needed some home comforts that only her mother's house could offer.

Oxford provided relief on Monday in the familiar smells and colours of her childhood. The river bubbled away her self-preoccupation as she lunched with her mother at the Jumping Trout, enjoying the first hint of early-summer sun. It tickled her that Mum could still turn heads in her floaty, bias-cut skirt and mauve jersey top, her short grey crop the height of fashion. Not that her mum noticed. Mum's attention was all hers, every Chanel-scented moment.

"So to what do I owe the pleasure?" Mum asked, untwisting the end of her long beaded necklace.

"Do I need a reason?"

"No, but you usually have one."

"Work just felt a bit full on, that's all. Needed a breather."

Mum took the hint and dutifully lightened the conversation to an appreciation of her latest roses which Helena rewarded by suggesting a rummage in the bookshops followed by afternoon tea in the precepts of the university. Helena adored those buildings for the sense of scale they provided. All was not ill with the world. Not all, whilst such beauty stood around her.

Helena was unaware that her mother had detected her brooding and was doing her utmost to deliver distraction. She was so good at it now, guiding Helena around one of her black moods. She had a film chosen already for their evening at home, a light romantic comedy that might bring a smile to her daughter's face, and perhaps hope into her daughter's heart, for she knew it was for a good relationship that Helena yearned. This love for her career was all very well, but it was give, give, give. She worried at the absence of a special someone, someone to give love back to her girl. Helena slept better than she had in weeks.

On Tuesday, Helena did her duty by her father. Lunch with him was comparably shorter as he had insisted on maintaining a busy career well past state retirement. Her parents had split up when she was seventeen. It was amicable, as far as divorce ever can be. She was old enough to have seen for herself that their lives were almost separate, that they had little left in common, and that even the once-usual tensions were non-existent. They had stayed together longer than anticipated, so as to least affect their daughter's turbulent teenage years, but they wanted things settled before she went to University so she would know how things stood. Logically, Helena couldn't fault them. They had done well by her, by one another. Her heart hurt for it nonetheless, wishing the dream of everlasting love might have won. Oh, well, she'd told herself, this way I get to give them undivided attention without either minding – which was what she did.

Mum had a treat in store when she returned to the house mid-afternoon. The University Drama Society was running a Pinter week and her mother had caught some late ticket sales. Distraction was maintained.

On Wednesday, Helena drove back home to Birmingham with a little more peace in her soul. As soon as she entered the flat she saw the green button flashing on her answering machine. She ignored it. She didn't want her world to catch up with her just yet. Instead, she cleaned, slowly reclaiming only her immediate world with hoover and duster and bleach. Bookshelf rearranged, angle of ornaments aligned, air-pine fresh, all agleam. Bag unpacked, laundry whirling in the machine, kettle on. Helena was going to reward herself with a cup of Earl Grey, then listen to her messages, before running a bath and planning the rest of her week off.

Brian was first, wishing her well, assuring her that her client list was sorted and that she mustn't think of them at all for the rest of the week. The dentist's receptionist was next, a courtesy call informing her that her check-up was overdue.

Jackie was next, hesitant, unusually. "Helena, I've done something that I hope you don't mind. I mean, it felt like it was okay to do. Shoot me if I was wrong. Only that girl, Kate, rang for you and got put through to me in your absence. She said it was nothing to worry about, just a personal call. And, well … I gave her your number. Anyway, if I've fucked up, just don't take the call. I know you always monitor anyway, and I'll call her back and sort it out. Okay? Oh, and Oxford good? Call me."

A bleep and the next message started up. "Helena?" The hairs on her neck suddenly tingled. She'd never heard Kate say her name. "Umm, well. I called work for you. But you're having a week off. So maybe that makes it possibly better timing … to meet up for that drink we talked about. I'll call again. Never can trust these machines. So, well, yeah, that's about it. I'll call again, just in case."

"Oh my God, she called me. She actually called me!" Helena did a little dance as she ran her bath.

That evening she curled up with A.S. Byatt's *Possession*, a novel Tessa had recommended, and the obligatory glass of Australian chardonnay. The TV was off, *Simply Red* was playing gently in the background. An inner smile kindled, died, re-kindled. It was around nine when the phone rang. The monitor picked up.

Tessa. "Wanted to know if you were home safely. Call if you want to go out this weekend. Call if you want to stay in."

Helena continued reading. Not two minutes later, the phone rang again.

"Hi, Helena. Thought you might be home by now." Kate continued talking, the message drawing close to an end.

Helena jumped to the phone, dispossessing herself of Byatt and her bookmark, and sending her wine to the floor in her haste. "Kate, hi. I was in the other room, just caught your voice. How are you?"

"I'm good, thanks. What about you? Where have you been, if it's not rude of me to ask?"

"No, no, no," she stammered girlishly. "It's not rude. I've been catching up with my parents, that's all."

"No major excitement, then? No overseas trips? No new romance?"

No new romance? Was Kate fishing? "No, just home grown fussing and spoiling. Does you good sometimes."

"It does. Look, do you have any plans for the rest of the week?"

"None yet, no, nothing, except ... oh yeah, Tessa and Jackie are harassing me to catch up. They're the two I was with last Friday when I, um, tripped over you."

"I remember it well. I thought I recognised them. They work at the unit too, don't they? I've seen them."

"Yes. It was Jackie who gave you my number. The dark one."

"Ah, so she told you I rang."

"Yep."

"And you got my message, the one I left on your phone, I mean?"

"Yes. I did."

There was a pause.

"Right. Well, if you haven't agreed on anything yet with your friends, how would you feel about meeting for that drink? If that's not too presumptuous."

"No. I mean, no it's not presumptuous, not no to the drink."

"Phew. I thought I was going to have to act all embarrassed or something. Where do you want to meet? It doesn't have to be Babes," she joked.

Helena thought quickly, unsure if she wanted to be in public on her first potential date with a woman, afraid she might show herself up by behaving awkwardly, afraid she'd look like a scared schoolgirl. "Actually, if you wouldn't mind, how would you feel about coming over here? I've not been feeling my most sociable this week."

"If you'd rather not meet, it's okay."

"No, no, Kate. I mean, no to me not wanting to go out with you, not the other no … you know."

"Sure, I understand. Whatever suits you."

"Great. Drinks here, tomorrow night okay?" And she gave her address and directions.

When she picked up her book again she saw that her

hands were shaking, and knew any pages read would have to be revisited. Her head was spinning. Putting the book down, she fetched some more wine and wandered to the mirror in the bathroom. She unbuttoned her pyjama top, turning sideways to look at the flash of cleavage. She piled her hair high, pulling out tendrils to hang by her face. "You look so old. Shit, what am I going to wear?"

Helena dashed to the bedroom and rifled through her wardrobe pulling out tidy skirts, smart trousers, a pair of cords and V-neck jumpers, and flung them aside. Suddenly everything looked too grown-up, passé, out-of-fashion, professional, tailored. Certainly not nineteen and trendy. She cursed her clothes, cursed her taste, cursed her curves that meant she couldn't do sportswear without looking a frump. The pile she threw across the room obliterated the bed before she caught hold of herself. "What are you doing? You know, she might just want friendship. And you know what, she's seen you in your work clothes before anyway. She's kind of got that picture already. Changing it now might be a mistake. And you'll look a damn fool if you rush out and buy something from Top Shop. Simple jeans will do. Cut across class, age, and money. Just pick a decent top." She calmed down.

Thursday was an insufferably long day. Everything lasted forever, especially the traffic through town, the queue at the supermarket till, and the old dear with coppers for everything at the post office. Helena had hoped these mundane tasks would occupy her butterfly brain and while away the day, yet on completion of their interminable irrelevance, she found that they'd been achieved in record time and only two hours in total had lapsed. Damn. She didn't feel like another walk in the hills. She didn't feel like reading her book. She finished the morning with daytime TV. At least its magazine style delivery gave her no time to tire of any given article. At lunchtime she indulged in a long bath, early, yes, but not without logic. She didn't want Kate arriving in a flat smelling of aromatic bath oils. That would imply that she had been fussing about how she looked, or worse, cleaning her body for a reason. She didn't want to look like she was up for it, not on a first date. If it was a first date. She wanted softly-sexy without looking like a tart, a come-on that was subtle enough to ignore, depending on how the night unfolded.

Helena chastised her mental ramblings. "This is ridiculous! You are behaving like you've got a hot date and you don't even know if she fancies you yet. Seriously got to calm down."

She determined that the afternoon would be spent covering work files. There were case notes and journals in her bag that would benefit from some attention. That should keep her mind occupied and nerves at bay.

Kate was due at eight. Helena had chosen the time specifically so that if things didn't go well, they could chat a while, stretch it 'til ten, and it would seem a respectable time to part without looking too painfully like an escape had been engineered. The last fifteen minutes of the twentieth hour of that day gave Helena too many opportunities: run to the mirror and query her appearance again; dash around the room rearranging cushions so the general ambience was one of casual nonchalance; disguise the fact that she hadn't made an effort to make herself and her place look nice this evening. Kate was kind enough not to prolong her suffering and arrived on the dot.

The beginning of the evening was stiff, uncomfortable. Helena opened the door in her jeans and neat jumper and found herself extending a hand to the lean young woman in loose cargo pants and a pretty fitted top. Before she could cringe at her formality, Kate took it with a wry smile. "Good evening."

"Um, hi," Helena muttered, shrugging off her stupidity, "Come on in. Glass of wine? White or red?"

"I'd prefer a beer if you have one?"

"Of course, yes." Helena led the way to the kitchen wanting to kick herself, for everything she did seemed to point to the almost ten years between them. A generation gap! In the living room, Helena hesitated in front of the armchair while looking at the sofa, trying to decide what was least awkward. Kate took the sofa with confidence and smiled so easily that Helena chose to join her there. Another silent moment was given to sipping their drinks.

"So," Kate started, "you already know everything about me. I guess it's your turn to talk."

Helena smiled. "What do you want to know?"

"Start with your early childhood," she parodied Helena's counsellor tone.

"Ouch."

"No, I didn't mean … I wasn't taking the piss."

Helena laughed and all tension in the room was gone.

She delivered a brief history; where she grew up, how she'd just been there to go shopping and to the theatre with her mum, her education and career choices. Autobiographical details divulged, there was nowhere else to go except to her relationship history. Well, they say you should never discuss exes on a first date, but nobody said this was a date and nothing yet suggested it might be. Helena didn't fancy her near-marriage as a topic right now, so used the hiatus to refill their drinks and put out some crisps and nibbles.

Kate took a bold lead. "Are you seeing someone at the moment, only, well, I'm not."

And there it was.

Helena bit the bullet. "I've never been with a woman

before."

"I guessed as much. Does it matter?"

"Only as much as our age gap and the fact that I was your counsellor."

"Age is only a problem if you make it one. I'm not seeing an old woman here." Kate slowly looked over Helena's body, then reached forward and took her hand. "You know what I want. I told you as much in our sessions. Love, honesty, fidelity, someone to hold and touch, and make love to. You're not my counsellor now. And it doesn't matter how we met, just that we did."

Helena gazed at the hand holding hers, mesmerised by its lightness of touch. "Is this an awful idea to you? You do find me attractive, don't you? Tell me I'm not imagining this."

"You're not imagining it."

Helena sighed the realisation into her bones.

"Okay." Kate stood up. "We both know what the other thinks. Time to sleep on it."

Helena thought Kate was inviting herself to stay and she wasn't ready with a response.

Kate provided it. "I'm going to go now, and I'll ring you sometime soon."

At the door, they stopped a minute, staring questioningly into one another's eyes, then, following a brief hug, Kate was gone. Pressing the door to a quiet close, Helena was stunned. What had she done? Why had Kate left? She ran an urgent rewind of the evening in her mind, then grinned to herself that at almost thirty, the world still held surprises for her.

"I want her. I want her." Sleep came peacefully.

In the morning Helena's world was sprinkled with magic. It

196

glistened and sparkled and smiled back at her.

A sleepy Jackie answered the phone. "Hey, you! Where have you been?"

"Oh, just pootling about. Saw Mum and Dad. Enjoyed a bit of me time."

"Feeling better?"

"Sure am. In fact, I've got something to tell you."

"Keep talking. It sounds interesting."

"Well, it is. But it might come as a bit of a shock. And I need your advice."

"Go on."

"You know you gave Kate my number." Helena proceeded to fill Jackie in on the phone call and last night's conversation.

"So how are you feeling about all this today?" Jackie's calm gave nothing away.

"I can only explain it by saying that I know this is something huge. I can feel this enormous opportunity sitting in front of me, and something inside knows that I have to take it. All I've been able to think of is how much I fancy her, how much I want to be with her."

"Like you felt when you wanted to marry Richard?"

"That's the truly bizarre thing. I didn't feel like this about Richard. Or anyone else for that matter. Yes, I fell in love with him, but it never felt like this. It was never this overwhelming thing, with a power way beyond me."

"Well, Helena, all I can say is, if you feel as strong as you do, go for it. Bloody hell, exciting or what?"

Helena burst into tears.

"What? What'd I say?"

"You're so good about it. I was afraid of what you'd say."

"Don't be so daft, girl. What did you think I'd say?"

"But she's a girl. And nineteen!"

"Details. You only live once."

"What about the client thing? My professional ethics?"

"Were you interested in her when you were counselling her?"

"No! It hadn't crossed my mind."

"There you are, then. What's there to talk about? Ex-client."

So much pleasure two days in a row. Helena didn't care to question how she got so lucky, and she all but ran to the ringing phone.

Could they meet again? Go out for a drink maybe?

Helena asked if she wouldn't mind coming to the flat again. It wasn't that she didn't want to be seen out with her. God no. "It's just that, well, it's easier to … to talk here."

In a soft-pink shirt and dark jeans, Kate was a picture. It was easy to smile and welcome her in.

Kate went straight for a kiss. "How's the thinking been going?"

"So, straight in there, hey?"

"I don't do straight," said Kate with a wicked smile.

"Well, lucky for you, I'm prepared to waver a little myself," Helena teased back.

"Seriously though, I have been pondering things." Helena grabbed Kate a beer from the fridge. Kate's fingers lingered on hers as she handed it over. "Do you agree with the fact that we both feel something is worth investigating?"

Kate pulled a face.

198

"You know what I mean." Helena turned to pour some wine. "Is it possible to move forward and start from a place that isn't counsellor and client?"

"You're the counsellor. Is it?"

"We're in a good position. We're not dumping anyone, breaking hearts and that stuff."

"Oh, I don't know." Kate faked a pause. "Perhaps there's someone out there pining for me."

"Thanks."

"Helena, stop analysing. Keep it simple. People have no idea what they want, or who they want to be with, and we suddenly encounter this. Us! I don't care what anyone thinks."

"Which is why I have to ask, how do you think your parents are going to take it?"

Kate put her hands in the air. "They love me. They'll want me to be happy."

And she said it with such resolve that Helena suppressed her response, the voice in her head that was replaying snippets of Kate's counselling sessions: they're very religious; church every Sunday, and Mum does the flowers; I couldn't wait to get away to university; everyone knows everyone around home; it's claustrophobic; it would never occur to them that I could be gay.

"I will tell them." It was as though Kate had read her mind. "More importantly, what will your parents think?"

There was an unbidden reminder of age, Helena's parents more likely of a generation that would still condemn homosexuality. She genuinely had no idea how they would handle it. They might be glad. They might be horrified. "I'm too old for them to care," she joked.

The two women sat on the sofa facing one another.

"So what now?" Helena posed.

"I want to kiss you again."

A schoolyard rush of pleasure threatened to make Helena giggle and run away, suddenly unsure as to the mechanics of a planned kiss with a girl. Kate leaned forward. Helena was intrigued discovering the difference of a woman's lips on hers. She had half expected it to be no different from any other kiss she'd experienced. She'd known gentle men, yet it was altogether lighter, kinder.

Kate pulled back and smiled. "Was that okay for you? Not too terrifying?"

"Not terrifying at all. Do you think you can do it again?"

"Oh, yes. I can do that again."

Many, many times more, 'til they were both lost in the exploration of tongues and the tantalising pleasure they could give and receive. Beautiful, delicious kisses.

Kate's hands held her close, pressed at the middle of her back, sliding up across her shoulders and down again. She wondered if Kate wanted to touch her more, and knew she tensed with the thought. She was afraid. Of what? Her ignorance? That her body might be a disappointment to one so young? Kate seemed to sense her apprehension, and the wandering hands stilled.

Helena had to make good, and ran her fingertips over Kate's face and around the back of her neck, into her hair as they kissed more. Kate drew her close, again, holding her head in the crook of her shoulder, her palm gently on Helena's cheek. "In time, it will all be fine in time."

They shared such faith in this thing.

Chapter Thirteen

The Pearsons

In meaningful glances beyond Kate's view, Mr and Mrs Pearson reminded one another of 'how they handle their children delivering bad news', which, of course, in this case, they assumed would involve the announcement of a pregnancy. They were fortunate. They had the guidance of their church. Whilst fornication beyond wedlock was itself sinful, it is the act that is unclean not the person.

Embrace your child and correct them. Punishment is the realm of God. As for the spawn of this erroneous path, the blame cannot be placed there. The infant is innocent of its parents' sin. The infant is a child of God. It must be drawn into the flock, protected and nurtured.

The Pearsons would cope. They were disappointed that their daughter had broken their moral code but they were not so naïve as to deny the terrible pressures on the young today to live a more physical relationship. In fact, they were truly quite proud that she'd been wise so long through her teenage years and the start of her university life, as had their other children. But surprised they were, that she had not exercised more wisdom and avoided the consequences of indulging her desires. They knew it wasn't hard to obtain birth control devices, of every sort.

"I'm not pregnant, Mum."

Mr and Mrs Pearson looked to one another in confusion as their planned defence strategy collapsed before them.

Flabbergasted, Mum put the question to her daughter, "So what is the problem, then? It's obvious something's wrong."

Kate had made a spontaneous visit then stayed in on

Saturday evening, alone with her parents when her brothers and sister were all heading out, and with that, they'd known something was very wrong.

Kate shuddered at the word *wrong*. It didn't set a helpful tone. "I'm gay."

Dad spluttered his mouthful of tea giving Mum the excuse to rise from the kitchen table and find some tissues, rub his back, make physical contact with her ally, and return.

"Kate, what are you talking about?" Dad tried a sympathetic smile and that parental voice that knew better than his troubled and misguided offspring.

"I'm gay. I thought you should know. I'm not attracted to men, never have been. I tried. But never will again. I need you to know."

Dad opened and closed his mouth in silent objection.

Mum's eyes welled and her disappointment shed unchecked down her face. "This is a mistake, Kate, a foolish mistake. You're too pretty to be a … a …" She could not speak the word, or any word for it. "You've always been popular with the boys, haven't you noticed? This is all just teenage anxiety and worry. You just haven't found the right man yet. These things take time. And anyway, have you ever really made time for boys? You're always too busy studying and training. That's all it is. And now you have time to notice other girls at uni with boyfriends and you're just wondering why you don't have one yet. What about Robin? I'm sure he's really keen on you. You're a late developer, that's all. It's a bit quick off the mark to call yourself …"

"Gay, Mum. Or lesbian."

"Oh, don't say that, Kate, don't say that."

"Now don't upset your mother like that."

"I'm not trying to upset anyone. I'm trying to be honest

with you." Kate rose to the whistling kettle, rose to create a breathing space, break the rising tide of hysteria.

Once all were seated again, nestling mugs for security, Dad restarted the discussion with a helpful, "What makes you think you're gay then?"

Although she had anticipated the question, she didn't feel she had a sufficient answer for her parents' understanding. What was she to say? 'All those years, Dad, of fascination with women's tennis. It wasn't the ball I was watching', is what she wanted to say. Instead she offered statements hoping they'd stand as facts.

"I always knew, really. I couldn't relate to gossip about blokes with the girls at training. I couldn't see what they found so interesting. I didn't want a boyfriend. I went through the motions but it was a disaster, and I never told you how much of a disaster, but you remember, Mum, it didn't go well. Even in my dreams, when I'm waiting for love, it's between women."

Mum drew a sharp breath. Dad's face turned scarlet.

"I know this is hard for you to hear, but best that you hear it from me."

"Why, who else would we hear it from? Do people know?"

"No one knows anything yet, Mum."

"Perhaps it's best, at least until you, umm, sort yourself out, you know, give yourself time to work through this whole idea. Maybe get some help."

"Help? This isn't a disease." Kate felt the tears threaten and the anger rise.

"But, Kate, you know your Bible." It was only a matter of time, and this was it. Dad started the religious line. "It says it's not normal, Kate."

"Listen to yourselves!" she screamed, storming to her

feet. "You're telling me that I don't know myself, that I have no idea what I want. That I'm stupid and confused. I'm a problem! I need fixing! That I'm not normal! Is that how you choose to see me? A problem? An abnormal aberration? God's mistake?"

Mr Pearson stood silently, his knuckles white where he held the edge of the table.

"Kate, that's not what your dad's saying."

"So what are you saying, Mum? That this is okay with you?"

"No."

"No? Exactly."

"Kate, wait." Mum was up on her feet too. "It's all a bit of a shock, you know. You can't be hard on us for that. And we need to be sure that you're sure. Lots of girls go through it, and boys. It's called *a phase.*"

"A phase. Trust me, this is no phase."

"But how can you be so sure?"

Kate glared at her father's question, her eyes burning with the truth.

"You're seeing someone, aren't you? A woman?"

"Yes, Dad, a woman."

"Don't, Kate," her mother warned.

Stand-off time.

Thirty seconds that felt like thirty minutes.

Three people standing around a table, locked in conflict. All emotional, none rational.

Mrs Pearson sat. "Who's the woman?"

"No one you know." Kate hadn't wanted to bring Helena into this at this stage. Not until her parents dealt with her own identity first.

"How long has this been going on?" Mrs Pearson continued.

"Not very long."

It was all the leeway Mum needed. "You see," she replied, her hands open like some consoling Jesus. "It's far too soon to call yourself gay. It might all blow over."

Kate slumped into her chair. "Don't you see, Mum? If it was something so trivial and passing, do you think I would put myself through this, put you both through this? You told me I'd know when I met the right one. And I think I know."

"Your mother meant men." Mr Pearson was the last to sit.

Kate ignored the comment and carried on. "This is different, Mum. This is special. I know she's the one."

"So who is she?"

Kate took this as a good sign that she had reached her mother's heart in some shape or form, perhaps her shared experience of finding love. "I was having counselling for a while, to straighten out my thoughts, to be more sure of myself. Helena was my counsellor."

"She was your counsellor?" Dad pushed his mug aside "Well, we're not having that! A counsellor has a duty to their patient. She had a duty to you, to treat you in confidence and with professional distance. She is in breach of her oath and regulations, her ethics, all of it. She's a disgrace to her profession. And trust me, my dear girl, I won't let her get away with it."

"Dad? Dad!"

This cycle of the argument was no calmer than the rest, and contained no more rational thought. Kate ran from the house, wretched at how badly she'd handled the situation. She stopped, panting, several streets away. Digging her phone from her pocket she called Helena, crying as she apologised, afraid that this might all be too much if Helena wasn't sure.

"I'm so sorry. It all went horribly wrong. I've buggered

everything up. I told them about you. I tried not to, I didn't mean to. Dad went off about breach of professional duty and threatened God knows what. I'm so sorry, Helena. I've made such a mess. "

"Calm down, Kate. You've had a horrible night. It's okay. Just remember, you're not my client any more. We've done nothing wrong."

It was relatively easy for Helena to sound controlled when Kate couldn't see her face. It wasn't so easy to feel it, alone in her flat, the phone now silent. "You'd better be right, Ms Callender. You'd better be right."

Mr Pearson was adamant that this woman be called to answer for her misdemeanour, her abuse and misguidance of his daughter's obvious trust and awe of her.

"I'm not sure we should take that line, Tony." Avril Pearson tried to dissipate her husband's anger. "Kate's already run off. What might she do if we push it any further?"

Tony was unmoved. "We might alienate her now, for a while, but we have to look at the pain we'd be saving her in the long run."

"I just think the whole thing might fade away quicker if we don't force her hand. By fighting her into a corner, she might dig in her heels. We might make things worse."

"No, flush it out now, before it has time to take root. She said it hasn't been going on long, so we can stop it going further. And that woman has to face consequences."

Round and round they went until only two things were decided: that this counsellor was in breach of her position, and that their daughter wasn't gay.

"We'll do this properly, above board, in a civilised fashion. It's a genuine grievance. I'll find out where she works. We'll take it from there."

Mrs Pearson agreed.

First thing Monday morning, Helena made an appointment to speak with Brian.

"Sounds important," he said.

"Oh, it is, Brian, very important. I'm seeing an ex-client. Kate Pearson."

"Kate?" Brian's face betrayed only a modicum of surprise. "I didn't realise that you …"

"Were gay? No, neither did I."

"It's not a problem." He was truthfully unfazed.

"I think it is. She's nineteen and was in therapy, with me."

"Were you seeing her during that time?"

"Of course not."

"Helena, she's over the age of consent, not that such a thing exists for lesbianism in the eye of the law. And she *was* in therapy. It's done. Your relationship is none of my business."

"Brian, thank you for taking that position. I appreciate it. But the reason it is a problem is because her parents are about to make it one."

"Explain."

"They have it in mind that the relationship started when she was in my care. They believe that I abused my position as a means to influence and manipulate Kate's feelings."

"I know you wouldn't do such a thing. Didn't you transfer Caroline for exactly that reason?"

"Exactly. But the Pearsons' stand is that I took advantage of their daughter's vulnerability when she was confused about her sexuality."

"And what are you telling me?"

"That it didn't cross my mind, the whole time. That I supported her professionally and at no time felt my boundaries were compromised. We had terminated on her instigation. I agreed as ample progress had been made. We ran into one another in town a week later, literally, and joked about meeting up sometime. She called, we met, and it went from there."

"Then my original position remains. Your relationship is beyond the parameters of your work and should remain there. What do you think the parents are going to do?"

"I'm pretty sure they're going to lodge a formal complaint to have me ousted."

"A bit harsh. What are they like? Do you know?"

"Religious. Homosexuality is a sin. Seems to me it's easier for them to scapegoat than deal with reality. They want to lash out and blame someone. I suppose it's better than lashing out at Kate."

"Okay. We'll have to wait and see what happens, won't we? I trust you, Helena. You've always been a woman of integrity. I'm satisfied with what you've said. If they get in touch, I'll deal with it. My advice, be careful in the staffroom. Tongues will wag. You're full of surprises." He added a wink. "Do your best to forget about it, after all, it might never happen."

Another two weeks lapsed before anything was heard from the Pearsons. For Helena, it was somewhat a relief when word finally broke. The acidity of anticipation bubbled away in her stomach each and every morning and remained longer throughout the day as time moved on. Apparently it was Mr Pearson who led the investigation. Having spoken with the Student Health Body at the university, and coerced them into breaking the rules of confidentiality with the insertion of the word 'malpractice' into his ranting, he was informed Kate had requested treatment off-campus and that their usual recommendation was the Youth Unit at Sutton Coldfield.

Brian kept Helena informed every step of the way. The initial phone call he took was quite heated. Mr Pearson was on a witch hunt. It wasn't a problem. Brian wasn't intimidated by inflated emotion, particularly when it involved the misplacement of righteous indignation. Brian agreed to meet the Pearsons face-to-face. The phone conversation concluded with Mr Pearson's announcement that he'd give that woman a piece of his mind, unaware that Brian had no intention of allowing him to do so. The appointment was made for the end of the week and Helena was instructed to absent.

"I'd rather be here. I'm more than willing to face them. It's my problem, Brian," Helena had argued.

Brian wouldn't have it.

"I'm just worried that if the Pearsons make a song and dance of it all, it could be blown out of all proportion and land in the local press. I'll resign before I bring the unit down."

"There'll be no talk of resignation. I want you to stay home for the morning. I'll meet them alone. I'll do this my way."

Helena's nights were bittersweet. Each evening with Kate clarified her purpose, validated her certainty that she must fight for what she believed. Platitudes of universal writings flooded her mind: the course of true love never runs smooth; better to have loved and lost than never to have loved at all; the greatest good is preceded by the greatest evil, and so on. But as soon as Kate was gone, she was flooded with doubt, trying to ignore the possibility that the Pearsons might have enough power over their daughter to pull her away, if they swayed their arguments in their favour. Time would tell, as it does, and if Kate walked away, then truly there could be no loss for it would mean that she was not of the substance she pertained. The only pain would be to Helena's dignity, with a serious question mark against her judgement, her intuition.

Wednesday evening was spent silently, limbs entwined, with a DVD to disguise the disinclination to talk about the fact that Mr and Mrs Pearson would be travelling up on Thursday. They had insisted on spending the evening with Kate before tackling Brian on the Friday. Kate wanted to be with Helena, but Helena thought it wise not to inflame the situation.

Helena would not be drawn on plans for the weekend. It wasn't possible when Friday could change all.

So there was nothing to talk about. *Scent Of A Woman* played to their silence.

Helena arrived in the unit at noon, feeling like a spy watching her own life. She waited quietly with a cup of coffee in one of the counselling rooms close to Brian's office. Helena swallowed down her nausea with a mouthful of lukewarm caffeine. It was the last one she could manage as she sat anxiously on the edge of her chair, the mug growing ever colder in her hands.

"Helena," Brian said. "Come into my office."

She followed, but couldn't sit, so Brian got straight to the point.

"Your suppositions were entirely correct. It was most helpful to have your insights beforehand, and your process notes.

I was well equipped. Initially Mr Pearson was furious that you would not be personally called to task. He definitely wanted his pound of flesh."

Helena cringed.

"Mrs Pearson, however, seemed relieved."

"Really?"

"Really. That's when I knew they'd give in eventually."

Helena collapsed into a chair, relief draining the blood from her limbs. Brian sat in front of her and took her hands.

"It's going to be fine. Okay? You were absolutely right about the approach they'd take. Salient details only. First, they tried to make an issue of their daughter's age and abuse of trust. I factually dismissed both counts as she is over eighteen and your professional relationship had concluded. They moved on to their religious stance which I carefully pointed out to be a personal dilemma and not one which had any bearing on the facts. Then they argued that Kate was not gay and never had been. I felt sorry for them, Helena. Mrs Pearson cried. We have to remember this is a big thing for them too. And yes, they wanted to believe that you had taken advantage of the doubts she expressed in her sessions to make a pass at her. I simply responded by reaffirming my confidence in your professionalism, as supported by your process notes."

"Brian, I am so sorry to have put you through this."

"You were just the scapegoat, Helena. You said it yourself. Their difficulty is in accepting their daughter's sexuality. This was going to happen for them one way or another. I tried to remind them what a difficult position they were placing both me and their daughter in by challenging knowledge acquired during confidential therapy. I afforded them one minor breach. I told them Kate did not come to counselling because she was querying her sexuality. From the outset, she was confident in her knowledge of who she was. It was issues around being gay that were her concern, that Kate came to us as a lesbian seeking emotional support. Mr Pearson suddenly threatened me with the press, but Mrs Pearson silenced him. She said, 'And where would that leave us, love? We'd be the ones to tell the world she's gay. She might never forgive us. Things are bad enough now, but we'd lose her for sure if we did that'."

"Wow. Good on the mum."

"I did grab my own counselling moment to elaborate on how difficult all this was for Kate, how she needed their support and acceptance, if they could find it in their hearts to give it. I told them the usual, that she needed to know they loved her, even if they didn't like or understand her behaviour. Five more minutes of that and the Pearsons left thanking me."

"Bloody hell, Brian. What a turnaround. You are amazing. I can't thank you enough."

"Well, it won't be plain sailing for you on a personal level, but you know that in terms of your career, your record is intact. Now go and enjoy your weekend."

Kate met with her mother and father after the meeting, unsure of just how much she hated them at that very moment. The noisy supermarket coffee shop was chosen more for its busy neutrality than convenience.

Her mother began. "We discussed the matter in detail. Mr Sharpe is quite convinced that nothing unprofessional occurred and that no further action on that front is possible or necessary. But if we should ever find out otherwise in the future, Kate, we will not ignore it. Is that clear?"

Kate looked at her father's frozen expression, the vein throbbing in his neck. She clenched back an urge to challenge him. It would only ignite more confrontation.

"Your father and I don't find this easy to understand. We have our doubts about your choice and they won't vanish overnight. We did what we believed was right. But you're nineteen, and capable of making your own decisions. At the end of the day, you are our daughter and we love you. We wouldn't want you staying away from home because of all this."

Kate couldn't imagine why she'd want to go home anytime soon.

Kate made a rabbiting phone call, babbling excitedly.

Helena shared the celebratory mood. "Wouldn't this conversation be easier face-to-face? Here? Later?"

Balmy. Not a word often used to describe an early English summer evening. Helena pushed at the windows of her living room, opening the room to the air from the small balcony. The city lights had only begun to twinkle, ill-defined against the twilight sky, with the last of the day's setting sun reflecting off the inch of canal she could see in the distance. Birmingham charmed her with its unique mix of high-grade partying, cosmopolitan culture and earthy humanism. She was glad to be living here, easier and more accommodating than the too upper-middle-classness of Oxford with its moralistic restraints. She moved to the bedroom. The view there afforded a screen of high oaks, marking the borders of the playing fields beyond, the greenery providing a rest from the urbane hustle and bustle. Helena opened this window too, and folded the duvet back. Tonight she wanted Kate to stay. They hadn't yet spent a night together, Helena too precious about her space, about sharing her morning

213

face.

Tonight was different. Those barriers that interrupted progress had been lifted. She felt Kate was hers now. Permission granted to go ahead. Not a blessing as such on their relationship. They had no need of that. But there was no doubt that the threat now removed from her career, and the accusation over her integrity revoked, the consequential euphoric relief provided an aphrodisiac.

Helena was aglow with it all, and dressed accordingly in loose cotton pants, a barely-buttoned white shirt, and a tight little camisole, bra-less beneath. She was happy in her skin tonight.

Kate registered the confidence on arrival. She too, was more relaxed this night, glad that the weight she had been trying to play down was finally lifted. The women embraced fully, inside the door, so glad to be in one another's reach. They kissed and laughed, and thanked the Lord, and kissed again without moving from the hallway. Finally, Helena took Kate's hand and led her through to the kitchen where the glasses stood waiting. She took a bottle of Veuve Clicquot from the fridge. Tonight was not a night for beer and chardonnay.

"I thought we deserved this tonight, don't you?"

"Great minds," said Kate as she went back to the hall to redeem the bag she'd left there. She pulled out a bottle of Moët. "This one needs the fridge too."

A pop, a hiss and a chink later, they stood in the living room toasting their future.

"You know, I think it might be warm enough for this little balcony tonight," Kate suggested. "Do you have chairs?"

"Two fold-up ones behind the kitchen door."

Two calico director's chairs were brought through and duly assembled. Concrete cooling already, Helena used the excuse to tuck her toes beneath Kate's thighs opposite her, as they

214

shared the details of how the day had unfolded for Brian, and for Kate with her folks. They talked quickly, over one another, laughing at what were now punch-lines, making light of the events. Scraping the chair across the balcony, Helena made to refill the glasses. A window slammed shut beneath them in the flat below.

Helena clinked her glass to Kate's. "Congratulations all round, it seems." She was feeling giddy already.

Kate's face took on an intensity, and she shifted from her chair and knelt before Helena. As she lifted her head, Helena saw the tears forming in Kate's eyes.

"I am so sorry, Helena. It could have gone so horribly wrong today. I'm sorry they put you through that. I'm sorry they threatened you that way. I hate that they made you sick with worry. You know nothing they could have done would change how I feel, don't you? I'd made up my mind. I wasn't going to give you up, no matter what they said or did, even if it meant losing them all." The tears tumbled onto her cheeks. "I asked myself so many questions, querying what was right, what was wrong. But I love you, Helena. That's what's right. All this shit they caused made that one thing clear to me. I'm in love with you, have been from the start."

Helena placed her glass to the ground so that she could take this beautiful face, so totally honest and open, in her hands. She kissed the eyelids, tasting salt. "Don't cry any more. I love you too." Running her hand across the shoulders, made bare except for the fine strap of the vest Kate wore, Helena hesitated. "Oh, honey, you have goose bumps. Are you getting cold?"

With a grin, Kate replied, "I could just say it was you. But that wouldn't be entirely true. Early summer evenings don't hold out very long, do they?"

Indoors, as Helena refilled their glasses, she had an idea.

215

"How about bubbles times two?"

"We haven't finished the first one yet, "Kate answered, mildly amused.

"No, bubbles *times two*. Champagne, bubble bath. Warm you up again."

"Excellent idea."

Helena went off to run the bath and light some aromatic candles. It had occurred to her in a flash that this might be an easier way for her to get naked with her girlfriend, a natural context for easing their bodies together.

Scene set, she went to the kitchen to open the second bottle of bubbly. She called to Kate, "I'm sorry, I don't have an ice-bucket for this," and took it through to the bathroom windowsill.

"I'm a student," came the reply. "What makes you think I expect an ice-bucket?" Kate joined Helena in the doorway of the bathroom. She'd brought the glasses from the lounge and placed them on the shelf. "So you love me, huh?" She spoke coyly as she stepped closer. "Gonna show me?"

Helena whispered between the playful lips and adventurous tongue, "Maybe."

Kate's tongue glided across Helena's lips once more before penetrating. In the same moment her hand travelled from hair, to her neck, and then under her shirt front to trace the outline of her breast. Kate felt the nipple harden to her palm as she pushed her tongue more forcefully into Helena.

The shirt was easily removed. Kate stepped back a moment to admire the woman before her. Tracing her collarbone with a fingertip, she raised her eyes to Helena. "You are so beautiful," she whispered, before their mouths found one another again.

The bath was a great idea. It worked exactly as Helena

had hoped. Kate, being taller, sat back first, and Helena laid herself between the long legs. Helena concentrated on the sensation of this female body that ran the length of hers. It was altogether smoother, with a different type of strength in the lean muscles, a gentle security and all too sensually beautiful. What pleased her most was the aesthetics, for there was no part of the female anatomy that was not a picture of beauty, in and of itself.

For Kate, it was a straightforward matter – the woman she loved was lying naked in her arms. It was blissful. More bubbles were imbibed and the women relaxed further into one another as they had hoped.

Helena was quiet, eyes closed, lost in the warmth of it all when Kate kissed the lobe of her ear and spoke softly.

"I want to make love to you." They bundled one another up in towels and kissed their way to the bedroom.

"Let me light some candles. I want to be able to see you." Helena, braver now that the bath had broken the ice, did not want the darkness to intrude on this magical experience. She wanted images that she could hold in her mind forever afterwards, no fumbling and groping to interrupt their harmony, no eyes shut tight that didn't truly want to see. Making love with Kate would be different in every way possible. Most particularly because she felt it so much.

Making love. Physical choreography of heartfelt emotions. Desire, to taste on the merest lick of a tongue. Breathing the scent of the one you wish to possess – mentally, physically. Working bodies simultaneously, seeking harmony, ecstasy.

Helena moaned quietly as Kate suckled gently at her breast, playing with the auburn tresses strewn across her midriff. Butterfly-kisses moved downward along her stomach. Kate pressed with the weight of her palm, pushing Helena's thighs apart and a single omnipotent finger found its way inside.

The utter, utter softness of it. Bubbles times three.

In the early morning light, Kate stroked her sleeping lover, indulging in the memory of the night before. Helena's complicity was so complete that Kate thought herself foolish for ever wondering if the woman she loved might not really be gay.

Chapter Fourteen

Everyone Has an Opinion

Jo Pearson was hanging off the top bunk talking to her pal Louise from her upside down mouth.

"Did you know, Louise? Did you ever look at our Kate and think, mmm, something funny about you?"

"Can't say it ever crossed my mind. It's not the kind of question you ask yourself about people, not unless you have some totally obvious reason for asking, like they have short hair and checked shirts and ask you out for a pint."

Jo swung herself upright and climbed down to sit nearer her friend. "That would never describe Kate. It's weird though, how you think you know someone, your own flesh and blood for God's sake, only to find out that you haven't a clue. We've slept in these beds for the last ten years at least, and I never knew. She never even hinted at it. I've been searching my memories for something, anything that may have given it away, some subtle hint or action that I might have missed. I can't come up with anything.

"We played together a lot when we were small. She had dolls, same as me, dressed them up, did their hair. It wasn't like she wanted the boys' toys or anything. I suppose there was a time when she was about six that she became fascinated by Tom and Dan and tortured them to go out with their friends and play adventures. She had a bit of a tomboy phase, but it passed. When we were coming up on eleven, maybe twelve, we used to nick Mum's make-up purse and sit in here putting on blusher and eye-shadow. She was as into it as I was. And we'd do our hair, and all that stuff you and I still do now. I suppose that sort of stopped when she got into her athletics in a big way. I presumed it was because it wasn't practical anymore. You don't see many runners glammed up to the eyeballs do you, except that Flo woman. Your make-up would run with all that sweat, wouldn't it? Do you remember when she pulled Lewis? God, everyone was after him. He was a right hunk. I know it didn't last or anything, but that was his fault. Kate told me about it the next night. She made me swear not to talk about it 'cos she didn't want Mum to go off on one. Kate said he spent the whole of their date trying to slip the hand down her shirt in the cinema, and when she blocked him he tried her thigh, and higher. And if that wasn't enough he put her hand on his you-know-what on top of his jeans, like, still in the cinema."

"You're kidding?"

"No I'm not. I don't blame her for being a bit pissed off with that on a first date."

"Me neither."

"But you'd have given Lewis a bit of a second chance, wouldn't you? Except that, get this, Kate said he tried to go even further, took her down some alleyway after the film, and tried to make her rub him off."

"Ewww. Creep."

"If my father had known he'd be after Lewis with a knife! It's no wonder Kate said nothing in the house. He was dumb, Lewis, wasn't he? If he had taken his time, she'd have come round to him, don't you think? They'd have made a lovely couple. She'd probably be happily shagging him now, knowing what a catch she had. Instead she's doing ... doing something with some older woman! Did I tell you she's nearly thirty? I can't think what's going on in her head. Very determined she is, according to Mum. I can't help but pray for her, you know, that God will hurry up and put the right man in front of her before she gets her head too screwed up. Louise, you're not afraid of *me* now, are you?"

Margaret was holding court in the corner of the staffroom. Natalie Preston made a coffee and arranged herself on the edge of the grouping to listen. Margaret was a trendy-looking, cropped grey-haired woman of fifty-three. Decked in a suitably mature version of recent fashion, she gave the impression of a woman in step with the time. Only it wasn't so. Behind the image was a woman stuck in the peak of her thirties, still swearing that Freud had it sussed, and that transactional analysis solved most people's emotional dilemmas. Margaret had plenty to say about Helena Callender.

"It's obvious when you look at her family background. Always is. Mum and dad divorced. I'd say that was when Helena was about four or five, slap-bang in the middle of her Oedipal-Electral phase. Just when she was supposed to be aligning her sexual urges through her dad to the opposite sex ... divorce! Breaks the safe transition, reattaches the girl to her mother. Add to that the fact that as an only child, she now feels responsible in some way for the breakup, and responsible for her mother's happiness. You can see it developing, can't you? Normal sexual progress aborted, over-identification with female parent, no doubt absorbing some hefty anti-male vibes to boot, and there you have the submergence of heterosexuality and an attachment to women instead. Of course, it's the submission then of child to parent in the subconscious so early on in life that caused the issue to remain buried so long. She didn't allow herself to indulge in teenage fun. The natural expression of sexuality was self-prohibited. Now, look at her relationship history. She moves into parent-adult mode and tries to satisfy societal norms, and the subconscious desire to correct her parents' failed marriage, which, naturally, doesn't work. Have you heard the story of how she was jilted? No? Well, another time.

"Interesting how she finds herself in psychology as a profession. It's like the ultimate smokescreen from herself. I mean, come on, you spend all your time sorting out other people's problems so you don't have to look at your own. And her own is so obvious. I'm surprised Brian wasn't onto it before. You only have to look at her. Have you ever seen a woman so sexy in form and manner who *isn't* sexy? Quite. I heard it all started with that last lesbian client she had – Caroline somebody. Apparently there was something going on there too. But Brian found out about it and transferred the girl to Jackie. It was only a matter of time before it raised its head again. I can't think what she must have told Brian to convince him to let her handle another lesbian. I believe she was experimenting with mini affairs of the mind, exploring sexual issues through these young women and reassuring herself of her lesbian viability in being the object of their affection and desire. I don't think she should be allowed to handle female clients from now on. And there'd be enough problems giving her males the way she looks. I think she needs some time off for therapy herself, maybe look at a career change."

"I thought she was sixteen when her parents divorced," Emily, another of her audience members, interrupted.

Margaret was unperturbed. "I should think you'll find that's incorrect."

Michelle managed to maintain her weekend training. It was easy. The campus was only an hour's drive, and whilst she lived away during the week, she was back at Damien's every Friday night. She didn't compete any more. She couldn't, didn't want to commit to the team on that level again, but it was good to keep in shape, and keep up with the local news. She'd heard little of Kate since she left – her visits home being sporadic – only that she was enjoying Birmingham to the fullest, getting on with her studies, the usual stuff. No news of a boyfriend, or anything.

Then one Saturday, late in June, Sarah was so full of it during their training break that there wasn't time to tell all. "You'll have to come for a beer after training. You have got to hear this."

Coach Colin had no idea why the girls were training so enthusiastically that night. Little did he know that they were rushing to the get to the end of their session. And showers in five made him ask, "Out on the town tonight, ladies?"

The parade of tracksuits and half-damp heads said otherwise.

"No," Linda offered. "Things to do. You know how it is." The last thing they wanted was Colin joining them in the pub. This was girls' talk.

Piled into a corner of The Black Swan, Sarah was ordered to hold the story until the beers were in. Once sorted, she began. "So my mum comes in from work the other day and she asks all out of the blue if I've heard how Kate's doing these days. She has this funny look on her face, like I know something I'm not telling her. So I say, 'Mum, haven't heard a thing in months'. And Mum says, 'Not surprising really. I think they're trying to cover it up'. Well, I was intrigued. I thought, whatever has our Kate gone and done? I mean, it's not like she ever put a foot wrong. So Mum tells me she heard from a friend of hers who knows a friend of a close friend of Kate's mum – and she wasn't supposed to say – that Kate was having counselling about thinking she was gay, then started up a relationship with the woman who was her counsellor. I hear she's in her thirties! Far as we know, this woman took a shine to Kate and decided to convince her that she *was* a lesbian, if you get my drift. Then, the Pearsons go up there in a total rage and try to get the woman sacked. I think she's been suspended or something, and has to look for another job."

Linda was mesmerised. "Are you sure this is true, Sarah? We've all known Kate for years. Every one of us has shared a room with her at some point. Had anyone guessed? Did she ever make a move on anyone?"

Diane spoke up. "I don't know. It doesn't seem fair talking about a mate like this. I always thought she was different somehow. I didn't know how though. I thought it was because she was really clever. A bit of a thinker, quietly in her head or something."

Abbie cut in with a dirty laugh. "Bet Lewis is hiding in shame now. Remember how he used to hang about our sessions watching Kate's every move and waiting for his chance to chat her up?"

"Well, he obviously thought she was up for it. Aren't guys supposed to know that sort of thing? Like, can't they sense a lesbian and avoid themselves the embarrassment? And she did go out with him." Diane was retracing her steps.

"Blokes can't tell," Michelle stated. Too clearly, it seemed, as all eyes turned on her. "I've had this conversation with Damien and he seems to think that unless women are big, butch types, you have no way of knowing." A pause hung heavy over the table.

Linda came back at her. "That's lucky for you, then."

Michelle looked around, at the averted eyes of Sarah, the half-turned face of Diane. "What do you mean?"

"Well, now that we're on the topic, it's not exactly a stranger to you, is it?"

"So you've had this sort of conversation before, I take it,

only I was the subject, is that it?" Michelle had walked right into this, and was frantically trying to decide which way to go. Should she challenge them with a guilt trip and deny all? Or should she pan it off as a teenage notion?

Sarah made the decision for her. "News travels, even when you're sure it has nowhere to go. Look at us now for God's sake. My brother was in Claire's brother's class at school. She slagged you off quite a bit back then."

Sarah asked with a knowing look, "So what did *you* think? Did you realise Kate was gay?"

Michelle conceded denial to be pointless. "It had crossed my mind in the way Diane said, but nothing I could put my finger on. Until our last meet, in Southampton, before Kate went off to university. We shared a room." She had their complete attention. "She was first for the bathroom. She stripped off naked in front of me and wandered in and out getting the water temperature right. I thought it was a bit brave of her, but we've shared showers before, all of us, so I didn't read anything into it. When she was done, she came out all wrapped in a big towel and sat down on the bed, chatting away as usual. She lifted her leg up in front of me to rub in moisturiser and gave me a full flash of her fanny. I'm sure it was deliberate."

"Well, she'd have known … I mean … that, maybe you'd be interested." Sarah shrugged her shoulders. "I'm only asking."

"I found out later how deliberate." Michelle downed the rest of her pint. She was going to give them exactly what they wanted to hear. "Halfway through my bath, I got bloody cramp didn't I, and had to come yelling from the water. I'd wrapped my towel round me and hopped up and down, as you do. Kate offered to rub it down for me, my hamstring. We've all done that for one another, haven't we?"

Wide-eyed nodding dogs stared back.

"Only, at the end, when she'd got the muscle under control, she slid her hand up to my bum, and it wasn't in a sports massage kind of way."

"What did you say to her?" Abbie obviously wasn't sure if her ears could take a lesbian sex scene.

"I told her things were going really well with Damien. That if she thought otherwise, that had been a long time before, and a phase when I was growing up. My mother blamed the athletics – too much bodily contact during puberty just confuses you. I think she was right. Things are great with Damien now."

"Did you tell her it was a phase that she'd get over too?" Abbie was still looking for a way out.

"No. Somehow it all seemed a bit more serious with her."

Photography was one of Robin's more inspired modules. Taken in the last term of this second year of study, he felt he could see his own maturity and development in the prints he had mastered, particularly the quirky close-ups of battered architecture, and the candid shots of street people. Inspired by the emotional reaction to his work, he wondered about the purpose of photography to ordinary people in everyday life. Very simply, photography was a flailing human attempt to capture their joy of the world, most often in the faces of the people they loved best.

Robin pulled the plastic carrier bags from the bottom of his wardrobe that contained glimpses of his existence thus far. He was going to make a montage of favourite moments, a collection he could frame on the wall as a constant reminder of his appreciation of the world.

In minutes his life surrounded him. Friends with funny faces, family in posed portraits, drunken lunacy at the Union Bar,

226

school plays, Paris. He lifted the set of his trip with Kate and pored over the shiny prints, revisiting the weight of his disappointment. Her smiling face would never be his. Replacing image after image, he recalled the hope he had felt as they ascended the Eiffel Tower.

The sound of her stereo across the hall sprung him back to the moment. He pictured her movements, unfolding herself out of bed, preparing to face the day, and remembering that she had found someone she loved. It was obvious. It had been since that night outside Babes. He'd seen a light in her eye, a glow in her face so apparent he'd hoped that woman knew it. He didn't want to see his dear Kate crushed. He hadn't been able to ask her about it. It made him feel raw. And in these last few weeks there had been no call to ask. He had only to look at her to know. She sang, constantly. She smiled at everyone. She danced around the kitchen. How could he feel bad when she was so happy?

He got up and banged on her door. "You decent?"

"Just about!" she roared back. She was doing up her jeans as she came into view.

"Take her to Paris, Kate."

"How about the Balti in Handsworth. Not beautiful, I know, but the food is to die for. Will you come, Helena, if you can tear yourself away for a night with an old chum?" Tessa had begged on the phone.

"Well, as you're so old, I might have to," Helena had joked.

Tessa suggested a Wednesday, so as not to encroach on their weekends, but Helena would have agreed to anything for she and Tessa hadn't managed an opportunity to talk in depth, alone, since the affair was made public. She couldn't help but feel nervous. These days she had to truly acknowledge that you never knew what was around the corner, which meant everything now had an element of uncertainty. She could not presume that Tessa was okay with her choices.

Walking between the tables at the Balti, the two bubbly chums turned heads as ever. This was Tessa's favourite eating place. It had once-velvet faded cloths on the tables, and ancient Venetian blinds at the windows.

"Who'd have thought, looking at us two gorgeous babes, that one of us was a raving lesbo?" Tessa kissed Helena on the lips before taking the seat the astonished waiter held for her. "That's so they think it's me," she whispered, and then to the waiter, "A bottle of the house white, please." She beamed as the waiter hurried away. "That ought to confuse him."

"We might *be* babes, but we're not *at* Babes so behave." Helena laughed.

In full theatrical whisper, Tessa told Helena a secret. "When I was about sixteen, my mum and dad asked to talk to me one night, alone. I thought I was in big shit, thought they'd found out I'd been smoking in my room. That wasn't it. They sat me down and started on about how much they valued their children and how they would hate them to feel there was anything they couldn't tell them, and blah, blah. And I'm thinking it's all a bit emotional for a smoking offence, when suddenly they came out with, 'We're aware how special Jennifer is to you'. Jennifer was my mate, at school. In fact, it was all her fault I started smoking. So they go on, 'We're happy that you have someone special like her. You know we're fond of her. We want you to know that you don't need to feel you must keep it a secret from us. We only want you to be happy. It's absolutely fine to be gay'."

"You're having me on."

"No, honest truth. This fluffy blonde is such a useful

cover-up." She smiled. "No, I started to laugh, until they looked hurt. I had to hug them both. I told them they were fabulous, and that I almost wished I was gay 'cos I'd be so lucky to have such incredibly supportive parents. I had to tell them that I was pretty sure I wasn't a lesbian, nor was Jennifer from the antics I'd seen."

"What absolute treasures."

"I know. I've felt a heterosexual disappointment to them ever since."

"Do you think we should shut up a minute? The waiter's coming and I want the wine before he decides we're drunk already and throws us out."

"Such wisdom, Ms Callender," Tessa mocked. "You can be the sensible one and order the food. So how are your folks about it all?"

The waiter placed the two glasses of wine at the centre of the table and poised his pen. "Your usual?" he asked. "Lamb Passanda, Chicken Biriyani, with vegetable rice?"

"And some onion bhajis, thanks."

"Certainly." The waiter moved on, but not before slipping the girls a sly smile.

"I think your act has him convinced, or at least intrigued."

"Too good an opportunity to waste. Gotta have some fun."

"So where were we?"

"Your folks."

"My folks. Well, Mum seems strangely uninterested. Said something about knowing I hadn't been myself lately, though she'd no idea *this* was what it was all about, then carried on as normal. No change. I wasn't really sure where she was at with it all. Then I saw Dad. He said Mum ranted about Richard and the wedding that never was. Apparently, it's not that she has

229

particular issues with the whole gay thing, but she has some preferred logic about what brought me to this point, and is disappointed that I won't be providing grandchildren."

"Were you ever going to?"

"What, grandchildren? Not if I could help it!"

"And your dad?"

"He's become so mellow these last couple of years. 'You seem happy to me, daughter dear', he says, 'enjoy your youth'. I'm not sure if that last bit was a pun."

"I agree with him. You do seem happy, happier than I've ever seen you with a bloke."

"Really?"

"Really. I'm not just saying it. But, can I ask you a question?"

"Sure."

"Don't you worry about it all a bit? Wonder where it all came from? I know it's a bit late for a phase, but did you really have no idea?"

"I've thought a lot about that. Of course it has worried me. I gave myself some serious analysis in case I'd hit some kind of crisis, or emotional breakdown of sorts. But I'm mentally intact. Initially, it's like I told Jackie and I know it sounds like romantic claptrap, but it was just there. In my gut I knew I was facing something huge, and Kate knew it too. Let's put it this way, we're all on the lookout for our perfect partner, aren't we? We all dream that one day we'll find them and our hearts will flip and we'll know the search is over. Well, there it was. Trust me, no one could be more surprised than me to find that she was a she. It was like part of me was thinking, it's you, I know it's you, and you never said you'd be a girl. I recognised this person, the person beyond the gender. I know she is my partner, so I'll have to deal with the girl thing. Does that sound stupid to you?"

The waiter delivered their food in little steel bowls, squashing them carefully onto the small table.

"Nope. Sounds pretty damn good actually. Don't know if it makes you gay though."

A bowl almost went flying to the floor. The waiter tidied the presentation then escaped.

"Stop it," Helena laughed.

"Couldn't resist."

"Well, maybe I am. Maybe I'm not. Does it really matter?"

"It might to Kate. Come on now, truth all the way. Did you even snog another girl before?"

"I've been searching my memory for anything I may have missed, or chosen to miss. I know my relationship history hasn't been brilliant, as Mum said, but it's hardly much of an argument. Think about it, does every man whose girlfriend dumps him, or every man whose wife ditches him head off into town saying, 'Right, I've had it with women, from now on it's only men I'm fucking'?"

Tessa almost choked with laughter, especially as the eavesdropping guy at the next table nearly popped his eyeballs.

"Seriously though, there are little things that make more sense to me now, like how I never had the posture of a lady, according to Dad. I always liked sitting with one ankle crossed high on the other thigh." Helena's attempt to demonstrate threatened the tablecloth with a colourful mixture of passanda and biriyani and had to be aborted. "Anyway, Dad used to tell me to sit nicely, and wouldn't accept that arranging my skirts over the resultant gap was enough to protect my decency. School friends thought I talked dirty, and directly, and not in a feminine or delicate way when it came to bodily matters. When I think about the boyfriends I had, especially when I was younger, it makes me laugh, and makes Kate absolutely my type. I always went for pretty boys. Fine-featured, smooth-skinned, broad-shouldered, narrow-hipped, gentle. Real men, the real masculine type always sort of scared me. I never bothered to analyse why. Add to that my exaggerated sense of indignation at the merest suggestion of sexism, and you get an interesting character sketch. I called myself a feminist, and left it at that. But there was one other thing. I had a friend when I was about fifteen. There was something about my feelings for her. It was an obsessive friendship, but not in a negative way. We couldn't spend enough time together. At one point, I remember it feeling almost physical. I wanted to touch her. The weirdest thing though, I just put the thought out of my head, didn't act on it, didn't think it again. From then on I went about doing what I was supposed to do, *i.e.* find a good man to settle down with. Doesn't amount to much, does it?"

"Maybe you're a classic case of suppression," Tessa offered. "One thing will tell all, that's for sure."

"What's that?"

"Sex. Have you done it yet?"

Helena squirmed like a teenager. "Yes."

"So how did it go?"

"I can't tell you here."

"Oh, get on with it. Who do you think's listening to us?"

Helena rolled her eyes. "I think we've been attracting our fair share of attention."

"Might as well finish the show then. Tell."

Helena chose the most innocent terminology she could muster to describe her nervous initiation into the world of lesbian sex, and how the excitement of feeling a body like hers took over so completely that she found out what orgasm really meant.

232

Tessa did not do a good job of disguising her shock, or her volume. "Hadn't you had an orgasm before?"

The waiter suddenly gave excessive attention to the adjacent tables.

Helena exploded into laughter at her face. "Faking it for years, girl. Thank you, Meg Ryan!"

"D'you know what? I think that says it all. You must be a lesbian ... except ... there's one final step to go."

"And what's that?"

"Well, it's all very well being able to shag a woman. Even I could do that. It's like masturbation, isn't it? So that makes us all naturals. But *muff-diving*, now that's the real test."

The waiter dropped a glass, and a cough and a napkin scuffle on the next table left the women in giggles.

"I haven't done that yet," Helena confessed.

"Yeah, but what do you think about it? Like I said, I can imagine kissing another woman and touching her, but I know for cert I couldn't go down on her. So, I couldn't be a lesbian, 'cos you can't have those kind of barriers."

"No, I suppose you're right. If I think about it, about Kate, my only negative reaction is nervousness, in case I don't quite know what to do, and I wouldn't want to feel like a prat and do it wrong."

"Best let her do it first then," Tessa suggested with all seriousness. "Well, thank you, Ms Callender. I think you've handled yourself very well. I'll give you a pass on that. Any chance of eating this food now? More wine?"

The waiter was tipped generously.

The Pearson brothers were at one another over the battered MG that was their money-eating hobby. Dan was agitated.

"Did you talk to them at all before they set off on their quest for truth, AKA mortal embarrassment?"

"What's embarrassing about protecting your daughter's honour?"

"Jesus! Listen to you! It's not the seventeenth century. We don't have to draw swords and fight any poor bastard to the death who happens to disagree with us."

"It's not about disagreement, it's about protecting the innocent."

"So you think our Kate is innocent in all this? Do you genuinely believe that she was misled by some old harridan that, by the way, just managed to get her knickers off?"

Tom was not impressed by his brother's crudity. "I don't need to imagine my sister having sex."

"Oh, get real will you? We all do it. None of us are kids anymore."

"That's all very well for you to say, but you have to remember that Mum and Dad still see us that way, and they sure as hell don't need our sex lives in their faces."

"Exactly, and that's what they were overreacting to – their baby girl having sex. I'm convinced they'd have been just as bad if she said she was moving in with a boyfriend, only they wouldn't have had the same excuse to create such a song and dance about it. Despite their religious beliefs, that one's too socially acceptable these days."

"Dan, you're being deliberately short-sighted. It does matter that the sex is with a woman. I heard them talking about it. They were totally shocked."

"You mean more terrified about what the church community will say about them, how they failed to pass on their spiritual values. The Bible doesn't say it's okay to be gay."

"Well, it's done now."

"So how have they been since the crusade? Did they drag Kate home kicking and screaming? Or has she seen the error of her ways and repented?"

"Stop giving them such a hard time. They did what any parent would do. They thought their child had been misguided by a person in whose trust she was placed. You have to admit, it's a bit suss."

"I might have thought that had I ignored the fact that my sister is not exactly your wimpy, easily influenced type, and the fact that she's gay."

"What d'you mean, fact?"

"She was always gay, Tom. When did you ever see Kate come on to a guy?"

"I thought she had it off with that dark-haired bloke."

"In Lewis' version of the story, yeah. I heard elsewhere that she'd have nothing to do with him, and she had a girlfriend after that."

"How do you know?"

"Seems the girlfriend wasn't keen to blow her cover either, stayed with her boyfriend throughout. I learned it from him, when he served his ultimatum and Kate got dumped."

"A bit shitty for Kate, that."

"Exactly. Which is why you could do with plucking your head out of your arse and keeping the olds sweet. Kate needs us on her side."

Margaret was seated at the drawing room table, surrounded by colourful notelets inviting every Tom, Dick and Harry to their summer barbecue, which had become something of an annual event. Keith, her husband of twenty-two years, was behind one of the daily broadsheets.

"We've got nearly fifty on the guest list this year. Quite the thing to be seen at our barbecue, you know."

"That lesbian's not on the list, is she?" he asked, eyes still focused on the print.

"She's always invited, along with the rest of the team from the unit. You know that."

"Not this year she isn't."

"Keith, that's not very PC, sweetheart."

"I don't give a fuck about PC."

It was not unusual for her husband to swear. Margaret put her pen down and turned her full attention towards him. "Keith. I don't want her here either. But how will I look if I don't—"

"I have two teenage daughters who love nothing better than to flaunt their figures in the sun. I'm not having that woman anywhere near them."

"Honey, it doesn't work like that. Being gay doesn't mean you're promiscuous."

"Don't bother turning your psycho-babble on me, Margaret. She obviously can't be trusted. You said she's seeing an eighteen-year-old. She's made her bed. I'll not be having her in my house. You don't even like her, so what's the problem?"

It wasn't posed as a question. It was rare for Keith to take that tone, but when he did, his position was non-negotiable.

Margaret went into work particularly early next morning so that she could pop the cards into the internal mail trays while there was a high chance they'd be covered up by the mail delivery. That way Helena wouldn't notice she didn't have one. Margaret reasoned there wouldn't be much chat about the barbecue now that it was a regular event, and as such, she might not be challenged on the omission of one particular invitation. Helena picked up Jackie's post to drop it off on the way to her own room. Anything smaller than A4 struggled to stay in the pile. The card was the first thing to fall on Jackie's desk.

"Thanks, sweetie," Jackie said as Helena plopped the batch on the desk. "Looks like barbie time," she added, quickly recognising Margaret's scrawl.

"Looks like it."

At lunchtime, Helena noticed similar cards scattered about tables, shouting their invitation from beneath plates and Tupperware boxes full of sandwiches. Helena checked her tray a second time. Nothing.

The weekend came and went. She made only the briefest mention of it to Kate, lest the girl should think it her fault. On Monday, Jackie stopped her as the post was dumped on her desk again. "Where were you on Saturday? Better things to do, eh?"

Interesting. It hadn't crossed Jackie's mind, and for a moment Helena wondered if she'd got it wrong, if the card had got stuck down the back of her tray or something. The dull weight beneath her ribs told her otherwise. "Seems I wasn't invited."

Jackie's cheerful countenance crumbled, the questions, the issues, the prejudices rushing forth for acknowledgement. "Helena, she's a narrow-minded, ignorant—"

"Whatever. Let's leave it." She went about her work, but it sat sore with her all day, aggravated by spontaneous silences which interrupted recollections of Saturday's events while she, the uninvited, was within earshot.

"Are we going out this weekend or what?" Elisabeth called to Usha. Pointless really, as she knew Usha couldn't hear a damned word over the waterfall that was the shower attachment on its third and hopefully final rinse of the Rich Plum colouring her hair.

Like many of their *verging-on-final-year* contemporaries, they'd stayed in Brum through the holidays. Digs had to be paid for if they were to be retained. Might as well use them. Homes and family suburban life did not hold the same attractions anymore.

"What are you shouting about?" Usha emerged, twisting an old multi-dyed towel onto the top of her head.

"Going out this weekend are we?"

"Too right we are. I want an excuse to show off my shiny new locks."

"Has it worked then?"

"I bloody hope so this time. I'm bored with black. Ha! Bit ironic, that." Usha suffered several failed attempts at colouring her native-Indian black hair. Rich Plum was her last resort before seeking bleached highlights which were guaranteed to work, though she feared the orangeness of those she'd seen badly managed by her friends.

Elisabeth got out the dryer and started to work on the back of Usha's head. "I think it's taken. Yes, it has."

"Excellent! So where are we going?"

"D'you think Kate would bring Helena out with us? I'd like to get to know her a bit myself. Wouldn't you?"

"It looks like Kate's pretty serious about it all, so yeah, I think it's about time we saw them out and about together."

"That first time Kate brought her round here, I was too worried about the state of the place to concentrate on her properly. I know Kate said she was really cool and everything, but she's still a professional woman, older I mean. Her standards are a bit above the average students, I would think."

"Oh, don't! D'you remember, we hadn't looked at our teapot in months until I gaily go and offer tea, turn the thing upside down in full view of everyone, and that alien, that globulous mass of furry growth plopped green and grey into the basin?"

Elisabeth screwed up her face at the memory. "Well, they seemed easy enough with one another. But it's different when you're out, isn't it? You have to trust an awful lot to get drunk and make a fool of yourself in front of them. Between you and me, I think it's a fair test of the age gap as well. We'll have to see if Helena can hold her own in a club. Because if she can't, it won't last, whatever Kate thinks at the moment."

"She is totally loved up, isn't she? I'm dead proud of her actually. I shouldn't think it's that easy to turn around to your mates and say, 'I know we've been close for a while now, but there's something I haven't told you'."

"It wasn't quite like that," Elisabeth corrected.

"No, I know, but it must have felt a bit like it, to her. But, hang on. If you want Helena to come too, are you suggesting we go to that gay bar again?"

"Yeah, why not? And I think we should let Kate choose a club too."

"Oh, Lis, don't make me go to a gay club. I don't think I'd like it."

"Give over! How do you know you won't like it? I hear they play really cool tunes, proper dance and sing your head off stuff. No prancing and posing for the gay boys. And, think about it, you can have a good old boogie to yourself without guys crashing your party all night, cracking on to you, or groping your arse. You've been complaining about blokes in town for ages. You've even threatened giving up those belts you call skirts."

"What if the women chat me up?"

"How gorgeous are you?" Elisabeth teased. "I don't know. Depends on how forward they are, doesn't it? I'd quite like

239

a woman to make a move on me. It must be the ultimate compliment when you think about it. Look at how critical we are about how we look, and what makes someone beautiful and all that. If a woman, a good-looking woman, chatted me up, I'd be flattered. You know what, I'd quite like to kiss a woman too."

"Don't look at me!"

"Doughnut! I wouldn't kiss you. I know you too well. But if some babe was turning on the charm, I'd probably go along with it. Get a taste of the whole lesbian experience for myself."

Usha shook her head in horror. "Come on though, at the end of the day, going the whole hog, would the sex not be dissatisfying? I know we always criticise blokes for not doing enough foreplay, and from that point of view lesbian sex must be really exciting and have you really gagging for it. But then what? Surely the job's not finished until you have a good hard cock thumping inside of you?"

Elisabeth whacked the top of Usha's head. "You are so lucky Kate's not here to hear you. Now go and look at your purple hair."

In the old wooden building, sparsely decorated with candles and the odd cross, the circle of chairs was broken and the small congregation began to disperse. Mrs Pearson had moved five minutes previously to take up her place by the urn, ready to serve morning coffee.

"An excellent sermon, don't you think, Avril?" Frances Nisbet addressed Mrs Pearson over the extended cup, her nails chewed to the quick, her tight hat pushed down onto her greying bun. "Mr Tennant is so right to speak out about the abominable trash the media churns out as entertainment these days. What on earth is the attraction to watch people terrified out of their wits as gory murders go on all around them? It's no wonder there's so much violence in the world when the media hands it to our children on a plate."

"We can't always assume that children absorb this stuff. Surely a lot of blame rests with the parents if they don't exercise control over what their children do?"

Frances raised an eyebrow and added pointedly, "Apparently, that sort of control isn't within the reach of *all* parents."

Unsure of the meaning of the jibe, if it was a jibe, Avril let it go. Frances had more to say.

"Of course, I think the way sex is thrown about so casually is a more serious threat to our young. They are shown that morals and values have no place in the world, that sex is recreational and you can do what you like regardless of the consequences."

Avril felt herself colour. She'd taken the line of education with her offspring. She and her husband had openly discussed all the issues that normal sex elicited, including disease and pregnancy, then left their well-informed children to apply their knowledge. At times, she felt a failure in the eyes of God for her liberal stance, but she hadn't felt a failure as a parent, until now. Frances was still talking and Avril directed the queue around her, passing on cups with a serviceable smile.

"Mr Nisbet and myself decided to do a survey of television programmes last week to check exactly what was being offered to our teenagers. Truly, five minutes of *Sex And The City* was more than enough to terrify us. The programme simply advocates getting out and sleeping with as many people as possible, in the shortest time possible."

"It's hardly a helpful role model for young people," Avril agreed, wishing Frances would take her ranting elsewhere for a while. It wasn't that she disagreed with the woman, but Frances was like a terrier with something between its teeth, and one sermon a day was quite enough to mull over.

"But, you know, Avril, that wasn't the worst of it. There were holiday programmes encouraging young people to go out, spend all their time drunk and almost naked. And have you noticed the amount of coverage homosexuality gets? It's frightening. Don't people know why Sodom and Gomorrah were destroyed? I thought it was illegal to promote homosexuality. Isn't it? Truly, people break their covenant with God without a thought as to how they will suffer for it."

Frances was maliciously herding Avril into a very difficult position. How could she reconcile the teachings of the Bible with her daughter's sexual preference? In processing this dilemma, Avril had moved away from the Old Testament (nothing but punishment there) and turned to Jesus. She was not yet convinced that He offered solace. In fairness, He was generous with his love, caring deeply for the likes of Mary Magdalene. But she stumbled with the problem of repentance. One had to feel remorse for one's wrongdoings, recognise that they are wrongdoings, before Jesus could lead the sinner back to God. Therein lay a conundrum. Avril came to the preferred conclusion that it was not her daughter's intent to do wrong, that her heart was pure and genuinely seeking love, which was exactly what Jesus represented; love and forgiveness. He would forgive Kate her foolishness if her heart remained earnest. Avril prayed that it would be so.

"Your children, Avril, all well I hope?"

Avril looked Frances calmly in the eye. "Very well thank you, Frances. Yours?"

Brian Sharpe paced the length of his narrow office, heels clicking softly on the parquet floor. The situation was not good. Brian lauded himself for his ability to manage stress and dissipate the concerns of others. For some reason, on this occasion these skills eluded him. In several recent case conferences different staff members displayed reluctance to allocate new clients, new female clients, to Helena's list. Reacting prickly to the first instance, he assumed he was being over sensitive, and passed it by. On the second occasion he confronted it bluntly, and reminded his team that ignorance and prejudice, however subtle, had no place in his unit. It seemed he only served to push it underground.

Individuals negotiated case lists prior to the weekly meetings, then presented him a fait accompli. One by one he began calling on his colleagues, inviting them to discuss their concerns. By each person, prejudice on the grounds of sexuality was denied, though Brian could see when this was not entirely true. Sad to see a person's true colours when faced with a situation they purport to be above. The real difficulty was the doubt expressed about Helena's ability to maintain boundaries. Brian explained time and time again that he was more than happy with Helena's structures. But he was told, not once by an indignant Margaret, that whilst they might have been stronger at the time, how were they now that she was in this vulnerable position of exploring her own sexuality and thereby her whole manner of relating to the world? It was not a point that Brian could satisfactorily dismiss. After much contemplation, Brian came to the conclusion that the cohesion of his team was under serious threat. The unit had to be protected. They thrived on the intimacy and trust of the relationships within, and it was falling apart. As much as he hated the inevitable, Helena would have to go.

Yet Brian wasn't prepared to simply abandon her. He'd done his research. He'd been on the phone, and a transfer to a similar unit in the city was open, a position dealing with addiction, attached to the Adult Rehabilitation Centre. He knew Helena wouldn't like it, but it was better than a handshake.

The appointment with Helena was for ten o'clock. He stopped pacing and sat waiting.

"Helena, take a seat. I've had a message through from George Street, Aston. They are in need of a well-qualified, well-grounded counsellor to fill a gap in the Rehab Unit. I thought it would be a nice one for you. I have the details here. It would be a promotion too. You'd head your own team. Have a look." He passed the papers over.

Helena took the papers in silence, glancing at them while her thoughts raced. Brian was not at ease. She could sense that much, in the same way she sensed the tensions around her almost every day now. There was no point in avoiding it.

"Brian, what are you trying to say?"

He looked at her, and shook his head. "Why am I trying to play tactics with you when we know one another so well?"

"Quite. So what's the deal?"

"The very thing I hoped wouldn't happen, has. I've been watching the shifting sands, Helena, and your role here is being undermined."

"By whom?"

"You know I can't say, and you know it isn't me. But compromise has crept in, and I can't stand by and watch your client list peter out until your skills are wasted."

"I know. I've watched it coming. Margaret has been busy," she added pointedly. "I hoped I was wrong."

Brian was relieved that his counsellor was as sharp as ever. It was what he admired about her; her clarity, her fortitude. "I can't bear to see you squeezed out, which is why I am making this offer. I know it's not what you want, but at least we can make a big noise about you being snapped up for promotion."

"I'm grateful for your allegiance, Brian. I said from the start that I wouldn't compromise the unit. Arrange the transfer."

Chapter Fifteen

Julian

Danielle washed and dried her neatly manicured hands, smoothed her navy A-line skirt against her knees, and again brushed the symmetrical bob of her black hair. The soft clatter of mail dropping onto the carpet drew her from the bathroom. Lifting the bundle of brown envelopes, she exhaled a snort of irony. "With a name like Flood you'd think he'd be prolific."

She told herself that's not the attitude and headed to the kitchen to make her husband a cup of tea, a morning ritual which included placing the cup on the bedside table by his head. She perched carefully on the edge of the bed so as not to crease her suit.

"Julian," she coaxed as she pulled the duvet back from where she expected to find his head. A blonde tuft, streaked now with premature grey, jerked in response to the change of temperature. He snuffled and grunted his routine comments about having a good day and not working too hard.

She placed a kiss on the visible forehead. "Are you going to the studio today?" More indistinguishable grunts. "I'll see you later." She maintained a note of kindness, so left the flat proud of her self-control.

Julian rose at eleven. After a long piss, his first job was the fastidious washing of the teacup, ensuring no trace of the skin-scumline remained. Julian didn't bother to wash himself. He hadn't exerted himself enough to build up sweat in need of removal, and there were no plans to go anywhere where he'd be seen. His joggers, his baggy t-shirt, his wavy hair almost vertical in its need for a cut, didn't matter. Except that they didn't quite fit in the pristine flat of theirs. Her flat.

A vision in his head of last night scratched at his apathy.

"Julian, Julian." Danielle had spoken his name quietly, like a disappointed parent. "This cannot go on. You haven't been to the studio today, have you? You haven't been sketching and drawing here either, have you, Julian? What else am I to do for you? I was there to encourage you when you needed it most. I propped you up. I rescued you. You were virtually destitute when we met, living in the back of that old studio, visiting friends when you wanted a hot shower. You had nothing, Julian, nothing but your talent. I've tried to give that back to you. I've given you a home, a stable environment so you have nothing to worry about but your art. And where has it gone, Julian? Where has it gone?"

Julian was ashamed, ashamed he brought this dedicated creature unhappiness, and that he disappointed her continually. He heard again her plaintive request.

"I cannot afford to support us both much longer. We need you to make some money. Go to the studio tomorrow. Try to work. Produce something, anything, even if you throw it away later. You must make it happen soon, Julian. Or we will have to find another way to get by."

They had slept at opposite sides of the bed, each clinging to the edge of the mattress.

Julian collected his bike from the communal sheds and rode down to the canal towards the studio. At that time of year there were more narrow boats around, and Julian wondered if they moored up for winter, like mobile homes abandoned at the seaside. At the studio, he didn't put his key in the lock. Propping the bike against the door, he instead walked along the towpath. He wanted to see the people who lived in those boats. He wanted to understand why they gave up bricks and mortar to live in perpetual motion, awake and asleep, forever rocking. Some of the boats held families, who, from their inappropriate t-shirts and flipflops, and brand new wood-burning stoves, were obvious wage-earners, their boats a holiday or hobby. They held no interest for Julian.

A couple in their forties, hippies of sorts with straggling long hair left grey and unruly, shouted orders and snapped back at one another. Their voices were in contradiction to the coordinated tasks that maintained their boat. An older couple, late sixties, sat in silence with coffee and newspapers at a steel table aft. Looking closely, Julian saw their bare feet intertwined beneath. It seemed they had, in their lives, the marriage that he eternally sought, their solidity of companionship balancing the fluidity of their lifestyle. That's what he wanted to paint, the contradiction: head versus heart; normality versus absurdity; individuality versus solidarity; idealism versus reality.

Clear of mind and with a satisfactory subject, Julian walked back along the towpath to the old army hut that was his studio and put the key in the lock. Oil and turpentine hung heavy in the still, warm air. Paints sweated their oily intestines onto the palette he'd abandoned uncleaned. The room was stifling. Julian opened windows and doors, praying the air might move. It didn't. It approached midday. It would worsen. He moved about waving cloths to create a draft. His efforts made some improvement, but he still couldn't bear to stay inside. He left the windows ajar and headed out back to the canal with a sketchpad and a box of charcoal, and sat by the water making notes of what he observed. All afternoon he tried to meet his promise. His hands defied him. Too often he stared at the passing world, forgetting to commit his view to paper. Around four, he'd had enough of the sun.

Another failed day. He rode home, sullen and defeated.

As he finished locking up his bike, Julian heard a swallowed sob. In his peripheral vision he caught movement heading into the flats. Seconds later he was behind her on the stairs. She sobbed again.

"Helena? Helena! Wait. Whatever's the matter?"

She paused mid-step. "It's nothing."

Julian placed his hand gently on the skin of her forearm.

"I'm sorry, Julian. Not as bad as it seems, honest. Just work stuff."

He smiled warmly. "I'm a good listener."

"That's kind. I appreciate it. Yes, come up."

Julian followed Helena up a further flight of stairs, past his door.

In her hallway she gestured to the sitting room on the right. "You probably know your way around. I'm guessing the layouts are identical in this building."

Julian admired the bright blues and matching creams of her flat. "Yes, but it's interesting how different colour schemes can make a place look," he said, picturing the neutral beige and taupe Danielle had chosen downstairs.

Helena grabbed two icy bottles from the fridge, handed Julian one saying, "I don't normally drink so early in the day, but I feel a beer is in order."

She led him through to the balcony, to the crisp air and the clearer view. "Frankly, it's nice to have the company of a fresh face just now. I'm so worn out trying to interpret everything going on around me."

"Funny to be a fresh face when we've been neighbours for, what, two years now?"

"Our paths don't often cross. I'm guessing you're not restricted to office hours, then. What do you do?"

Julian peered down at his grubby clothes, and smiled to himself. "No, definitely no office. An artist. A painter."

"Wow. I'd love to have a talent."

"Talents don't always pay, unfortunately."

"Things aren't working out right now? Sorry. Don't answer that. It was a bit forward."

"Not at all. And the answer is no. I was supposed to be at the top of my game by now and instead I am uninspired and mediocre."

"Don't all artists feel that at some point?"

"I'm sure they do. Perhaps I feel it more because I was apparently destined for big things." Julian looked at the floor as he said, "I fell in love with drawing as a child, with chunky crayons and rolls of old wallpaper. It stayed with me all the way through school and teachers believed in me. I got into St. Martins, and from there, a scholarship to the Sorbonne."

"Paris? You must have been really good."

"The problem's the expectations that come with it, the expectations you have of yourself and the expectations of others. Right now, I can't find myself. And it's disappointing everyone."

"I'm sorry."

"Hey, Helena, no, I'm sorry. We're supposed to be talking about you. And as I don't know, what is it that you do?"

"I'm a Clinical Psychologist."

"And I've just dumped on you, while you were having a bad day. Good one."

Helena smiled. "The distraction was just what I needed. I don't know any artists." She raised her bottle to the light. It was almost empty. "Another?"

"If you're not in a hurry."

"Not at all," she sighed.

Julian followed her back inside and asked what had

upset her so much. Helena hesitated, for a second, grabbed two fresh drinks and headed into the lounge. Julian interpreted the shift of her legs, the slump into the sofa, the gulp from the bottle as a need to unload.

"I am being obliged to leave a job that I love, where I work with good friends, and get huge satisfaction from supporting my clients."

"What's obliging you to leave?"

Helena's eyes filled at the question which Julian quickly retracted. "You don't have to talk about it if you don't want to."

It was his tone that encouraged her to go on. "I fell in love. It's not quite how I planned it, but it feels so real that I had to take the risk. In the few months we've been together, I've had opposition from the most surprising places and it saddens me terribly. The hardest part has been the demise in professional relationships that I trusted in, completely. I can't believe that just because there's been a big personal change for me, that my record to date can be overlooked." She paused and looked to Julian's expression. She seemed to soften somewhat, as if concluding he was non-judgemental. "I feel like an idiot to have misread people so badly, and their prejudices, especially as I'm trained to ensure I don't. Sorry, I should explain. My new love is a woman."

"I can see why you're so disappointed, and why you would expect more of people in your line of work."

"Exactly."

"Are you getting any support?"

"My friends have been amazing. I thought they may have challenged me when I've been straight all my life, but no, they just want me to pursue the dream and be happy."

"Now you're smiling. Perhaps you should focus on them. And in time there might be many more like them. Me for instance."

251

"Thanks, Julian. Enough whingeing from me. I'd love to know more about your painting. Is your wife an artist too?" She glanced at the ring on his left hand.

"No, she's not." He looked at his watch. "And she'll be home already. I'm supposed to be cooking."

Helena apologised profusely for delaying him, but with lots of thanks, assured him it was worth it, as she hadn't wanted to pass her worries on to Kate, her Kate who would be arriving soon, and Julian had provided the perfect ear.

"Looks like we both need to get a move on." Helena stood to see Julian out and giggled. "I think I'm a little squiffy."

"Well, you're certainly happier than before."

Danielle was not impressed with the smell of beer on her husband's breath as he approached in the kitchen. She had started the cooking, chopping onions with ferocity. "Where have you been?"

"At the studio, 'til about fourish. I met Helena from upstairs on the way in. She was upset about something, so we had a few beers and a chat. I didn't realise the time. Sorry."

The studio? Now that was good news. "Tell me what you've been working on."

They settled into a comfortable evening, disappointment abated. Danielle opened a merlot to go with the stroganoff for dinner, pleased at Julian's efforts. After discussing the news, they wandered apart to read in distant harmony. Julian's preference was to lie on the bed with his books, sprawling amongst them while interacting with their suggestions. Danielle, the librarian, preferred to sit up, back straight, avoiding tension in the neck muscles or strain to the eyes. The windows were open and Julian was glad for once, of the pale environment, cooling as it was on the sticky evening.

A chuckle floated on the warm air. Followed by another, and another, then a shriek and hurried footsteps that thundered and stopped above his head. He was pleased to know Helena's misery had ceased for the interim, that perhaps he had helped.

The laughter fell silent and he held his breath, afraid he hoped too soon. The silence elongated. Then a sound, quiet, muffled. Please don't let it be tears, again.

It wasn't tears. Julian sighed and relaxed.

The whimpers continued to rise in volume and frequency, interspersed with a deeper moaning. He had no idea whose voice was whose. Julian checked himself, shocked that he was attentively listening to two women making love, concentrating on the crescendo of their union. Still, he listened further. He was impressed by their rhythm, and pleased when he heard its climax and its fall to silence. He rolled over onto his front with his book and found he was stimulated. He ventured through the flat, to his wife. It had been a while. He stroked her glossy hair and took the book from her hands. "Come to the bedroom with me."

Julian was buzzing in the morning. While Danielle showered, he prepared a bowl of fruit salad with fresh strawberries and natural yoghurt. There was no tea to be delivered to his bedside today. He was ready to leave at the same time as Danielle, ready to cycle to the studio. On the way, he detoured to an electrical goods shop and acquired a fan, to make ready for work. It was a gorgeous day, full of air and warmth and movement and colour. He painted the battle of love. He painted prejudice. He painted tears. He painted sex. Huge canvases, six feet wide, strewn with cadmium red and raw sienna and deep Prussian blue. He packed up his work around four in the hope he'd meet Helena on the stairs again, to say thank you.

No luck. No matter, the dam had broken.

Danielle was delighted with her husband's exertions. She didn't enjoy telling him off, giving him ultimatums. But ends determine means. It had worked. She was glad he hated hurting her, that her pain stirred him. She was glad he saw out his promise this time. Danielle was particularly happy that this surge in creativity had brought with it a rush of expression that made him physically attentive to her again. She had been feeling starved. She was almost in need.

Julian opened the door of his flat to put out the rubbish as she came home. "Hi, Helena. How have you been? How's work?"

"Well, I agreed to the transfer and finish at Sutton Coldfield next week. I'm okay with it. I'm looking forward to Aston and new challenges, hence the books." She nodded towards her elbow. "Research. I want to be totally up-to-speed."

Julian looked at the titles: Wilson, Viktor Frankl, Jung. "Fascinating," he said, and described his interest in the human condition. The conversation took off, right there on the stairs.

Helena couldn't comfortably manage her bag and books to continue. "Come on up if you're not cooking."

"I'm not, but let me return your hospitality," and he popped back indoors to fetch a bottle of wine.

They enjoyed some rather excellent discussion with Julian borrowing the Frankl, finished the wine, and were called to stop talking when Helena's doorbell rang. It was Kate. Julian was excited to meet the object of such driving passion, but a trifle uneasy that he may have overstayed his welcome.

"Not at all," Helena said. "Kate's not interested in this

stuff, are you, darling?"

Kate pulled a welcoming face – permission to continue granted.

Danielle was late home. Julian knew that, before he had opened his door, bin bag in hand. He knew he had time on his hands to talk.

When Danielle finally came home, Julian served dinner.

"It's so useful having a psychologist upstairs. She's helping me unravel ideas from my reading, to free my expression on canvas."

"That's great. I'm glad she's a help to your work." She didn't mean it. She had no intention of making love to him that night, there was a film she wanted to watch.

He went to bed without her.

Something was bothering Danielle. She felt a curdling in her stomach and she knew the source was that woman upstairs. She had seen her many times, watched how she walked and moved. She was often behind her when she got to her car in the mornings. Danielle found it childish how she held the keys in her teeth while putting her bag on the seat. She saw how she swung her thighs together when she wore her shorter skirts, how she created the impression of one containing her sensuality. She used to admire Helena's hair, how she knotted it casually in the summer heat, but now, she saw how the auburn looked brassy in the sunlight. Danielle found it hard to believe the woman was gay. She wondered what game she was playing. She wished Julian was not so intrigued. For the moment, she had no choice. She needed him to work. If Helena helped to stimulate his imagination, she had to sit with it. She would allow him a few weeks more, until there were enough paintings.

Time and again Julian eavesdropped on their lovemaking. He always knew when Kate was around. Helena was noisier then. Music played, films boomed, there was activity. Alone, Helena was quiet, more still. Reading no doubt, and working. Except at weekends when women's laughter was heard, from the friends he had learned of. As he listened, he began to draw. He wanted to capture their energy, to relay it in colour the next day. Work was going well. It was as he hoped it would be, a vibrant experience, demanding, challenging, energetic, satisfying. In the studio Helena was with him constantly as he spread his fingers through the paint, pushing texture into formation, causing passion to explode from the medium. He stopped to admire the plethora of fresh pieces hung on the walls about him. The poignancy of the raw emotion punched his gut as he stroked the piece titled *Desire*.

Julian barked the sobs that emitted from his baser instincts. "I love you, Helena. I want you."

Julian's voice fell casual from the balcony where he had tended Danielle's window boxes. "Do you have time to talk about Viktor Frankl? Astounding!"

He was at the front door as she approached. "Why not come in here? Danielle's working 'til ten. No duties for me to forget."

It was the first time their meeting place was in his home. Julian offered coffee. Helena wondered if it was being in his own home that caused him to be so stiff and serious. If that was the case, she was unhappy for him. Who would wish to contain an artist? She noticed the sterile environment of this over-tidy lounge and suspected the conforming was done already. Julian was reluctant to begin the conversation, so Helena lifted Viktor Frankl's book and made ready to speak. As she raised her eyes she saw his head hanging. He seemed unhappy, and she had to ask why, though a bolt of alarm shot through her as she did. He was painfully slow to respond.

"I think you know," was all he offered.

Scales fell from her eyes. She feared what she started to see. She wanted to walk away, to say she didn't know anything. Helena allowed her brain to take over. Perhaps she didn't know anything, had assumed wrong. In any event, she would not guess for him. "I am not sure what it is you are trying to say, Julian."

He raised his head. "I am in love with you, Helena. You must see that."

She felt a fool, for up 'til now, she did not. She saw only Kate.

"I am a married man. I don't want to hurt my wife. I don't want my heart divided like this. But I love you. That is how it is. I don't know what to do with it."

Helena was confused. The man was not making a pass at her, per se. He did not claim that his wife didn't understand him so what harm could an affair cause. The man was in pain. Helena felt it. She asked herself what it was that he wanted her to say, wanted her to do. But it was all of no consequence. There was no mutuality in this situation.

"I am in a gay relationship, Julian, and I love my girlfriend very much."

"I know," he replied, but waited.

For what?

"I'm going to go now," she said.

Now in the quiet of her own place, she closed her door behind her and growled. "What the hell was that about? It's his problem if he's convinced himself he's in love with me. Not mine. He wants to be looking at his marriage if he's finding himself with feelings for someone else. It's got nothing to do with me.

What did he think I was going to do? How dare he try to hand this to me? What is it with men anyway? They declare they're in love with you, then they make it your problem, your responsibility. Well, tough, Julian. Your feelings are your responsibility, and you'll just have to get over them."

Julian was very disappointed. He had been certain there was a connection there, a meeting of souls. She must have seen that they sparked off one another, touched things that others, in the main, did not. She even had said herself that Kate wouldn't talk to her like he did. And she knew Danielle didn't inspire him as she had. What made her think that a physical union was more important than what had grown between them? For that's all she had with Kate, a physical union that was new, different and exciting. It would pass. It always passes. Then what would she have? Normality. Practicality. A comfortable thing that was no longer cherished.

Julian was so caught up in his ruminations that he didn't hear Danielle come home. He was unaware that she stood behind him in the kitchen, a lipstick-marked mug in his hand, poised over the sink.

"Removing the evidence?"

For one horrible moment Julian feared she had read his thoughts. He turned to her, guilty.

"The lipstick, Julian. Had company? Here? In my home?" In a flare, she tore around the flat. Indentations on the sofa cushions, an open book, facedown on the coffee table. Too, too innocent. She threw open the bedroom door, tugged at the duvet that hadn't moved since morning.

"Danielle."

She spun around, enraged as her foot slipped on a

258

sketchpad poking from beneath the bed. She snatched it up and flicked through the pages. The accusations flew.

"What exactly is your fascination with this woman?" Her rampage was stopped by the image of writhing female bodies on the page. She closed her eyes. When they opened again, they burned. "I have tried to ignore this, Julian, for the sake of your work, our future. I am not stupid. I understand how passions must be played with in the mind for art to be created. But why, Julian, why her? I am always here for you. I would do anything you asked of me to stimulate your work. You don't even look at me that way. Explain it to me. Explain how your devoted, supporting wife fails to ignite you, and some floozy of a lesbian, if she is one, can do it instead. Is she a lesbian, Julian, or is that just a clever cover? Or, or is it not the sex at all? She's not physically interested in you, is she? Why is that better for you? Are you frigid, Julian? Is sex beyond your remit?"

She stopped. She saw where her logic took her. "My God, Julian, you're in love with her!" She threw the pad at him and stormed out the front door, and to Julian's horror, up the stairs.

She banged on Helena's door.

Helena had been cooking and chatting in the kitchen with Kate. She was unprepared for the fury on her threshold. She recognised the red and angry face to be Julian's wife. She opened her mouth. It was only Danielle's voice that was heard.

"What the hell do you think you're doing with my husband? Everything was just fine until you befriended him, if that's what you want to call it. You've changed him. You've made him behave like a fool!"

"If anyone is behaving the fool it's you, screaming like this." Helena spoke with quiet conviction. "Stop shouting or I close my door."

Danielle took a pained breath and lowered her voice to a

threatening rumble. "I know your type, you women who pretend to be unaware, but use your wiles, your sex to get men where you want them. Do you still need a quick cock on the side to satisfy you when your little girl can't? Is that your game? Is he your occasional screw? Well, you can forget it. He's my husband. And if I see you anywhere near him again, I'll see you ruined."

Danielle turned slowly and calmly and stepped pointedly down the stairs.

Helena turned, leaning back into the closed door.

Kate stood in the kitchen doorway, her face ashen. "I'm going home."

Kate stomped through the streets rather than take the bus. Tears rolled, dropping from her face. *She said she loved me.*

On autopilot, she found herself near the Broadway. Elisabeth and Usha had their digs two streets away. It was only nine o'clock. They couldn't have gone anywhere yet. She banged on their door. Usha answered with a beaming grin that lasted a split second.

"Oh, honey, what's the matter?" She drew Kate indoors with an arm already around her shoulder.

Elisabeth looked up from the television and guessed the worst. "You haven't split up, have you?"

"No, not yet, but we might as well." Kate retold of the unexpected arrival at Helena's door, and how it quickly transpired that she was the wife of the man in the flat below. She told how the woman was in a screaming rage, accusing Helena of an affair with her husband because she still needs a bit of cock on the side. Usha was quick off the mark to curse Helena and her dirty tricks. Elisabeth remained rational.

"Kate, has she been seeing this man?"

"She said he was just a friend, that they talked about books, psychology and stuff. He was there the other night when I arrived, and I, like a mug, said it was alright that he stay and keep chatting."

Elisabeth was determined to make her think clearly. "Why are you doubting Helena? Why do you want to think they are anything but friends?"

"She's been straight all her life, hasn't she? Didn't even wonder if she was gay. Never crossed her mind until I came along. Not much of a track record is it? She'd been having a spate of bad relationships. Maybe she thought she'd try something new. She's not going to tell me *that*, is she? And she doesn't exactly look gay, all make-up and tight shirts. It's hardly any wonder men continue to chat her up. I mean, when do men genuinely want friendship with a woman? After they've shagged her, maybe. After they've had a crush on her."

Usha was finally on the ball. "Wait up, Kate. It's unfair to slag her off because of how she looks. You wouldn't have looked twice yourself if she was all masculine and wearing dungarees. And as for the friends thing, look at Robin. Sure, he had a terrible crush on you, but you're best mates now. The important thing there was that you didn't fancy him, so it went nowhere. Maybe Helena is in the same boat."

"His wife seemed pretty convinced something was going on." Kate was still questioning.

"Think about it. Your husband has this female friend that he chats to a lot."

"And drinks wine with, and beer." Kate wanted them to deal with the whole picture.

"And drinks booze with," Elisabeth allowed. "We'd all take a while to be comfortable with that, wouldn't we?"

Nods of agreement.

261

"Then you notice that your husband-slash-partner is talking about that friend more, arranging to see them more often, that sort of thing. It would be natural to start worrying. Then, what if, for whatever reason, you find cause to believe that they've actually got the hots for this other woman. Then what would you do?"

Usha answered, "You'd tell your husband to get it back between his legs, and not to see her any more, or else."

"Thanks for the graphics, Ush," said Kate.

Elisabeth sounded like a detective, or an amateur psychologist herself. "Yes, but, if you challenge your husband you will bring yourself face-to-face with a problem in the relationship. You'll have to acknowledge that if he is fancying someone else, then something isn't right. Maybe the something that isn't right is the wife. Get it?"

"So far." Kate began to see signs of hope.

"I think it's a scapegoat situation. I think there are problems between them and rather than deal with it the wife has blamed it all on Helena."

Usha patted Elisabeth between the shoulders. "Dead clever, you are. So, Kate, any room for that line of thought?"

"If Helena's been telling the truth, I suppose so."

"Do you have any reason to doubt that the truth is what you get?"

"No, it's something we've talked about, and share a big thing about."

Usha probed further. "Does she tell you she loves you? Is she comfortable in bed with you? 'Cos that must have been an adjustment."

Kate grinned. "That's all really good, she's a natural. We have a great time. And yes, she says she loves me."

Elisabeth found her bag and rummaged for her car keys.

"I think we should get you over there. Get this sorted out."

When the door opened, it was obvious Helena had been crying. Kate hurt to see her that way, and cried too.

"I'm sorry. I'm sorry. I was stupid to run off like that. I know you haven't been doing anything. I was dumb. I overreacted to the witch on the doorstep."

She enveloped Helena in her arms until her sobs subsided. They went and sat together and Kate explained why she was so irrational, and how, fortunately, she ended up at Usha and Elisabeth's door who knew her well enough to make her see sense.

"But you didn't trust me." Helena was smarting.

"I had a moment of weakness. I suddenly thought of all those blokes you've been with before me and I panicked. I thought maybe you weren't gay after all, that I was just wishing you were, for my sake. It wasn't really about you, or not trusting you, because I do, Helena, I do."

Emotion and adrenaline at an ebb, the women made contact and kissed gently.

Kate asked, "What are you going to do about those two downstairs?"

"I'm swinging between going down there and slapping her face, and his too, if he doesn't put her in her place, and then moving out. Can you imagine how awkward it's going to be bumping into either of them on the stairs? The thought makes me shudder."

"Maybe moving would be a good idea."

"A sign of defeat though."

"Not if it's a move forward. Not if we move in together."

Their lovemaking that night was tender beyond belief,

their vulnerabilities opening a channel to deepening connections.

In the room below, Danielle hovered uncomfortably on the edge of her bed, unable to feel the heat of her husband's body, so far removed. Above them they could hear the muffled sounds of love.

Chapter Sixteen

Preston Vs Pearson

Sutton Coldfield's Youth Unit was not the same without Helena Callender. It was strange for Natalie Preston to admit this. Her feelings and opinions with regards to Helena were of no fixed abode. Sometimes admiration won, for she certainly had a way with her clients. She got results. It was what they all sought to achieve. And she was humble about it, an endearing quality. Yet a distance remained between them. They never made it past acquaintance or colleague. Natalie minded this. She minded that Helena attracted people and could be choosey about who she responded to. And Natalie was never one of them.

Helena represented the 'in crowd', the group that Natalie was excluded from. It bothered her most because she knew it was not deliberate. She was not of that much consequence. She was an oversight. Nonetheless, she had kept a watchful eye on Ms Callender, her fascination fed in those last few months with rumour and speculation. She had enjoyed analysing the pretty woman's body language, her sexual signals, trying to decide for herself if she was indeed capable of making love to another woman. She had not reached her conclusions when the powers that be aborted her game. It was unfair. There was aimlessness left. So what now? Perhaps her brother could step in and offer some entertainment.

She didn't bother to call first. No need. She had her own key to Hal's Starter Home. He bought it three years ago and kept it impeccably. Army training paid off in more ways than one. Since then, he'd been seeking an opportunity to fill it. In some ways Natalie was glad he hadn't. She enjoyed being with her brother. A wife would change all that.

"Hal!" she sang out as she closed the door.

"Up here!" he called from the shower.

Natalie wandered up and stood in the doorway of the bathroom. "I'm bored."

"You're always bored." Water off, he stepped into full view from behind the shower screen, and flexed his shoulders. "How am I looking?" he posed, sexy-model style, long limp dick along his thigh.

"Excellent, as always," she answered off pat. He always asked, because he had no need to. She admired his exceptional physique as he rubbed himself down with a towel. She shared his desire for physical perfection, but for all her attendance at the gym, had not yet convinced herself she was in his league.

"I've got a fresh bottle of Jack Daniel's and a new brown package from Germany that I haven't had a look at yet." He flashed a wicked grin.

Natalie didn't really understand his interest in pornography, not when he could have whatever he wanted, and pretty much whenever. It had always been fun to share it with him though. They shared everything, and he certainly was an education.

"Anything for a laugh," she said.

Hal was an accomplished host. He poured a drink as if he was head barman at the Hilton, somehow delivering the very best of its flavour and alcoholic aplomb, whatever the content. He'd put on a dressing-gown; classic, in white towelling. No need to dress to stay in. He set the video up and sat on the sofa so Natalie could stretch her legs across his lap.

The bourbon was delicious. "Mmm, nice one, bro."

The viewing began. It was the same as always. Random strangers meeting in a public environment, this time on a long haul coach-journey. They made eye contact, suggestive licking of lips and positioning of hands on breasts, and genitals, until the message, I want to fuck you, was absolutely clear. The characters retired to the back of the bus, which was conveniently free. No one else bothered to look as they performed every sexual act imaginable from fellatio on his over-sized and eternally-stiff cock, to full anal sex that the woman took without a whimper. Only the driver was aware of them, from the scene in his rear view mirror. He successfully wanked off with one hand, while maintaining control of the wheel with the other.

Hal shifted slightly under Natalie's legs. She saw the unmistakable bulge beneath the fabric of his robe.

"I don't know how this stuff turns you on, Hal." She smiled as she reached to rub the hardened knob. "Haven't you had it in a while?"

"No. It's all this celibacy since the horniest woman I know went lezzer on me."

"Yeah, right." Natalie knew nothing would keep her brother celibate for longer than three days.

"Any news on the woman? Any goss?" He poured them both another drink.

"Funny you should ask. I was thinking about her earlier. I actually miss her about the place."

"Get away! You didn't even like her."

"That's not strictly true. It was a bit of a love-hate thing. Any decent bitch has to hate a woman who has men salivating on sight when she doesn't even make the effort to bring it about."

"Course she makes the effort. She's sex on legs, that one."

"Not in the way you would think, Hal. I used to watch her. And I agree with you on one level. She's made up, she knows how to dress to accentuate her figure. She's very sexy, she's got

267

great boobs."

"My, you *have* been watching closely, haven't you?" Hal tickled his sister in the ribs. She squirmed but didn't bother to blush. They were too close for that nonsense.

"Yes, I admit it. She kinda fascinated me. Anyone who could hold your interest so long would be bound to." She adopted a slightly sarcastic tone, but still smiled.

"You're trying to change direction, Nat," he teased. "Go back to the fascinated bit."

"It's the whole idea of a woman who has screwed men for years suddenly deciding to try it with a woman. It kinda indicates that anybody could change sides if they took a fancy to it. Got me thinking. I'd be quite up for it myself. It would be interesting to have sex from a man's perspective, feeling what it's like to squeeze a breast, put your teeth on a nipple, finger another woman's clit." She took another look at the rising bump in his robe. "Hal, it seems I am better than the video."

Hal adjusted himself with a firm hand. "It's interesting to listen to you, very interesting."

"So it seems. But let me clarify. I haven't been wandering around eyeing up women that I imagine might be a good fuck. It was just her. It was her sexuality that intrigued me. She seems so unaware of it. I have this fantasy that when her present relationship folds, I'll have the chance to move in."

"Thanks very much. Cuckolded by my own sister. When do I get to shag her?"

"After me." Natalie laughed. "I want the experience, not a relationship. I could warm her up for you."

"Now I like the sound of that. God, I've imagined fucking that woman so many times."

"Oh, yeah? And what's she like in your head, big boy?" Natalie was closely aware that her brother's hard-on had refused

268

to diminish.

"Well, I agree with you that her tits have a special quality."

"What's special to a bloke then?"

"I don't do the giant jugs thing. Yuck. Big turn off, fear of suffocation, frankly. But Helena's, they're sort of round enough and grope-size enough to be the perfect handful."

"I think I know what you mean there. So how would you take her?"

"She strikes me as the sort of woman who would like a lot of handling first. Lots of touching."

"What woman doesn't?" Natalie unbuttoned her shirt a notch and slipped her hand inside.

"Behave, or I won't continue," Hal threatened.

"As if." She knew him too well.

"Perhaps a massage and lots of tongue work. Let's put it like this, I imagine she's a tiger in bed. I reckon if she decides she likes you enough to screw you then she has already taken a view about you, she has already chosen to trust you. If you respond in kind, she'll drop her guard. She'll really go for it."

"I think you have our Helena pretty well sussed."

"Yeah, but in all honesty, do you really think she is gay?" Hal remained unsure of the final analysis.

There was a pause, a long pause during which Natalie pondered, lost in her bourbon.

Hal loved watching her like this. It meant she was hatching something. Anything could happen. He savoured his drink and waited. A smile, both wicked and enchanting worked its way across her face to joyous completion.

"I have the best idea. After nearly thirty years, okay, fourteen actively sexual ones, where the woman has done the done thing and shagged blokes, she, apparently out of the blue, has it off with a woman. This must, of course, lead to particular questioning on her part about the nature of her sexuality. Yes?"

Hal nodded.

"She must therefore be in need of proof herself as to the truth of the situation. How is she to find it? Is one relationship, sex with one woman, enough to convince her she's actually gay? Come on, perhaps it's a one off. Genuine. But a one-hit-wonder. How will she know? Maybe she hasn't met the right man yet, with the right sensitivities, the right technique." She winked at Hal. "How can she be sure?" Natalie paused, a judge about to pass sentence after a long deliberation, and sipped on her JD to elongate the wait.

Hal was barely breathing. His sister was capable of going anywhere with this.

"We could offer her the way. We could provide the means by which she will know herself. And satisfy our own wicked curiosity on the way." Natalie chuckled. It grew into full-hearted, full-bellied laughter.

"Let me in on it, sis. Come on."

"Are you a gambling man, brother dear?"

"How much?"

"Fifty. No, dammit, a hundred."

"You have it. What's the deal?"

"We've got, let's say, one month, in which we each have to make a move on Helena. Whichever one of us manages to fuck her first establishes her sexuality and wins the bet. Deal?"

"Too fucking right it is. You are brilliant! Gonna finish this video?"

"If you top me up, I will." Natalie was thoroughly self-satisfied, and a little damp. By the end of the film she was totally relaxed.

"You staying then?" Hal asked of the stretching, languid

270

figure beside him.

"Course I am. Couldn't drive now, could I?" She smiled a lazy smile.

Hal turned off the television and the lamps. Natalie followed him upstairs, going straight to the bathroom. She washed her face, and in the mirror, she could see his bedroom door, where he dropped his robe to his feet and climbed naked beneath the duvet. She undressed where she was, in front of the wash-basin. She dumped her clothes and ran one hand from her neck, across her breast, down her stomach, to push it between her legs. She was very wet.

She slipped into bed behind him. "Are you going to shag me then, or what?"

"Don't I always?"

Natalie rolled over and let her legs fall wide.

"Don't you think it's a bit premature, love?" Avril Pearson was horrified at her daughter's phone call informing her of her plans to find a flat with Helena. She had constantly prayed it would all go away, that one weekend her beautiful Kate would come home and say, 'Thanks for standing by me, Mum, Dad, you were right. It was something I had to go through. It's over now'.

"Helena is getting grief from one of her neighbours," Kate explained.

Avril felt an un-Christian pang of *serves her right*.

"And it would make sense for me to be in a more settled environment for my finals. I'm likely to get more work done if I'm not in a student house."

"You could move back into halls," Avril retorted.

"And waste time to-ing and fro-ing. This offers the least compromise on the things that matter."

"I still think it's too soon. Your father won't like it."

"It was going to happen sometime, Mum. I'll call you in a couple of days."

Avril went to the kitchen, automatically putting on the kettle. So far, she had only talked to Josie, her closest friend, a sensible woman, about Kate's sexuality crisis. She'd advised Avril to be prepared for the possibility that Kate could stay gay.

Avril refused to discuss the matter with her other children, all of who were taking it too matter-of-factly for her liking. She thought the boys, at least, might have tackled Kate and talked her out of the nonsense with the assistance of a few nice looking friends. They were all too casual about it.

Previews of future conversations flashed before her eyes: goodly neighbours enquiring as to the advancement of the marriage course of her coming-of-age children; how odd it was that university makes them fussy these days when it was always considered the breeding ground for a good husband or wife; the question of whether Kate would return to work around Norwich, settle here as the others seem to have done. How long could she lie? She had not broken breath of it with her own brothers and sisters. Kate was now forcing her hand.

Avril said nothing to her husband over supper. She was fearful of angry conversation that would undoubtedly tug on her loyalties. So she waited for the dark of the bedroom and offered the information like a passing comment. "Kate phoned today. She's talking about moving in with that woman."

"Already?" he snapped.

She sighed inwardly, then sniffed back her worry. "I'm not happy about it either."

He must have sensed her apprehension. "Well, we just let her get on with it. All the advice in the world isn't going to stop her. We give her enough rope to hang herself."

"An unfortunate metaphor," Avril chided.

"I mean simply, that I have no faith in this relationship. From the sound of it, neither of them is sure what they're up to right now. That woman is none of our concern. I still think she's too old and it won't last. We do have to face the fact that Kate may decide she is gay regardless of what happens with that Helena, so it's our job to hang on, and pray for her happiness, pray that it all comes right in the end. We'll let her get on with this. She has to learn her own way."

At a quarter to midnight Helena's phone rang. In her dreams it was an alarm clock, one she couldn't turn off. She finally felt for the receiver beside the bed.

"Mm. Hello?" There was no reply. She expected it was Kate on a payphone, or on a friend's dodgy mobile, out on the town, missing her, as she does.

"Hello?" No answer.

The line went dead. Helena groaned. She was wide awake after that, which is just as well for Kate was bound to try again within twenty minutes, the length of a taxi ride home to a reliable phone. Helena fetched a glass of water and jumped back into bed with a book on modern psychosis. The phone didn't ring again.

"Were you trying to call me last night?"

"No, I was at the pictures 'til late, with Robin and Mick. Did I say I'd call? I'm sorry, I forgot." Kate tried to remember the promise she broken.

"No, no. You didn't say you would. You're not supposed to for a couple of days. You said you had assignments to get in."

"So why are you asking?"

Helena told her of the late call, her presumption. "No one else would call so late midweek, not without trying to say something. But no worries. Probably a wrong number. See you at the weekend."

"Missing you already."

George St. Rehab Unit had its own car park. Helena reminded herself it was supposed to be a bonus. She didn't feel so fortunate. It gave her no time to delay her entry to the building. Rumours had beaten her to the door.

One kindly colleague thought it best that Helena be informed of the sort of thing that was being said. She'd called in to her office, a conspiratorial good friend who, of course, didn't believe any of the gossip herself. It was all too plain Helena's every minute reaction would be reported back.

Helena smiled a false gratitude, letting nothing slip, pointing out to the woman that she was well trained and very, very aware.

In supervising her own team, Helena spent most of her time in one-to-one situations with each counsellor, and on administrative tasks. It appeared to keep the peace and she was saved from the weight of the group siding against her. Days moved slowly. One Thursday, Helena told the secretary she was heading out to lunch. The idea sounded good, a change of scenery, alone, nothing more. She stopped to pick up the late internal mail on her way back through. Her name was spoken in a cheerful voice, one that lifted a momentary hope in her heart.

"Helena, Hi! I was hoping I might run into you."

Natalie Preston may not have been a friend at Sutton Coldfield, but she was a potential ally in the midst of this invisible subterranean hostility.

"Natalie. It's good to see you." She meant it. "What are you doing over here?"

"Linking up a session with first time users and our older addicts. A warning session, if you like."

"Of course, of course."

"Look, I've got to get into this meeting now." Natalie looked at her watch. "Are you dashing off after work?"

"No. Nothing planned."

"Why don't we go for a bite to eat? Catch up?"

"I'd really like that, Natalie." Helena meant this too.

At five o'clock they discovered the vicinity didn't offer much in the line of decent restaurants. Helena was quick with an alternative; a well-loved Chinese place near her home that would deliver. "We can pick up some wine on the way."

Over noodles and chicken, Helena asked for news from the unit. "It's rotten being on a different schedule from Jackie and Tessa. It's weird not knowing the little stuff that makes up their days, stuff we used to do together."

"I can imagine. Well, nobody's pregnant, nobody's up to anything exciting. Same old stuff."

Helena considered asking if the gossip about her had died down. She would have liked to know the details, how far wrong it had evolved. She decided to leave it. It might have put a damper on the evening which, to her delight and surprise, was an unexpected pleasure. Natalie was engaging, entertaining. How had she not seen that before?

Natalie repeated the thought with a coy turn to the corner of her mouth. "How did we not come to know one another better at Sutton?"

Helena felt the sting of a blush in the apple of her cheek. Before that day, she was severely guilty of less favourable assessments of the woman.

"You had no time for me, always busy dashing about getting things done, playing safe and selective." An acidity hung over the last word, dissipated by the broad grin Natalie offered as she finished, "See what you were missing?"

Beguiled, Helena reached out and rubbed Natalie's shoulder. "Sorry. I didn't realise you were such fun."

Natalie held her gaze. Something fluttered. "It's funny what you don't see when you forget to look."

Helena didn't want to be first to look away. Natalie made her wait. Conversation resumed normally as the women tidied away the foil containers. It was Helena's turn to describe people at George St. and how different everything seemed in her new workplace. A matter of time, she supposed, though she wished her team was more cohesive. They finished in the kitchen and returned to the lounge, glasses in hand. Natalie took the sofa, and Helena was unsure where to sit. The chair opposite implied formality, and next to her on the sofa, an intimacy that did not yet exist. It was a schoolyard moment.

Natalie saw it. "For goodness sake, be comfortable. I don't bite." Her eyes flashed as she patted the cushion next to her, where Helena obediently arranged herself, lotus position, and turned so she faced her companion.

"So come on then, tell me about this woman of yours. I've been ignoring any gossip. It's bound to be untrue. Such is the nature of the beast."

"Kate is amazing. She is tall and slim and beautiful. And she's so grounded. She knows what she wants, that girl. She's so mature, emotionally I mean."

"Sounds like a good deal to me. How did you get together? As in, what happened when your sessions were over?"

That little hint of trust was all Helena needed to share

her romance. She was animated, forthcoming, open. Natalie was tactile in her reception of the detail. Her smiles, her touch, her constant wide-eyed contact were all affirmations. She encouraged the flow. Helena unfolded her legs from beneath her, brushing Natalie's as she stretched by. Her apology was dismissed by a pat on the thigh. It was like static electricity.

Natalie commended, "I think you're really brave to push the boundaries of your own life. And look at the reward. You've got something new and wonderful. Hats off to you, I say, truly." Her admiration showed in the glow of her face, the expanse of her pupils.

Natalie swept her hair up off the back of her shoulders to hold it in a loose pile on top of her head. She was aware that the position lifted her breasts to accentuate the cleavage now visible at the V of her top. Late September permitted the last weeks of bare legs; maximisation of a fading tan. "I need the toilet."

They tried to stand at the same time. The coffee table, too many limbs at once, tripped them up. They fell awkwardly back onto the sofa. Natalie pressed herself into Helena in her attempt to right herself. "Try that again, shall we?"

The saucy smile invited Helena to ask herself which part exactly they should retry. She knew then and there she was being toyed with.

"You first, Natalie." Helena remained seated and took full stock of the female form before her. Natalie indisputably showed a fine figure.

She followed, directing Natalie to the bathroom, stopping in front of the hall mirror where she adjusted her hair, her clothing, smiled to herself with the knowledge that Natalie was flirting with her. Helena was flattered. Natalie was a fit, attractive, intelligent woman of thirty. The encounter was allaying some of Helena's niggling fears. It was not just a heroine-worship kind of thing then, with Kate. She was also attractive to her own age group. She was attractive to women who may not have considered a woman before. There was an advantage in breaking the stereotype. Perhaps Helena was more accessible to other women this way. Helena was comforted, confident of her sexuality for the first time. That's what it was about now.

She opened a second bottle and poured another glass of wine. The game was too much fun to end just yet. It was time to reciprocate. Ironically, Helena had to use the rules for flirting she'd learned from toying with men: playful glancing poised against elongated gazing; subtle self-stroking, on the neck, the thigh; thoughtless twisting of strands of hair; the tip of the tongue frequently moistening the lips; constant engaging conversation throughout.

It turned out to be a different game with a woman.

Natalie mirrored her.

Natalie had watched how her flattering attention and a bit more wine had dissolved the last of Helena's defences. She was proud of her progress. It proved easier than she thought it might. The girl must have been a fling after all, but from her eager response to this flirtation, her body language, the fling was not with homosexuality. Natalie pondered that the time may have been ripe to make a more direct move. But Helena's next comment threw her.

"My God! Is that the time? I normally keep more careful hours on a weeknight. The price of having a good time. I'd better organise a taxi for you."

Natalie underestimated her counterpart. She hadn't seen that Helena recognised it as a game. It was no longer clear whether she stood a chance. She was hearing Hal telling her she probably didn't. This was unacceptable. She'd end this interlude on her own terms.

"Actually, if you don't mind making me a coffee, I'm fit to drive home. It's not far."

"If you're sure." Both moved back to the kitchen. Natalie leaned with her back to the work surface, thrusting her hip forward. She wanted to create conversation that would keep Helena sweet a while longer. "Have you thought of moving Kate in?"

"Actually, we are talking about looking at a new place together. Keeps the power balance equal if it belongs to both."

"Of course." Natalie believed she was on track again. Helena was relaxing. "Can I be forward?" The coy twinkle was replaced with an innocence. "If you weren't with Kate, would you find me attractive?" Natalie lowered her head a degree, implying a girly shyness.

"You are a very attractive woman, Natalie. You have a great figure, you're intelligent, and you're fabulous fun. I'd say you'd be quite a catch."

Natalie stepped up to receive her coffee cup. She placed her hands around Helena's on the cup. Her face was close enough to share breath. "And if you weren't with Kate, would you kiss me?"

She was tantalising. Helena knew that the merest adjustment would let her taste that mouth. That's all it would have taken to change everything she had, Kate included. "Maybe." She lifted the cup to the waiting lips and withdrew her hands.

Natalie maintained the banter for her last ten minutes in the flat. She would not concede defeat until the door was closed behind her.

Her denim jacket donned, she paused in the hall to thank Helena for an enjoyable night, one she very much hoped they would do again. Helena offered an embrace. Natalie took a step out of the flat on her goodbye, then turned to place a slow deliberate kiss on Helena's cheek, catching the corner of her mouth. "Call me," she quipped from the second stair.

At the foot of the flight, Danielle was bent double at her front door, placing milk bottles on the mat. She took a good look at Natalie skipping down the stairs, raised an accusing eyebrow at her neighbour, and retreated, shutting her door firmly.

Helena was washing her face when the phone rang. It had gone eleven.

"Hello," she expected Kate, of course. In the silence of the open phone line, it was Danielle's face she saw. Is that bitch trying to wind me up? She wouldn't put it past her.

"Hello! Hello? Who is this?" intimating in her tone that she had her suspicions. A click.

Seething quietly, she went to her room to don her bedclothes. The bedroom extension rang anew. What the hell is she doing, following my footsteps on her ceiling?

"Hello!" Her voice was sharp this time.

"Whoops. Did I wake the sleeping monster?" Kate.

"Sorry, darling. Sorry."

Natalie pushed hard against the increased weight on the chest-press. "It's uplift I'm after, not pecs," she warned Hal, who was clearly considering adding another ten kilograms.

Natalie benefitted from a reduced membership rate at Hal's gym, contained as it was within the Sports Centre. It had been their most regular source of contact since he started working there, and there was always the preferential treatment she received as the revered manager's kid sister. It would be a good place to pull, this gym, if Natalie could see past her brother. Today she was here to report on her attempt at ensnaring Helena.

"Helena was flirting with me from the outset. Come on, takeaway? That was just to get me in her home. And I saw how she mentally undressed me on my way to the loo. She even admitted that if she wasn't with Kate, and who knows how long *that* will last, she would have been asking me to stay." Natalie crossed to the lat-pull machine.

"That's a no-score for you, sis."

"What d'you mean, no-score? I thought it was a damn close thing myself. It certifies her sexuality if you ask me."

"The deal is the first to shag her. Touchy feely moments and a peck on the cheek don't even get close."

"Fine. Your turn." Natalie skulked. She hated losing to her brother. "I don't know how you're going to get away with turning up out of the blue, though."

"*You* are going to make it possible."

"I am not."

"Don't be a sore loser, Nat. I'll make it worth your while." Hal ran his palms down the underside of her upstretched arms, along her ribcage, and rested them on her waist, then let go as he watched the goose-bumps rise across her shoulders.

"What do you want?" she resigned.

"You said she was pissed off with her team, didn't you? So offer my services, sister dear. It's an obvious follow-on from your conversation, isn't it?"

Natalie had to admit that her brother was a smooth mover. Helena would be so grateful for the assistance of his team-building skills. She was bound to go for it.

"Then you'll ask her out for a drink afterwards?" she presumed.

"Oh, Natalie, you disappoint me. More class, more clever than that, if you please." He winked, mischievous and knowing, divulging nothing.

Two days after that interesting night with Natalie, Helena picked up a written phone message left on her desk. It read: Don't forget Hal has a service that may be of use to you right now. Give him a call. Nat.

Of course! You absolute sweetheart, Natalie. Helena made a mental note to call to thank her, and smiled to herself that there really are no coincidences. She arranged the secretary to call Hal right away, to book an appointment during which they might discuss options. Time was of the essence if any semblance of team spirit was to be achieved under Helena's auspices. Any course they attempt must happen soon. She prayed Hal was available.

To avoid the anticipated rumblings about the daft ideas of a new manager, Helena arranged that the course would run on a Thursday and Friday as part of the week's regular hours, so no one could shout 'extra-curricular' or 'voluntary'. Everyone from her eight-strong team would be obliged to attend. The last week of September was decided upon, before the weather broke.

Hal applied his exquisite charm and skill in his introductory session. "Whilst the activities you will participate in are physical, no one is expected to qualify for the Olympics or the Territorial Army."

Only a little laughter rang out. Hal scanned the team and noticed a few characters were very fixed in nature. One rigid, overly tidy man of about forty-five, and a matronly woman with neat grey hair and a pinched mouth, were two he suspected to have issues with a young female boss, never mind a gay one, if she really was gay. Hal was thrilled. Two challenges rolled into one, and he was certain he'd win both. What excellent promise this course held.

Hal set to work: a combination of army training and personal motivational exercises; problem-solving; decision-making tasks; a dollop of healthy humiliation where necessary. He arranged it so Helena worked with her staff in different combinations, experiencing first-hand their individual strengths and weaknesses, and their relationships with others. Hal's reward was the pleasurable view of Helena in shorts, feeding his imagination of the moment when he finally got to see more.

By the time they packed up on Friday, Helena was satisfied that she had a whole new mass of raw material to mould. Spirits were high, communication was quick-fire. The bar was nominated for their closing ceremony. It was the first time she had been invited to drink with the staff. Adrenaline ran so high, one beer was enough. Helena left while the mood was up.

Hal was ready.

Her first pleasant drive home since the transfer, Helena was no longer lamenting the list of complaints that had been plaguing her. Rather, she was thinking forward, planning her next move, daring to feel hopeful that George St. had a future for her after all. She parked, grabbed her bags and skipped up the stairs, forgetting to feel the habitual dread as she approached Julian's door. A radio played within and she truly hoped they were having a pleasant evening.

Her hand was in her bag, distractedly rummaging for her key. "Damn!" The keys didn't come quickly to her fingers. She dropped the sports bag to the floor and opened her shoulder bag wide to see the contents rather than just feel them. She pushed around notebooks, and compacts when a voice said, "Looking for these?"

Hal smiled. A helpful boy scout, keys suspended in the

air. "I found them on the floor of the changing-room. Your guys were still in the bar. Process of elimination made them yours."

"Hal, that was so good of you to drive here and save me coming back. I'm not even on your way home, am I? Look, come in, at least let me offer you a beer."

"Cheers, wouldn't say no," he replied, as he silently acknowledged his earlier sleight of hand, when acquiring her keys from her bag during their afternoon break. He didn't bother to check if the rest of the team was still there when he left. He had his other goal to pursue.

He stood in the lounge, admiring the view from the window. Helena clinked bottles in the kitchen. She brought them through.

"Cheers, Hal. You may have just saved my career, as well as my temper."

He raised his bottle to hers and sat. "Tell me how you think it went. What do you think they got out of it?" An answer would take her a while, of course. Psychologists love to analyse. It would give him plenty of time.

Helena was still talking about the progress made when the phone rang. "Let the machine get it," she said, and moved to take another gulp from her now-empty bottle. Jackie's voice chattered in the background. "This goes down well after a lot of clambering about, doesn't it? Another?"

"Great."

She was off. In the kitchen, Helena contemplated how grateful she was for the opportunity to put her connection with Hal on a professional footing. Natalie had made no reference to the old crush he'd had on her. She was happy it had passed. She returned to the living room and together they further assessed the day's achievements.

"I'm impressed you can read them so well."

"People come to my team-building thinking they have it all worked out. But it's always a revelation. Sometimes, I'm astounded at a group and just can't imagine why someone put them together and expected it to work." Hal watched how she moved. His clients were always physically freer after a few days with him. He moved them back into their bodies, reminded them what it was to use them.

Helena sat opposite, with knees apart and thighs disappearing into her shorts. Her elbows rested lazily on her legs, and she leaned forward in eager communication. It was a masculine position. Perhaps Natalie was right. But he enjoyed the feminine cleavage, courtesy of the t-shirt draping away from her as she leaned.

The wind rose. Helena closed the windows around the room. She reached past Hal where he was seated. Hal placed a hand on the back of her thigh and stroked. She shot round to face him.

"Hal!"

He dropped his hand and apologised.

Helena wondered if she should make him go. She reasoned it would leave him embarrassed with no way of making it right. Natalie would step away again. In any event, perhaps she was wrong. The apology suggested so. Hal handled people all day. He's handled her in the past. He probably slipped up, that's all. She decided it was wiser to be adult, to pursue further conversation so the mistake would be absorbed.

Hal humoured her for a few minutes but was tiring of the talk. It wasn't getting him anywhere. He needed to be taking action. He stood and faced the window. "You can see a lot of the area from here, can't you?"

Helena took to her feet and pointed out various neighbourhoods, the reservoir to the left, the hint of the canal to the north, the city to the east. He allowed her to move and turn beside him. Mid-flow, he swivelled and caught her into his arms pushing his mouth fully onto hers so she could no longer speak. He held her there for a long moment, an uncomfortable, unwanted long moment.

On separation of their lips, she spoke calmly in her best counsellor voice. "Hal, I don't want this. I thought you'd moved on. If I've done anything to make you think otherwise, I'm sorry. It was not my intention."

Hal didn't release his hold. "Not your intention? You've been sitting in front of me with your legs spread all this time. I'd say that was a pretty obvious invitation. Wouldn't you, counsellor? And are you unaware that your t-shirt gapes when you lean forward? Bet you do." He looked down on her breasts, a perfect view from his height, a perfect sensation as he pressed them closer to him.

Helena squirmed. "Hal, it's nothing personal. You're a great guy. It's just that I'm—"

"Gay? My sister told me of your recent change of direction. She seemed quite convinced of it herself. I, on the other hand, am not. Look at you." He held her firmly across her back with one arm. His hand he placed directly onto her breast, squeezing before moving it around to her bum to squeeze that too.

His voice heated. "This is a woman's body, Helena, a very luscious, very inviting woman's body." He drew her against him again pressing his hardened penis to her stomach. "Correct me if I'm wrong, but sexually, isn't a woman's body designed to take a man?"

Helena pushed at his chest and leaned her head back to look up. She opened her mouth to answer, to fight, to chastise, but his hand was in the back of her hair, pulling it taut so her

286

neck couldn't move. His face was upon hers again, his tongue pushing into her mouth. She couldn't break free from his vice. His arms were hard and steely about her. His face, his mouth, denied her breath, until she gasped. It made him smile.

"That's more like it. Stop fighting. You know you've been missing it." Hal lifted her across the room and threw her onto the sofa, followed her down, and laid on top, pinning her motionless.

"Hal! Hal! Stop it!" She turned her head this way and that, avoiding the mouth he wanted to press on her more. Her hair tangled and caught on her tongue. She pushed her wrists hard against his grasp praying she might expand the vice-like hold, break it. She couldn't. She was puny beside him.

She tried to kick.

He placed a heavy thigh across her shin, immobilising.

"Hal, I don't want to have sex with you!" she screamed.

Downstairs, the radio was turned up louder.

"But I want to have sex with you," he replied calmly as he freed a hand to unbutton her shorts, pulling them sharply away, burning the skin on her ass as he yanked them down.

"God, no, no!" She forced her every energy into a furious wriggle that got her nowhere, aware that he was freeing himself to take her.

A hard and violent thrust, and he succeeded. Again and again he rammed himself into her. He was too big for her small frame. It was hard, and sore. She didn't speak. Twice more. She felt the heat of it, and he pulled out. Leaning back, he looked at her face, at the tear running across her temple.

"You really didn't like that, did you?" He sounded

surprised. "Natalie must be right."

A noise. Elsewhere in the flat. A key. In the door.

Hal stepped up, away from her. "Expecting someone?"

He smiled and casually zipped his shorts, turning to face the living room door as he smoothed his hair, nodding a greeting to Kate as she entered.

"I'd best be off then." Hal strolled out.

Kate wanted to stop the flood of possibilities before they consumed her very mind. She watched the back of Hal's head before he closed the door, and looked back to see her dishevelled girlfriend pulling her shorts up onto her bum. She couldn't take in the scene. She did not want to. The deception, the stupidity, the agonising display of it all crushed the breath from her. She could only whisper, "Helena?"

Tears streamed down Helena's face as she stared expressionless at her lover. Kate had no room for Helena's regrets. The tears increased. Helena buckled in rasping howling sobs. She slid onto her knees and vomited onto the carpet.

The truth slapped Kate in the face. The rank odour of the room was not sex, but fear.

"Helena? Dear God, what's happened? What happened here?" She knelt to draw the sobbing mess into her arms.

"He raped me. He raped me." It was all she could say.

Kate wrapped Helena in a blanket, and gave her a glass of water, nothing else. She insisted that nothing be moved, touched, cleaned, until they decided what to do. Kate had the phone in her hand ready to call the police. Helena pleaded for her to wait, to look at the situation, think on what they would say, look at how hard reporting this rape would be.

Helena rocked in the chair as she described the facts objectively, her voice surreally calm.

"I invited him in. It's Friday night. We've spent two very physical days together. Touching, guiding hands. We are scantily dressed for a September evening. I offer him beer. The suggestion of the possibility of it going further is already there. So why was he here in the first place? Being gallant. I'd dropped my keys at the sports centre."

"When did you drop your keys?"

"I don't know. I ... I wasn't aware. It must have been when I put my bags in the locker."

"The keys were in your bag?"

Helena heard the suggestion, the thought of this being planned, a motive, a design, some twisted logic. Was that easier to handle? "I don't know. I don't know how they fell. There is history. A few years back, Natalie his sister, my work colleague, intimated that he fancied me. But I was with someone else. When that broke up, Hal waited a discreet couple of months then sent me a bouquet of roses. He'll be described as thoughtful, romantic, genuinely in love with me all this time. I won't be the aim of a cheap fuck. No, I'll be blamed for leading this sensitive soul on!"

Kate stroked Helena's tangled hair. "You're not that kind of person, Helena. A court would see that."

"The law on rape, Kate, might sound like protection for women, but it is applied as protection for men. I've seen it. I had a private client once, a woman of forty-five, raped by her cousin. Court overturned it on the fact that she'd invited him to stay at her house for the weekend. After he'd driven all the way from the south coast, what else was she to do? But no, that didn't count, wasn't even considered. She tortured herself when he was acquitted. She examined every movement, every word and gesture, convinced by the court that she was giving him some sort of sexual signals. That's exactly what they'll use against me. They won't let me get away with saying I'm a lesbian. No, they'll have a laugh as defence asks, 'Isn't it true you've been a lesbian for only six months?' They'll imply some sort of sexual confusion that will work to Hal's advantage. My God! If this got out, Danielle and Julian could really stick the knife in. They'd bring up your parents and their investigation into my professional misconduct, and I'd be annihilated. That bastard would walk away laughing. He already has." Her tears ran afresh, dropping steadily onto the blanket. "It's not just me, Kate. Think how this affects us. We'd be public property. All of the gory details would be bandied about the local press, maybe worse. You'd get questioned, and everything you say will be twisted or torn apart. The Gay Woman Cries Rape story would be everywhere. You'd have no privacy left. I can't drag you through this. I can't do that to you." She reached out and gently touched Kate's face.

It was Kate's turn to cry. "Darling, I am already in this. First on the scene, a key witness. I have no illusions about how ugly this could all become. Helena, it's already ugly. Look what he's done to you. Do you want him to get away with it?"

"No!" Helena sobbed. "I want the bastard to pay!"

Both women jumped sharply as the phone rang.

"Probably Jackie again."

"That's not Jackie's voice."

"Helena? Helena! Pick up. It's Natalie. Jesus, Helena, talk to me. I've just spoken to Hal. Shit! I know … I mean, he said … fuck! He wasn't supposed to take it that far … Helena! Helena? Are you all right? He didn't mean to hurt you. Shit!"

Helena's eyes widened as she tried to make sense of it.

Kate surveyed the room: covers and cushions askew on the sofa; a bottle knocked over on the coffee table; a pool of vomit; the tear-stained, dishevelled woman in front of her; the red beacon on the answering machine.

She kissed her lover gently on the cheek. "I'm not afraid of this, Helena. We can do this. We'll get through it. And when it's all over, we'll go away somewhere, just you and me. A bit of breathing space, before finding our new flat. Dublin is supposed to be a great place to visit."

Helena nodded, a child in her hands. Kate wrapped the blanket closer around Helena's shoulders. "Ready now?"

She picked up the phone.